SEARCHING FOR JANE

Sequel to *The K Code*

a Novel by Lorna Makinen

Searching for Jane

ISBN-13:978-1511572170
ISBN-10:1511572175
Also available in eBook

Cover Image Credit: http://www.123rf.com/profile_jojjik
Cover Design: Elizabeth E. Little, Hyliian Graphic Design
Interior Book Design: The Author's Mentor,
www.LittleRoniPublishers.com

PUBLISHED IN THE UNITED STATES OF AMERICA

This book is dedicated
to my editors. Without their
support and encouragement this book
would have had way too many ellipses and
commas. Plus, all the stuff authors should know.
I'm indebted to them.

Cast of Characters

(in alphabetical order by first name)

1. Alex McGraw – rogue inspector in prison
2. Bobbie Grantwood – Inspector for Scotland Yard. She heads the photography lab at the Yard. Huge supporter of the Dream Team and wants to be a member. She's also girlfriend of Dennis Ross.
3. Chief O'Doul – Head of Scotland Yard and grudgingly supports the female Dream Team Task Force.
4. Dennis Ross – Lead inspector for Scotland Yard. Called Ross much of the time, is responsible for the solving the case of The K Code. He's also the reason for this story in that Jane, Alex's wife, is missing.
5. Edward Edse – Medical doctor. He conspires with Alex McGraw.
6. Elizabeth Hennessey – Inspector for Scotland Yard and newest member of the Dream Team Better known as Hennessey
7. Father James Turnbull – Anglican Church priest. He operates an orphanage in Bedrule, Scotland.
8. Henry Peckham – defense attorney for Alex McGraw.
9. Jane – wife of Alex McGraw, dear friend to Dennis Ross and his belated wife Lizzy. Her disappearance is the basis of the story. Question being is she alive or….
10. JoAnne Barr – goes by Jo….Inspector for Scotland Yard. Has a degree in surgical nursing and is a member of the Dream Team.
11. Karen Cogar – Inspector for Scotland Yard and member of the Dream Team. Holds a degree in Criminal Psychology.
12. Kitty Carroll – Inspector for Scotland Yard and Dream Team's creator. Her background is a career in the Navy that was interrupted by the powers that be at Scotland Yard.

13. Linda - Lead inspector for Scotland Yard and a first member of the Dream Team Task Force. She brings to the table her ability to strategize under pressure.
14. Michael Doone – defense attorney for Alex McGraw and business partner to Henry Peckham.
15. Neil Ghent –brother of Peter Ghent, an associate of Alex McGraw and who was in The K Code. Like his brother, Neil works for Interpol.
16. Patti D. –inspector for Scotland Yard and a member the Dream Team with questionable status in both groups because she can't pass shooting fire arms or martial arts. She is, however, brilliant with computers, and has a keen sense about most tactical devices. She runs the Dream Team's brain trust.
17. Theresa –Inspector for Scotland Yard and one of the first members of the Dream Team.
18. Zilpha Peckham - Mother of Henry Peckham and associate of Alex McGraw.

Prologue

The case of the "K Code" was stamped CLOSED in red ink and again below that in big black bold letters CLASSIFIED. This case could be listed as one of the top ten mysteries solved at Scotland Yard; however, there was no media coverage, no bonus given with time off for the lead inspector, no fanfare because according to the governments involved, the case, the incident, the murders never happened. In all his twenty years at the Yard, this was by far the biggest and worst case for the lead inspector, Dennis Ross.

Almost a year had passed and Ross still battled sleepless nights, recurring nightmares of that night at the Braun estate. It was inconceivable his partner, Alex McGraw, could become a suspect, let alone a murderer for hire. How does one come to terms with a twenty year relationship working day in and day out together, even saving each other's life several times, only to discover such duplicity? How had he missed it?

Then another shocking development surfaced. It wouldn't be a factor in the case itself, but very important to Dennis. Alex's wife Jane had disappeared. Their wives were like sisters, they were so close. Jane was always there to help him take care of Lizzy up to the day Lizzy passed away. Dennis feared the worst, wondering if Alex had anything to do with her disappearance.

The Yard went on with its routine, but Dennis couldn't drop the case. For his sake and for Lizzy's, he had to know Jane was alive somewhere.

Chapter 1

Ross's home

It had gone on four in the morning when a crash of thunder and streak of lightning lit up the bedroom. Pouring with sweat, Dennis jolted up in bed grabbing his leg where the bullet pierced. The gun shot rang in his head. His arm pointing to the wall, he woke up yelling, "Don't Alex, you can't win."

The bed was a mess with the sheet and comforter every which way. He dropped his head. *When is this going to stop? How many times can I be shot? Where is Jane? Alex couldn't have killed her. I must find out if Jane is alive.*

He sat on the side of his bed wiping the sweat off his face with the bed sheet. *Bobbie was right; I'm letting this put me over the edge. I've no one now. Lizzy is dead, and Bobbie can't even be in the same room with me. She thinks I'm obsessing over Jane. I'm a criminal psychologist for God's sake.* He slung his pillow across the room. *Why can't I deal with this?*

Flinching at a huge flash of lightning followed by another blast of thunder that shook the room, he stood to shut the window. Lightning lit up the yard as he peered out. The barrage of flashes fed his mental state resulting in flash backs to the shooting spree at the Brauns. As he stood, he saw in the window glass a reflection of a woman behind him in the bedroom doorway. His heart stopped. *Oh my God!* "Jane!" He whirled around as another flash of light ripped across the walls but no one was there. He stared breathing deeply and swallowing hard. *There has to be an explanation. That was Jane. I can't be dreaming. Maybe she's trying to find me or lead me to her. It looked like she was saying something...What was she holding. It was one of those empty boxes we found.* "Ross, quit it! You're making yourself crazy. You'll be committed if you're not careful."

With a slight limp he walked to the bathroom, peeling off his soaked undershirt and pajama bottoms. Throwing them into a hamper, he got into the shower. The water was freezing. Leaning his head against the wall, he obsessed yet another time over the last meeting with Alex. He was standing in the prisoner's waiting room when Alex was brought in wearing chains on his ankles up to his one remaining wrist. His arm had been amputated as a result of that horrible night at the Braun estate. The guard pulled out a chair but Alex just stood. Ross turned from staring out into the courtyard, glancing at the guard's report showing a list of visitations from Alex's attorneys, his daily activities that included a lot of exercise and then into Alex's staring eyes. The same stare before Ross was shot by his partner. *He wanted to kill me.* "I brought you something. We found several of these by the creek behind that shack of yours. So far we've found six of them. They were empty." Ross watched every twinge on Alex's face as he shoved the box across the table toward his partner, asking "Did Jane empty them?"

The pupil in Alex's eye couldn't be controlled as he cocked his head and turned motioning to the guard he was ready to leave. "Dennis, are you brain dead? I was tried already for killing her. Remember! And you caught me. You're the hero. What else do you want?"

Dennis grabbed Alex's arm. "Then where's her body?"

Then he whispered into Alex's ear. "I think she's alive and is hiding because she has more than your money."

The guard moved as Alex pushed away from Ross's grip. Ross signaled he was fine to the guard. Alex smirked at the guard and then glared at Dennis. "Don't come back here again."

Dennis hit the shower wall. *I want to know Jane is alive! She has to be alive. His eyes told me. Whatever she's taken is what's keeping her alive.*

The storm continued to be as relentless as his nightmare. After a twenty minute shower, he stood before the mirror tying his tie, wondering why Alex's attorneys visited at least once every other week. *For a year?* The third ring of his house phone jolted him. "Chief, is there a problem?"

"I'm afraid there is, Dennis. You're not going to like this anymore than I did a few minutes ago when I got a call from Admiral Benjamin. It seems the evidence the Americans said couldn't be used in the K Code case has allowed more loop holes for Alex's and Edse's defense. If I understand this right, the time served is all they're getting."

Dennis shook his head. "Tell me I'm not having another nightmare."

"I wish I could. I know what you're going through. We all have seen what this case has done to you. What's worse is that you, being the lead inspector in the case, have to go out and sign off on Alex's release. I'm sorry, Dennis, but it is this afternoon at three o'clock."

Dennis sank into a chair next to the phone stand in the hall, the phone bouncing on the floor.

"Dennis! Dennis! What was that noise? Are you okay? Dennis, pick up the phone."

"I'm here. Chief, Jane has got to be alive. I'm sure of it. Now her life is in danger. I've got to find her."

"That's what you keep saying. How do you know she's alive?"

"Trust me, she has to be. The last visit I had with Alex I shoved one of the empty boxes we found at his place in front of him and asked if Jane had taken the contents. He said she was dead and he'd been tried for her murder. His eyes didn't lie, Chief. The pupils lit up like Christmas trees."

"Dennis, Alex was given a lie detector test and those questions were asked. He was convicted really on circumstantial evidence and the attempted murder of the Admiral."

Dennis heard the Chief talking with someone. "Dennis, I appreciate what you're saying, and to ease the situation, I will put a special detail to follow Alex beginning today."

I know whatever she's taken is what is keeping her alive only until he finds her. "You know he'll spot anyone you have."

"Maybe not. I'll give Inspector Carroll a call and see if she can assign some of her girls. Alex knows nothing about the Dream Team

Task Force."

"Chief, you can't. The man's a psychopathic murderer. He would have killed me had it not been for the Braun dog."

"We'll work it out. You just get yourself together and handle the release. Come to the office when you've finished."

Dennis sat mumbling holding the phone until he heard "If you'd like to place a call…"

He replaced the receiver and hesitated. "Bloody Hell. There's water on the floor" He looked up at the ceiling. *The roof isn't even three years old. What now!*

Chapter 2

Scotland Yard – Chief Inspector's office

Chief Inspector O'Doul stood as Inspectors Kitty Carroll and Bobbie Grantwood entered. "Ladies, please have a seat." The chief handed each a folder marked classified. "You've both worked on parts of this case and as you read, you'll see we're faced with an unexpected situation. I'm hoping you can help."

Inspector Carroll frowned holding the file. "I don't understand…the K Code was solved a year ago."

Bobbie nudged her friend and pointed to the last paragraph. Kitty read aloud. "Time served…released July eighth, nineteen ninety-five at three pm…" Wide eyed, she exclaimed, "My God, that's today! How can that be? That man murdered and master-minded major…"

The Chief cringed taking a couple of quick puffs on his pipe. *Bloody Hell.* "Yes, yes,… but, you both know all the evidence of the Dream Team's having saved the American Admiral is classified. McGraw was tried and convicted on impersonating an officer, attempting the murder of his wife and booby-trapping his property. Anything even remotely associated with Robert Braun was excluded. The legal teams for Edse and McGraw continued to find loop holes."

Kitty shook her head, "And that is justice."

Bobbie blurted out. “Chief, what if Dennis is right and Jane is alive? She’d be in grave danger.”

Chief O’Doul rubbed his forehead. “Bobbie, please don’t make me wonder about you too. Tell me, besides Alex’s eyes lighting up like Christmas trees, what other evidence supports your theory?”

Bobbie looked a bit strained at the Chief. “My guess is there was a lot of money in those boxes and Jane found out about it, and perhaps how he got it. If Alex thinks she took whatever is so important, then yes, I think he’d stop at nothing until he got it back.”

Before the Chief could respond, she leaned forward pointing her folder at him. “What’s even more puzzling to me is we don’t have any background information about Jane McGraw. There’s not a shred of information about this woman in this file or anywhere else. I thought all of us had to submit family histories to qualify for the yard training?”

The Chief saw his other inspector nodding. “What do you think, Inspector Carroll?”

“I’m in full agreement with Bobbie. We need to find out more about Jane. I realize we don’t have much time available. Still, I would do a background check on her if I were you. In the meantime, I can assign one of my girls to follow Alex McGraw as soon as he’s released.”

The Chief agreed. “I’ll go along with that only with the understanding she makes no contact with him whatsoever. Ross has made it very clear that Alex kills without hesitation. So you’ve got to put your best on this. I hope this isn’t a first for you.”

Inspector Carroll rose with a weak smile. “No sir, we’ve trained under every conceivable circumstance. I better get a move on this. Coldingley Prison is a good hour’s drive from here.” *Right now our rookie is the only one available, Hennessy.*

Bobbie sensed her concern. “I’ll be leaving as well, sir. Let me know if there’s anything I can do.”

Out in the hall, Bobbie took hold of Carroll’s jacket. “Kitty, what’s the matter? Are you worried your girls can’t handle this?”

They stopped to wait for the elevator. “Not at all. The Dream Team has made quite an impression, thanks to you. Right now we seem to be spread pretty thin. I really don’t like having my girls work alone. I've trained them to work together in teams always having a back-up. The team available has one out sick and that leaves Hennessy to work alone and she's my rookie."

Bobbie shook her head. "I wish I could help you, but Alex would spot me in a flash."

Kitty smiled. "Actually you can help me. The girls check in every hour. If you could handle the control booth, then I can go with Hennessy. There's a log book for each team. When they call in, they will give you a quick draft of what's happened during the hour."

"I can do that."

Chapter 3

Coldingley Prison in Surrey County

Ross looked at his watch and then at the clock on the wall. *Two fifty five. It's no longer just a dream but a real live nightmare. I should be watching an execution instead of seeing him walk out the door a free... monster. Twenty years fooled! That bullet was meant for my heart. I pray the Chief isn't making a mistake having the girls on that Dream Team follow Alex. This is not the man I thought I kn...*

The door opened and Alex walked in without chains. He laughed, "I wondered if you'd come. But, I guess you'd have to be the one since you were the big cheese. Hey, what do you think of this?"

Alex showed off his prosthesis. "Pretty cool. Don't feel so bad now. Signed up for that guinea pig med school program in Surrey. They finished it just in time."

Ross ignored the gestures and signed the paper, handing it to the guard. "It's okay, we're good here."

Alone with Alex, Ross closed his brief case. "I don't need to give you the drill. I'm sure you know the routine." He walked to the door.

Alex grabbed his bag of stuff and put out his new hand to shake hands with Ross. "I want you to know I really didn't want to shoot you. We're even now. You're alive and I'm free. Let's keep it that way. Just stay out of my life, or... I won't miss the second time."

Ross reached past Alex's hand for the door knob. "Jane better be alive, Alex."

Alex stepped back. "All this *concern!* Could it be my dear wife was sleeping in two beds, maybe three?" He started to laugh.

Ross grabbed him by the throat and smashed him into the door. "You bastard, that woman adored you! She better be alive, Alex, or you'll wish you hadn't missed killing me."

Ross started to open the door, hesitated, stepped back and flexed his fist, punching Alex hard in the jaw, knocking him against the wall and to the floor. "We're not *even. Not* by a long shot." He wiped his hand on his suit coat, nodding his head, glaring at Alex. "That's your first payback."

Chapter 4

Chief O'Doul's office

"Chief, Inspector Ross is here, it's five thirty, take your pills, change your suit, your wife will meet you at the Palace for the State dinner, at six thirty. Chief…I'm leaving! Did you get all that?"

O'Doul shook his head grizzling as he pressed the button. "Send him in and *yes I got all that*!"

Ross walked in and got waved to a chair while the Chief continued. "Mrs. Gipson, where did you put my suit and shoes?"

"Where I always do, in your bathroom, Sir. I gave Inspector Ross a report that was just delivered. Take your pills and I'll see you in the morning…Good night, I'm leaving. Remember six thirty. Your car will be out front at six fifteen."

As he sat, Ross handed him the folder. "She's been your secretary for a lot of years. As long as I've been here."

The Chief stared at the outer office door. "Thirty years. She treats me like a child. Every year I threaten to fire her."

Ross smiled, "Does that help?"

"*No*…she just thanks me for such gratifying news and goes on working." The Chief handed a copy of the papers to Ross. "I'm sure there's a conspiracy with Mrs. O'Doul…You can wipe that grin off your face…"

He leaned back in his executive chair stoking his pipe. "By the way, Ross, I've already heard you made an impression at the prison."

Ross quickly changed from a knowing grin to a frown. "How's that, sir?"

"It seems Alex's attorney filed a grievance against you. He claims you punched Alex so hard that you may have broken his jaw!"

"I can explain that…"

The Chief stared at Ross as he tried to interrupt. "I was told, *Dennis,* the attorney asked to see the tape that monitored the room you were in with Alex. It showed you signing the release, handing it to the guard, and that was all."

He peered at Ross over the rim of his glasses. "Now, was there something you wanted to say?"

Ross lowered his head to concentrate on the papers he held. *I'll take a big bottle of gin over to the prison tomorrow.* Ross cleared his throat. "What is this information about Jane McGraw? I couldn't help but read the cover of the file I gave you."

O'Doul explained his meeting with Carroll and Bobbie.

Ross jerked his head. "Bobbie was here?"

"Yes, she has aligned with the Dream Team for the time being. Carroll asked her to attend due to her knowledge of the whole case. They want to help but noted that very little is known about Alex's wife." He looked at the clock on his desk and stood. "If I'm late for this State dinner I will have two Ladies in Waiting! I can assure you a beheading won't compare to the chastisement I'll get from my wife."

Ross stood. "I understand. I will study these and maybe get an idea what caused her disappearance."

O'Doul stopped at the bathroom door frowning. "Dennis, you realize, you must come up with admissible facts, not speculation, or you'll be laughed out of court. And,… it could mean the end of your career. There are two more folders on the desk for Carroll and Bobbie. Before you leave the Yard, could you drop those off at their offices?"

Ross didn't need another reason. He grabbed the folders and off he went. "See you tomorrow, sir. My best to your royal highnesses." *Now, I hope I can find her.*

Chapter 5

Carroll and Hennessy in Woking, Surrey, England

"Bobbie, Hennessy and I are at our check points. Alex McGraw was picked up by his attorney and they have gotten on the A322. Our GPS data indicates he is headed for his home in Woking."

"I think you're right. That is where he lives. It's a shack back in the woods about five hundred feet behind the house he and Jane first lived in. It won't be easy for you to watch. I was in that shack and almost got Ross and me killed, but that's another story. I'll fill you in another time. What's your disguise this time?"

"Woking is all of ten minutes away from the prison. Being that close, it is surprising that Woking is rather large, maybe thirty thousand people, and mostly blue collar workers. I thought we should blend into the area so I asked Hennessy what she thought… Well, we are enjoying a ride on two gorgeous BMW touring bikes. James Bond would eat his heart out… Lucky for us there's a Rooster's chicken fast food two side streets east of where McGraw's car turned to go to his home. There're detailed maps in my file cabinet. You can plot where we are. We're just pulling in. It must be popular. The parking lot is huge. I'll get back to you in a few minutes. We want to get these leather jackets off."

Bobbie laughed. "If training on motorcycles is part of the deal, I want to join the Dream Team. Hey. are you expecting anyone? Someone's knocking on your office door."

Kitty turned into the parking lot. "Wow, this place is jammed with motorcycles. There must be a rally somewhere. Works for us.

Hennessy and I are going to split up and see what's going on in the area. These aren't just kids here. Very interesting. You better answer the door. It may be a courier bringing the resume on Jane McGraw the Chief said he'd send."

Bobbie went to the door leaving the microphone on. Seeing Ross, she caught her breath. "Well, this is a surprise! Part time job being a courier?"

He glowed and reached out to her. When she didn't resist, he gently took her in his arms and kissed her. "Bobbie, my life isn't the same anymore without you in it. I didn't mean to push you away."

Bobbie smiled with tears in her eyes and kissed him. "I know. It was time for me to back off and give you space."

The speakers on each side of the control booth emitted a giggle and then a snoring sound. "Oh, Lord… *The craziness of love hath no age…* Shakespeare? No Chatterton."

Bobbie got back to her seat. Pushing the intercom button, she chuckled, "Ha, Ha, Ha…You were right. It was a courier."

Dennis was wide eyed. "*A courier*?"

Kitty laughed. "Hi Dennis, you didn't know you're one of many. I'll let Bobbie fill you in on this stake out. Wow, more bikers are arriving. I'll check in later."

Hennessy and Carroll moved around the Rooster's parking lot talking to the other bikers while watching the street. At least fifty bikes had made the restaurant a rest stop. They couldn't have planned a better set up. There were people of all ages and backgrounds. Hennessy found out that Woking was a first stop of this group. She came out of the restaurant with two coffees. Handing one to her boss, "I just heard inside there are six other groups this size making a circle around London. It's a big charity drive to help the families of those miners killed in the Liverpool accident…" She looked around. "Glad I'm not on duty in London today."

Kitty shook her head. "*Three hundred fifty bikes!* Where is the meeting place?"

Hennessy giggled. "Would you believe…Buckingham Square, outside the Palace."

With eyes like saucers, Kitty pulled out her cell phone. "We better let the Yard dispatcher know…"

Hennessy put her hand on Kitty's arm. "Saw a couple of women I know from my school days. They told me this is an organized rally and the city is expecting them. Guess some of the rock groups have jumped on the band wagon giving a concert at midnight. I don't know how true this is, but I overheard someone say Prince Harry was helping in the effort."

Kitty sipped her coffee. "Back to business. You better mingle some more on the other side of the lot over by that side street. We don't want to be distracted by all these people either. It's six thirty and I doubt if this group will be here more than an hour. It's going to be a long night so we need to find some other places we can watch from. Once they leave we'll stand out like…"

"Looks like Jane has several last names." Bobbie showed the folder to Ross.

Ross quickly opened the other folder. "I can't believe that. My gosh, she has. Wainright, then Peterson and Wiggins, but no McGraw. She was raised at St. Mary's orphanage in Scotland. She did have some schooling. Left Scotland and came to England in the early nineteen seventies… *She hasn't any siblings, no sister*."

Ross stared off at the wall and then turned to Bobbie. "Do you remember the first time we..."

Bobbie quickly shut off the microphone. "You mean the day you hemmed and hawed about your feelings for me?" She chuckled. "Why is that so important?"

"I was so happy that day I mentally set aside the case as I wanted so much to share with Alex and Jane the news about us. When he came to my office, he could see I was bursting with delight. I told him I wanted them to meet you and he regretted they couldn't have dinner with us because Jane was helping her sister in Ireland. *She hasn't a sister!* Yet he said it without hesitation. It just flowed from his mouth."

Bobbie put her hand on his leg. "Remember those old men at Alex's house? You didn't want to believe them. Dennis, if their story is true, then Jane's been missing nine years now."

Bobbie looked at her watch. Another hour had passed. She turned back to the intercom to accept each of the Dream Team's checking in. "Kitty, it's seven o'clock. The others have checked in. Haven't heard from you or Hennessy."

"All's quiet. We're assuming the attorney is still with Alex, unless Alex has a secret way out. According to our maps, there's only one entrance to Alex's place and this fast food place is sitting kitty corner to it. I figure we'll have to move with the bikers when they leave. Looks like there's a MacDonald's three or four blocks further east of where we are now. We can hole up there for the rest of the evening."

Bobbie opened her folder again to catch up with Dennis. "Did you see the arrest record? She was arrested for soliciting and shop lifting. My gosh, look who was the arresting officer Alex McGraw."

"What's the date on that?" He flipped to the last page. "Nineteen seventy four, my first year at the Yard." Ross sat on the edge of the desk staring down at the folder. *Lizzy and I were already married five years. That was the year she had another miscarriage. Alex must have been living with Jane. They never married. This doesn't make sense. I can't believe she was part of his...*

"Dennis!" Bobbie shook his arm. "My God, where were you?"

"I'm sorry. I got caught up remembering twenty years ago." He waved the folder at her. "You realize this could mean Jane was nothing more than an accomplice." *No, that's impossible. She was shy when Lizzy and I first met her. Then she blossomed into the sister Lizzy never had. Lizzy didn't make friends very easily. This had to be genuine.* "Bobbie, how long will you be here?"

Ross looked at his watch, "It's after seven. Are you hungry?"

Bobbie half smiled. "I'm here...maybe for the night. I brought a sandwich. Kitty will let me know when I can leave." She motioned to a cot in the corner. "I can stretch out if I need to."

Ross grinned. "It's been a day for me. Unless you want company..."

They suddenly heard the intercom. "Check the street, Boss. I'm at the corner of the parking lot and the side street. A taxi is going past. See it? Can't see in it. I'm kneeling down to tie my boot. It's making a right turn and will go past you. Any bets? Yep. The cab turned down McGraw's street. Have an idea. Be back in a few."

Ross quickly took a chair next to Bobbie at the desk listening.

Kitty, carrying a coffee back to her bike, shook her head. "Damn,

I hate it when they just take off without clearing it with me."

Bobbie pushed the button. "What happened? Are you okay?"

"Yeah. I'm on the other side of the parking lot and Hennessy is very close to the main road. Without asking, she had an idea how to get a better view. Some girl jumped on the back of her bike and they took off."

"Boss, a man got out of the cab carrying a suitcase. My friend lives just down the street from the path. I dropped her off and now I'm parking my bike. I've turned on the record function, so I can go in her house and not look obvious. Soon as my friend gets her stuff, we'll be back."

"You haven't dropped your cover? YOU can't put that girl in harm's way. Hennessy! You've got fifteen minutes to get back here." *Oh Lord, this one has a mind of her own.*

Soon Kitty was able to see on her screen what Hennessy was recording from her bike camera. "Bobbie, that cab number is 113324728. I've a list of cab companies hanging on the wall above the file cabinet. I think the first three digits identify the company. You'd think there's only one company since they all look the same. Maybe you can find out where this man was picked up and maybe a name."

Bobbie pressed the button, "I'll get right on it."

"Dennis, will you man the intercom, while I deal with this?"

While the two inspectors talked about the stake out, Bobbie called the cab company. She hung up a good twenty minutes later frowning. "Well, we do have some news. The man in question is Henry Bartholomew Peckham. Seems he's one of McGraw's attorneys. I'm sure there's a reason but the cab picked him up at Heathrow and delivered him to McGraw's house."

Ross pulled a face. "Okay, what's the rest of it? I get the look."

Bobbie grinned, as she pressed the button. "It seems Mr. Peckham was on a return flight from Johannesburg, South Africa."

Ross gawked as he addressed the microphone. "The obvious is that Edward Edse is involved somehow with this new development."

Kitty jumped in on his comment. "That's a given. The bikers are beginning to break up now. Hennessy has about two minutes to get back here before…saved by the bell, here she…, they come. I'll get back to you. We've got our hands full now. Oh, Bobbie, could you find out which teams can be called off their details? I'm thinking we'll need a full crew now to handle this case."

Ross sarcastically barked at the intercom. "What case? Before I left the Chief's office, he warned me about hard facts and double jeopardy. Well, the hard fact is Alex is home having company from South Africa. Since when is having company a crime?"

Bobbie shoved his hand off the button and looked sharply at him. "Dennis, stop this now! Get hold of yourself. You know as well as we do that something is being organized. This time we will be patient, we are prepared and we will get the hard facts we need to put that bastard away forever."

Startled by Bobbie's use of profanity, Dennis rose. Bobbie put her hand on his arm. "Sometimes, you have to use words to awaken someone you care about. You're exhausted. I bet you haven't slept since..." She smiled, then looked to see if the intercom was on. "...since we were together."

He turned to leave. *She's right. I can't go on like this or I will lose her.* She stopped him. "Get something to eat and then come back. You could stretch out on the cot until I'm done. Would that work?"

He kissed her. "Thanks, you're an angel."

While she waited for the teams to check in, Bobbie got out several maps showing the surrounding areas. *There's something wrong about all of this. Why...*

Just as she was putting the map back in the file, her eye stopped abruptly at a file titled Trains and Bus routes. She pressed the intercom. "Kitty, can you talk?"

She could tell Kitty and Hennessy were on the move; there was a lot of motor noise in the background. "The rally bikers have left and we couldn't stay at that place. Too conspicuous. Give me a minute and I'll call you back. I can hear you but we're just arriving at our next check point."

During the next ten minutes, Bobbie chewed her sandwich quickly while studying the maps she had spread out on the Inspector's desk.

"I can talk now. Have been to the loo while Hennessy watched Alex's street. What's your concern?"

Bobbie gulped her last bite taking a sip of tea, pushing the intercom button down with her napkin. "I don't know if this will make any sense to you, but I think Alex wants us to know what he's doing."

"You're right…it doesn't make sense. What does Dennis think?"

Bobbie had just finished explaining her little episode with Dennis when he returned looking a little better. *It's amazing what a hug and a few kisses can do.* "Hi, have a seat. Hmm, looks like you brought dessert."

Dennis smiled and kissed her gently.

"I think I heard that. Now that Dennis is back, tell us both why you think Alex wants us to know what he doing."

Dennis frowned and stared at Bobbie. "How'd you come up with that?"

"Kitty, I have two maps out on your desk. One is a local street map and the other is a map of bus routes to London and to Heathrow from Woking. My question to you both is, which is traceable, a bus or a cab? The obvious answer being the cab."

She showed Dennis the easy routes one could take to Alex's place via both means of transportation. He sat on the edge of the desk and responded almost simultaneously with Kitty. "You're right…but…Why?"

"Okay, then, are we making a mistake having the Dream Team risk being recognized or should we have an inspector out there to play into Alex's hand?"

Dennis pushed the intercom button. "Kitty, I think Bobbie may have something here. You still have daylight. Can you and Hennessy leave now? According to the map you can get on the M25 in less than a mile from where you are. In the meantime, I'll assign an inspector for the area. Can't hurt. We'll let Alex think he's being watched."

They heard Kitty call to Hennessey. "We're going back to London…I'll explain on the way."

"Bobbie, we'll be on our way and see you both in the morning at my office. Eight o'clock sharp."

Dennis shut off the intercom and looked at Bobbie. "I hope you're right. I must admit, the obvious sure got covered up. What should we do now?"

Bobbie smiled and handed him the phone. "While I clean up here, you're going to call and ask for a surveillance of Alex's place, and then I'm taking you home to my place."

Chapter 6

Alex McGraw's shack in the woods at Woking

Alex and his attorney, Michael Doone, sat on tree stumps in his back yard, having a beer. The associate attorney had arrived in the last hour and they were waiting for him to join them.

The porch screen door screeched as it opened and a somewhat weary-eyed tall lanky man stood looking at them. Alex grinned. "Henry! Grab a beer out of the refrig and…" He looked over at Michael, who was showing an empty. "Correction, grab three and come out here for our board meeting."

Handing the beers out, Henry chuckled. "Mike, we should have sent a crew out here to make this place livable." He handed a beer to Alex. "Sorry about this mess. We had no idea…"

Alex pulled the tab on the beer can. "Not to worry, I don't intend staying here. There aren't that many cob webs thanks to the bomb squad." He smirked. "You see, I had enough explosives around this place inside and out to blow up the entire neighborhood. I'm sure they've been here several times looking for clues. My guess is they were out recently to bug the place. That's if they had time. My release must have floored a few at the Yard." Alex chuckled and gently rubbed his chin. "I can certainly vouch for one."

Mike shook his head. "I don't see how they could. I got the judge's ruling late last night."

Alex raised his beer to Michael. "Trust me. The Yard is very thorough. Besides, they could have bugged the place long ago for other reasons. They could suspect I had more than Charlie and Peter working for me. Maybe they thought you're involved, or maybe they thought--" squinting and biting his lip, Alex looked toward the creek, *"Jane* would come back.*"*

Henry blurted without thinking. "Uncle Charlie said you're a different sort of..." He saw a very stern look coming from Alex and sat down, *man with no sense of humor.*

Alex took a long drink. "Your Uncle Charlie was my best friend." He saluted both of the young men with his beer can. "And that is the only reason you both are here."

He scuffed the ground with his shoe. "Did you know Charlie and I met in Korea?" He snapped his fingers. "Just like that, our psyches clicked. I could trust him with my life, and many times it was just that on some of the jobs we did together. Charlie was a genius."

Henry watched Michael roll his eyes listening to Alex reminisce. Both quickly became attentive as Alex sternly concluded. "So if you're anything like him, we'll get along fine and I'll make you both rich. Henry, your eyes give you away, but you're right. I have no sense of humor."

Henry flushed.

Alex cleared his throat. "Charlie spoiled me. He had every conceivable detection device known to man to handle anything we needed to do. Really miss him. He never missed a beat. So, not to take any chances, we'll discuss the problem at hand out here."

Michael smiled boldly. "Alex, I really don't think you need to worry. We both understand and we're ready and able to handle this problem."

Alex choked on his swallow. "Oh, and just what do you think my problem is?" *You little shit bag...*

Michael and Henry sat up very straight frowning at one another.

Henry swallowed hard. "Of course it's to find Jane before anyone else does."

Alex glared at them shaking one good fist. "Do you really think you have the skills to track down that bitch who took all my money and has been able to hide from me for three years now? That's if you ever leave that fancy office with its plush decor. Are you prepared to make her talk when you find her? Or were you thinking she'd hand over my money after a cup of tea and scones?"

Alex stood and pointed his beer at Henry and Michael. "Yeah, you two look like you know all about being persuasive... That's a great word..." He put his foot on a stump and leaned his prosthetic on his knee. "I remember a time Charlie and I were working a drug case together. The Yard had asked the help of Interpol because they suspected a charter service that had taken over an abandoned air field outside of Windsor might be either making cocaine and shipping it or just shipping it across the borders. After we did our preliminary work finding out the drugs were being made there, Charlie had the idea we could make some money on the side if we made contact first with the seller."

Alex stood back laughing. He wheeled around to look at Henry and Michael. "Would you believe this asshole wouldn't agree to a sixty forty percent agreement with us? We thought letting him know when a raid was coming was worth sixty percent of his take."

Henry cringed. "Sixty percent is quite a lot, Alex. I mean that guy was making the stuff."

Alex pointed his bottle at him. "Yes, but if a raid puts him in jail and busts up the operation...Anyway, this is when we decided to persuade him to see it our way. Well, we didn't have much time to get this guy to agree. We still had to set up a raid. When we pointed this out to him, he laughed and told us to get lost. Leave it to my partner. Charlie had an idea."

Alex started to laugh.

Henry leaned forward. "What was the idea?"

Alex bit his lip and frowned. "Are you sure you want to know?"

The look he got from Alex, Henry hesitated. *How bad can it be? They roughed him up. So big deal...* "Yeah, I'm sure."

Alex opened another can of beer. "The guy agreed to our terms alright...It was funny. Charlie brought in a contraption he'd rigged up and put it on the guy's head and shoulders. Mind you his arms and legs were tied to a post. The good part was when he clamped this fool's mouth wide open. It's hard to describe. Can you picture this thing holding your mouth open?" Alex squinted... "Then he showed this dude a bag of squirming live stuff like a garden snake, baby mice, worms, spiders, and..."

Henry jumped up. “We get the picture!” He bent over touching his knees. *I think I’m going to be sick.* He gagged a bit and then straightened looking at Michael and back to Alex, breathing hard.

“Okay, good, you know what persuasion means… Then you’re prepared to kill anyone who gets in your way?” He drew out a gun. “Because, it wouldn’t bother me one stitch to kill either one of you right now.”

He tilted his head and glared as he holstered his gun. “So… Michael, Henry…old cliché, put your money where your mouth is. Want to change your mind? Think sitting behind a big desk rattling papers around is going to handle my problem? Here’s my point, gentlemen. Make sure you mean every word you say because I take every word I hear very seriously.”

Alex threw his can up into the air, drawing his gun from his left side he rapidly shot at the can making it dance in the air until it fell to the ground. *Not bad considering I used to be right handed.* He grinned at them and held out the gun. “Would you like to try? Or better yet, how about another beer?”

Henry’s eyes bolted toward Michael. He jumped up. “Sure! Beers all around. I’ll get them.” His tall lanky legs almost leaped to the porch in one step. *Holy fuck, Uncle Charlie loved this guy? He’s off the charts. What have I agreed to? What kind of work did these two do?*

Alex chuckled, holstering the gun as Henry handed him a bottle of lager beer. “No more cans?”

Henry shook his head as he handed a bottle to his partner.

Alex wiped his mouth. “Well then, I guess we can get down to business. Correct me if I’m wrong, Henry. You did meet with Edward Edse? You’ve brought me a package from him?” He looked at Henry with searching eyes to make sure he was listening and raised his eyebrows. “You did follow that?”

Henry responded quickly. “Yes sir, the package is in my suitcase.”

He looked at Michael. “What have you to report?”

Michael put his beer down and pulled a small note book out of his shirt pocket. “I got two tickets for you and Henry for Johannesburg. It’s an eight o’clock morning flight out of Heathrow on July 12th. As you ordered, I've had the prosthesis added to your passport information."

Turning to a new page in his book, he tore it out and handed it to Alex. "Those are the mental institutions where you asked me to show your wife's picture, but there's no record of a Jane McGraw. However, you said she had been married before, and I did find a place called Arnold Lodge in Leicester that had a Jane Wainright admitted in 1983 and released in 1986."

Alex took a swig of beer. "That place, I know. I put her there after Ross's wife unfortunately had to die. All she did was cry over Lizzy's death. When the neighbors started asking questions, I knew I had to do something."

Unfortunately had to die, echoed in Michael's mind as he handed the paper slowly to Alex. *Don't even go there. Keep talking.* "I'm still working on it, but that's all I have right now. Perhaps when you get back from Johannesburg, I'll have more."

Alex stared at him rubbing his chin. "Did you ever meet Henry's Uncle Charlie?"

The fixed glare in Alex's eyes made Michael feel uncomfortable. *We have to remain calm. Don't say anything to set him off.* "Yes. I did. He came to the office soon after Henry and I started the firm. I must admit he made quite an impression. He asked a lot of questions. I was surprised when he asked to see the entire office."

"You didn't stop him from looking around, did you?"

Michael shook his head recalling the incident. "No. You knew immediately he was a no nonsense person."

Alex stared at them. "No nonsense is a good description for him. Let me add to that, you never, ever heard him say *Perhaps*, or *Maybe* I would get something from him. We dealt only in the completed action. Does that make sense, or should I clarify some more?"

Michael cleared his throat. "I understand completely." *My God this isn't a good situation.*

Henry frowned. "We never saw him after that one time. Yet when he'd stop by to see my mum, I got the feeling he knew how well I was doing. I just figured she told him."

Alex chuckled. "Knowing him as well as I did, I don't need to bet. I know every phone in your office is bugged as well as the office walls. You don't think you got so popular over night because of your good looks and flashy law degrees? Charlie not only directed clients to you but laundered a lot of our money through your dealings for our benefit. He set you up in style."

Michael dropped his head in his hands. "Then according to you and Charlie, we've been working for you all along."

Alex laughed. "Yeah, I guess you have. You wouldn't have known had Charlie not been murdered by Robert Braun's men. Now, since Charlie is gone, I have to reorganize the business."

"So what's it going to be gentlemen, business as usual or do you want to leave and call it quits."

Henry nudged Michael who looked like he had just been hung. "Of course we want to continue with the arrangement, don't we, Michael?"

Michael had his eyes shut. "Yes, we do." *I had no idea. We're dead and it's only going to get worse. This man is insane and we can't do anything about it.* "I think I've had too much to drink in this sun." Michael got up quickly and threw up by a bush.

Henry knew it wasn't the beer. "Alex, I think…I mean know where Uncle Charlie kept all of his stuff."

Alex, amused by Michael's sudden terror, turned to listen. *So far I can't imagine what Charlie saw in this kid, but I'll extend the rope a bit more.* "Where could that be?"

"I just remembered. Every time Uncle Charlie had to take a long trip, he'd come over and give mum an envelope. She would never open it, but told him she'd keep it for him. Once I was in the room with them when he gave her the envelope. After he left, she put it in her desk drawer. I'm assuming that's where it is now."

"Henry, Charlie's been dead a year now. That's one big fuckin' assumption."

Henry boldly spoke back to Alex. "No it isn't. I know her! Charlie meant the world to her. She hasn't touched anything in the bedroom he used when he stayed with us. Fact is, no one is allowed in his room. She even lied to the Scotland Yard inspectors when they came to ask questions about him."

Alex almost smiled. *Maybe I should be asking his mom to work with me.* "What sort of questions?"

"They told her that Interpol had us listed as his next of kin. She acted like he was a stranger and we had very little contact with him. Then she asked me to vouch for it. I was so stunned I just nodded my head."

Alex grinned at Michael sitting on the ground, leaning against the tree stump, white as a sheet. "Well, Michael, do you think we should ask Henry's mum to join our new organization or…perhaps take your place?"

Hearing the word *Perhaps,* Michael knew Alex was making his point. To stir the pot more, Alex turned enough to show the butt of his gun. Michael began to sweat. "Sure. I'd ask her to join up with us. I've met her a few times. She's nice looking and definitely could handle herself. She's not afraid to get in your face. I will say that for her."

Looking at the dust covered screening on the porch, filthy windows and missing shingles on the roof, he smirked, "You may want to reconsider bringing Mrs. Peckham here. She's a neat freak."

Henry chuckled. "Yep she is that. If you want to ask her out here, then I better start cleaning up." His eyes glowed with enthusiasm. "She's a firm believer in judging a book by its cover."

Alex frowned. *I like her already.* "What's her name?"

Michael grinned. "Would you believe, Zilpha."

Alex raised his brow. "Zilpha Peckham? *That's one to envision. Though Charlie was a fairly good looking man and Henry isn't too bad.* He shrugged his shoulders. "Sure, give her a call and see if she can come out tomorrow night. If she agrees, then start cleaning. Oh… ask her to bring Charlie's envelope."

Shortly Henry reappeared on the porch, "She said to apologize for not being able to make it, has another appointment." Henry jumped to the ground. "I know it doesn't help now, but she did say to give our address, and you're welcome to stop to see Charlie's things after your trip to Africa."

Before Henry had finished his remark, all in one motion Alex jumped up, tossed his gun to Michael, then launched his bottle straight up into the air as hard as he could. He shouted at him. "Shoot it!"

Michael's heart pounded as he almost dropped the gun before he began firing away. The third bullet hit the target. *I should have aimed lower. Who would believe me? He's already got Henry and now Henry's mother in this. I think Henry would shoot me as well. I have no choice.* Ashen and sweating, Michael reeled to face Alex. Hand shaking, he gave the gun to Alex. "I hope that amused you." He walked slowly to the porch steps and turned around. "Let me remind you, Alex, those flashy degrees found the loop holes in your case that got you out of prison."

Alex laughed. "You're a bit delusional. Had it not been for the Americans, I'd still be in jail."

Henry shook his head. "You're way wrong on this. Edse's team wouldn't work with us after the exclusion of the American files. They as much as told us to take a hike. That's when the trials became separate. We found an exception to the law dealing with time limits on admissible evidence. It was pretty cool. Michael found it. It had to do with your partner being the lead Inspector and lending credibility to the American evidence. Thus, anything Ross could produce was associated with the American's case and…became inadmissible."

Alex frowned. "Jane had nothing to do with the Brauns. "

Henry's eyes enlarged. He eagerly explained. "Exactly, but Ross had it in his report you were responsible for her disappearance. Therefore, because Ross's name was on the American list of inadmissible evidence, anything remotely associated with Ross the American guidelines classified as inadmissible. Thus the accusation that you impersonated an officer wasn't admissible nor was being charged with Jane's disappearance. The prosecution could not produce any evidence unrelated to Ross's investigation. That's what reduced your sentence to time spent…"

Alex smirked. *I wonder if Ross knows all this. . . He would die a thousand times to think he's responsible for my release.* "So what you're saying is that if and when I do find Jane, I could kill her and not be tried a second time. That would be Double Jeopardy."

Henry hesitated. "Not exactly, a body was never found. With additional evidence, you could be tried for murder… Alex, I know you and Dr. Edse are friends, but I never went to any prison to talk with him. I met him at his home, which was very plush at that."

Alex stared at Henry silently. *That's not the story I heard from Edse's father.*

Henry met Michael at the porch door. Henry held the door open as Michael came out holding his suit coat and brief case.

Alex got up. "Where are you going?"

Michael slung his jacket on his back. "I need to show you that a flashy degree is just as important as being able to handle a gun. Finding your wife is your main concern. Right? I better get started." He was still pouring with sweat. "I'll pick you up Thursday at six in the morning to take you both to the airport."

Alex stepped back. T*hese two have got balls, once you shake them up. So far they don't know what I've got planned. I'll decide after this trip if they will fit in.* "Okay. That's fair. I'll walk you to your car."

They heard a vacuum cleaner as they walked past the house. Alex hesitated at the window. "It must run in the family." He chuckled. "His mother isn't coming and he's still cleaning. Charlie was a neat freak too. He never talked about his past much. He told me once his father was a drunk and I assumed it was bad enough that Charlie and his sister ran away. There was considerable difference in their ages so he essentially raised her."

They reached Michael's car at the end of the path. Alex noticed a car parked down the street. He smiled. *Like clockwork, Ross thinks I'm going to lead him to Jane. Won't he be surprised to find out he's going to do all the leading.* Alex opened the car door for Michael. "I hope I haven't made a mistake about you guys. You're not at all like Charlie. To be honest, I can't imagine what he saw in you two. I guess we'll just have to see!"

Michael got in his Mercedes and pressed the window button. "Alex, you know what sickens me is that Charlie isn't around to tell you that Henry and I have earned every penny we've made in our law firm. So, Charlie brought us clients. Their cases still had to be won."

Michael stared at Alex. "And, they were, every one of them, including yours. You're one of our clients, and we will do whatever needs to be done to satisfy you. But, let me make this very clear, you… do not own us." He turned the key and put the car in reverse. "Be ready at six."

Alex turned to walk back to the house. He rubbed his hands in satisfaction. *Charlie made the right choice. I like him. He stood up to me.*

As he walked back to the house, a car horn interrupted his thoughts. He recognized the driver and turned back. It was Peter's brother Neil. *Peter and Charlie were in that massacre at the Braun estate.* Alex waved. *I miss those guys. Such teamwork. What one missed the other thought of.*

"How's Interpol treating you?"

Neil got out and gave Alex a handshake and hug. "It's not the same without my big brother." He squinted to hold back his emotion. "I miss my daily training drills, being yelled at for the screw ups. It's no fun anymore. I don't know if I can stay much longer."

Alex grabbed his shoulders. "Do me a favor and don't quit yet…I need your help."

Neil laughed. "What's with the card you sent? 'Harvesting hay at the farm. Come when you can'?"

"Sorry, old habits don't go away. Charlie and I had our own kind of language. Everything we did had a code. I wasn't sure if you'd understand my message. At least you had a laugh."

"You're right about that. It brought back some memories. Anyway, I'm here to help. By the way, you know you've got someone watching you."

Alex scoffed. "I'd be more surprised if they weren't there. After Thursday, with your help, I won't have to worry."

As they neared the house a window shade suddenly shot up. Neil's arm flinched to his gun. Alex touched his arm. "It's okay. One of my attorneys is here." He chuckled. "He's cleaning. Actually, you just might know him. He's Charlie's…"

At that point, Henry peeked out the window, "I thought I heard voices and wondered if Mike changed his mind." He recognized Neil and smiled from ear to ear. "I know you!" Like a leaping gazelle he was out of the window giving Neil a bear hug. "Oh, my gosh, it's been forever since I last saw you."

Neil beamed at his friend. "I think so. It's already over a year since we buried your uncle and my brother."

Alex led them to the back yard. "I'm sorry I wasn't there for you. I was in the prison hospital recovering from losing my arm. It took a while for me to remember what happened. The doctor told me I suffered from a form of post-traumatic stress being attacked by the dog. Even after a year I still have flash backs. Being attacked by an animal is far worse than by a human. They're unrelenting for the kill. The power that dog had was more than my body could resist. I passed out from the trauma. The doctor said there was little left of the arm to cut off. When they told me that Charlie and Peter had been killed…"

Neil frowned and bit his lip. "You mean murdered! Believe me, there's a payback on my list for those people."

Alex sneered. "The warden wouldn't let me attend the funerals as they weren't my blood relatives. That really pissed me off. So, when you're ready, count me in. I, too, have a score to settle not only for Charlie and Pete but with that dog."

Neil put his arm on Alex's shoulder. "We heard what happened to you. By comparison, you went through a horrific experience. At least Charlie and Pete didn't suffer."

Henry scurried to the porch and brought out a cooler full of beer cans and bottles. "I want to help too. Let's drink to it."

Wiping his mouth, Alex grinned, "How'd you two become such good friends? You're about as different as night and day."

Neil chuckled. "Don't they say opposites attract?"

Henry swallowed hard. "Uncle Pete came over to the house a lot to work with Uncle Charlie on projects for Interpol."

Neil explained. "Since Pete was fifteen years older, he usually had to babysit me while mom and dad worked. They had night jobs…Charlie and Pete never let either of us watch them work, so High Pockets and I played together and became the best of friends. Because of you, Alex, I've hardly seen him this year."

Alex frowned. "How is it my fault?"

Pointing his bottle of beer at Alex, Neil jumped onto a tree stump to equal Henry's height, and put his arm around his best friend's shoulder. "I suppose you should thank Mrs. Peckham, because she taught this guy that dedication and perfection win the prize." Neil rubbed Henry's head and jumped down. "While he worked on your case, he hardly ever went home. You couldn't talk to him about anything as his mind was locked into law books, case studies… He never knew I even called. So yes, it is your fault. H.P. and I have to catch up now."

Alex smiled at them. “There’s a nickname. Truth be known, those projects Pete and Charlie worked on weren’t for Interpol. They were solving major problems for me. I would come up with the damnedest ideas and they would bring them to life. A day doesn’t go by that I don’t think of them.”

While Alex left them to order some pizzas to be delivered, the two young men recapped their activities of the past year, laughing and carrying on.

By the time the food was delivered, Alex had a fire going in the middle of the surrounding tree stumps. He paid the man. “On your way back, would you give this smaller pizza to the guy sitting in the black sedan at the corner of the street?”

Alex reached into the cooler. “Give him this beer too. Tell him we won’t squeal. Here are a couple pound notes more for the delivery.”

Neil had a mouthful. “Well, I know you didn’t ask me out here for this reunion. So what’s the deal?”

Alex wiped his mouth with his shirt sleeve. “You’re right about that. I do have a deal for you.” He looked at Henry and paused.

Henry frowned. “Alex, it’s called attorney client privilege. I can’t repeat anything I hear you say in a court of law or otherwise. It’s the law. Besides, I will be travelling with you and should be apprised of what’s going on.”

Henry stood straight and tall and continued with a concentrated stare at them rubbing his chin. “There is, however, one exception to that rule and that is if you should admit to or confess to a…”

Neil shrugged his shoulders at Alex mumbling. “Always the attorney.” He stood on a tree stump next to his friend and chuckled putting his arm around him. “HP! Cool it. We get it.”

Alex grinned. *This works out perfectly. Charlie and Pete are watching over me.* “ No, let him finish.”

Henry proudly smiled at his chum. Pointing his finger at Alex he began to pace. “There isn’t much more to that. It is an American law that is becoming more accepted internationally, except in dictatorships.”

Neil cleared his throat and motioned to speed it up.

Flushed, Henry stopped his pacing. “The rest of it is, we would lose the privilege if you should divulge to me your intent to commit a crime or fraud. But, since you're going to South Africa to get a new face…"

"Actually, that's only half true. Henry, go in and bring me the box that Edse gave you."

Alex soon had the box opened and pulled out two facial masks. "I'm sure by tomorrow Ross will know that Henry and I will be flying to Johannesburg. That said, I believe we will be followed. That is exactly what I want…" Standing up, Alex held a mask under his chin looking just like himself. "Anyone you know?"

Alex grinned at their amazement. "When you and Michael told me there was a good chance I would be getting out of prison and soon, I knew the only way I could find Jane and my money was to disappear. That's why I sent you to Edse with that letter. Neil, with your Interpol badge, you can go almost anywhere. Henry will give you the gate number we take off from. I can almost feel the surge of adrenalin Ross will be feeling when he finds out about this trip and won't want to believe it. You can bet he will be there to watch me leave."

The crackling of the fire was all that could be heard for the longest time. Henry looked at Neil and frowned. "You and Alex are the same build. Why do you want Neil to pose as you?"

Neil squirmed a bit staring at Alex. "Jesus, Alex, you could have started out with something easy. How in the fuck are we going to make the switch?"

Alex put his hand up. "Neil, just relax. Tomorrow go over to Heathrow and check this out. I'm sure there's a men's room adjacent to the gate. My passport says I have the prosthesis. Ross will follow me to the gate. Just as they show the boarding light, I'll come into the men's room and we'll switch. You go out in my place. Wear exactly what you have on now. I'll wear the same black suit. Here's my old passport, no prosthesis, who will know. I will have gone through the security. You won't be checked. You'll stay in South Africa until I let you know I've done what I need to do."

Neil shook his head. "Aren't you going to need our help finding your wife?"

Alex sneered. "That bitch isn't my wife. I took her off the streets and trained her to be my decoy. After meeting Dennis and Lizzy Ross, she got funny. Thought she could have the same kind of life and told me she wanted us to get married and have kids...Well that was the last straw...I thought Lizzy dying would straighten her out, but instead she got worse. So I put her in a mental hospital. I messed her up a bit. She's got a scar now down her left cheek. At that time my badge covered me and the hospital staff believed my story that I saved her from committing suicide."

Alex threw the pizza box on the fire.

Henry opened another beer. "According to Ross's statement, she was missing for eight years. So that's three off. What happened then?"

Alex shook his head and motioned to Henry. "Toss me one of those... I split the property and sold off the house up front for more privacy. I didn't want anyone snooping down here so I put a fence around most of it. Then Jane came home for three years. It wasn't the same. For some reason, I felt she was playing along. I tried to figure it out, and then realized she was smarter than I thought. In actual fact, she was playing me. I had made a concrete safe in the ground down by the creek. I kept the money I made from my side line work and a list of my jobs in that safe. I hadn't told her about it, but obviously she must have followed me and watched. Little over two years ago, I went to put my deposit in and found the lock had been cut off and the safe was empty. There was a note...This is for Lizzy! You killed the only real person in my life. Now, it's your turn to pay!"

Henry grimaced. "So if Neil poses as you, who are you going to be?"

"Good question." Alex looked at the mask and opened the envelope. "Looks like Dr. Edse found a stiff at the morgue making me Mr. James Gibbons who lives in West Sussex country. I have a passport." He chuckled holding up some keys. "I even have a house in Shoreham-by-Sea. I think it's one of Edse's properties." *I bet Edse's worried I found out how his attorneys tried to screw me at the trial. Finding out my attorneys were just as good as his, he's trying to make life a bit easier. His sincerity sucks.*

Alex leaned toward the fire to check his watch. "It's getting late guys. I'm turning in. You can stay here or there's a motel about two blocks away if you want more comfort."

Henry and Neil smiled nodding to each other. Neil grabbed a six pack out of the cooler. “We can do that…What time do you want us back?”

The two men grabbed their stuff and took off. “We’ll bring breakfast around nine.”

Alex frowned at their enthusiasm, shook his head and let the squeaky screen door close. Already half way to the car, they heard Alex yell, “No later than that! You have a lot to learn. ”

Chapter 7

July 9, 1995 Inspector Carroll's office

Ross and Bobbie knocked on the door and heard "*Enter.*" They chuckled as they went in.

Ross put the coffee, tea and scones on the desk. "Have a feeling you've had some time in the service."

Inspector Carroll leaned back in her chair and swiveled. "Yes, sir, my family tree shows ten generations in the Navy and I followed suit."

Responding to another knock at the door, her commanding voice made Ross jump. Standing, she smiled at Bobbie laughing at Ross. The inspector towered over the courier as he handed her an envelope. Her posture and presence commanded respect. The young man backed up a bit before turning to leave her office.

"Such a treat, fresh scones. And still warm." She started to hand the envelope to Ross who already had a mouth full of scone. With jaw bulging, he talked out of the side of his mouth. "Can you read it, my fingers are sticky."

She laughed as she opened it... Her forehead wrinkled. "That's not your entire problem... swallow...I don't want you choking."

As he swallowed hard and drank some tea, she handed the paper to Bobbie. "Looks like tomorrow, your buddy is leaving for Johannesburg with his attorney. The return date as you can see is blank."

Ross paced a bit with his hands in his pockets. "Obviously he's up to something. Still, he's within his rights. He's not on probation so there are no restrictions on his whereabouts."

Bobbie poured more tea. "I still think he wants us to follow him. Our only ace is that he doesn't know about your girls."

"Bobbie, did you ask which teams are available now?"

Bobbie handed Kitty the day's report. "By the weekend they all are done with their assignments."

Carroll sat on the edge of her desk scanning the paper. "I think we should send a team tomorrow and then rotate each week for as long as we need to. The other teams will spend time looking for Jane here. At least Alex can't hurt her if he's away."

Ross pursed his lips. "That's true. Maybe he's got someone looking for her. He's so vindictive I doubt he'd let someone else do his dirty work for him. Still, having him away would give us more freedom to look for her."

Bobbie handed Carroll her tea refill. "You've a hard decision to make. Which team should go."

Carroll raised her brow and bit her lip. "Because of the danger factor, I can't really order who goes. This has to be their choice." She looked at the clock on the wall. "They should be arriving in another ten minutes."

Bobbie turned to Ross. "Have you had a report from your inspector watching Alex's property?"

He rolled his eyes. "Yeah, seems Alex treated him to a pizza and beer. The attorney's car left and another car arrived soon after. He wasn't able to make out the face. The man was fairly young and in pretty good shape."

Ross opened the door. "I better get out of here." *Not ready for a bunch of hens today.*

Carroll waved. "You're welcome to sit in on our meeting, Dennis."

He grabbed another scone, waved, and shut the door behind him.

Bobbie shook her head as the door closed. "This separation of the sexes still exists, doesn't it?"

Carroll stood as the members of her team walked in quietly and took seats. "Yes, unfortunately it does. So much so, I have a segment in their training on it. Most often the gender issue determines if women stay in the program. I'm surprised I've two women that are married and two with boyfriends."

Bobbie grinned. "Either you've trained your girls well enough that their partners are deathly afraid of them, or they've come to an understanding."

Carroll, dressed in a green watch plaid suit, took off the jacket and hung it on the back of her chair. A woman in her fifties, she wore her graying hair in a bun. Lifting her glasses on a chain around her neck, she put them on and motioned for Bobbie to take a seat.

She addressed the group. "Good morning, I want to get right to the point and will ask that you submit your reports for your last assignment in writing. First I want you to know that Bobbie Grantwood is at the moment a part of the team. She is acting as liaison between Chief O'Doul and me. The Yard would like us to investigate what could become a very dangerous situation. You recall our first assignment."

The six women chuckled. Inspector Grantwood raised her brow at the team's boss who also frowned at the amusement.

Theresa raised her hand. "They're laughing because of the nuns' outfits we had to wear."

Carroll smiled. "Yes, those outfits were a bit restricting. Though that case is closed, another element of the case has surfaced. The man convicted of kidnapping and torturing the Admiral, whom you saved, has been released on technicalities unimportant to us at this time. Inspector Ross believes this same man, Alex McGraw is resp…"

Carroll passed out pictures to each of the women, and then held up her copies… "responsible for the disappearance of his wife, Jane. On the back of his picture you'll find all the pertinent information about this case. This man is a killer for hire and could be responsible for at least a hundred murders. Pay particular attention to his skills and mind set. On the back of her picture you'll find what the department knows about her. Our task is not only to follow McGraw but also to find Jane and protect her."

Three of the women leaned forward whispering to one another and Linda Burr sat up and raised her hand. "Mum. Has she moved to South Africa?"

Carroll tightened her brow. "No, not that we know of…This is where it gets confusing because A: This whole case gets into classified information that we can't discuss. And B: Even if we could discuss it, it is so involved, we just don't have the time." She looked over at Bobbie for help.

Bobbie stood and spoke. "What can be said is that Jane posed as Alex's wife. After he was arrested for involvement in the Braun case, we found empty boxes in a cement vault on his property and she couldn't be found. Inspector Ross thinks there's a connection, explaining the urgency to find her before Alex does. Ross thinks she took more than money. Our investigation into the others involved with Alex indicated he had a gun for hire organization. Unfortunately no concrete records documenting this could be found. "

Theresa blurted out. "Then she's the only one who can fry his balls."

The women broke out in hilarious laughter.

Bobbie laughed shaking her head. "Yes, I guess you could say that…The Yard suspects McGraw is going to meet with one of his associates, a Doctor Edward Edse living in Johannesburg. You'll recall when you rescued the American Admiral, you found residue on the Admiral's face and hands. That and other evidence in that basement turned out to be the makings of a facial mask that this Doctor Edse made for Alex McGraw who impersonated that officer."

Inspector Carroll returned from her office holding a picture. "This is what Edward Edse looks like. I'll make copies before you leave."

Karen Cogar raised her hand. "Then, you think he's going to get another facial done to impersonate someone else to throw us off again?"

Bobbie nodded. "That's right, but this time, there will always be a prosthesis involved." *Thank goodness they haven't done arm transplants.* "So, following every move he makes is of the utmost importance. What is of more concern, he could be having facial reconstructive surgery and we'd be back to square one. You can surmise the importance of this task."

No more hands and the room got quiet.

Inspector Carroll held her hands behind her back staring at her teams. "As you know, I select only from those of you who choose to be on the case. I've filled you in on what's involved, so if you like we can take a break to discuss with your partners, or you can choose to leave and get other assignments."

No one moved or said anything. Kitty Carroll looked over the rim of her glasses at her group. "This could be life threatening." Still no one moved.

She glowed proudly at her team and then looked at Bobbie and almost whispered. "Now you know why I call them the Dream Team."

Carroll asked for ideas and suggestions. Linda Severance raised her hand. "Mum, since Bobbie is with us, that essentially gives another team if she works with you. Under the severity of the circumstance, I think we should have two teams follow McGraw to South Africa. When we found the Admiral, it was obvious the person who messed him up had to be psychotic."

Carroll saw several heads moving in agreement. Their boss looked down at Bobbie. "She does have a point. What do you think?"

Bobbie nodded. "As long as I don't have to man your control center."

Carroll grinned. "No, I can get one of the of Yard dispatchers to handle it."

"Okay, who wants to have the first free trip to Johannesburg, South Africa, following the target?"

She laughed, as all the hands went up, including Bobby's. She went to the blackboard behind her and pointed. "Write this down. Address and number for our Embassy in Johannesburg. You'll be staying at the Twelve Decades Art Hotel…"

Two heads looked up. Carroll put her pointer down. "Time and budget are factors. The Embassy made these arrangements. You will be met by one of their undercover people acting as a tour guide. We've sent them the pictures of McGraw, his attorney, Henry Peckham and Edward Edse. Your contact will already be watching Edse's house, which is located in the main part of the city and very near the business district."

Hennessy raised her hand. "Who or what are we posing as?"

"Anything but nuns!" Theresa shouted.

Carroll nodded. "Not this time. We thought two of you could be students from England attending the art exhibits and workshops that are part of the Art Convention. The other two would take part in the Metallurgy Institute Convention. The center for these activities is within walking distance of Edse's house. The rich people seem to live in and around the city and the poorer ones outside of the city. From the pictures, it's like a time zone effect – the cultural differences are amazing, going from the ultra-modern to the tribal wildlife in less than two kilometers."

Bobbie raised her forehead looking at the clock. "Kitty, the clock is getting away from us. You better decide who's going first."

Studying the roster, Kitty shoved it over to her friend. "Feel almost like we're playing chess. Do I send my most seasoned girls first or last? Out guessing a psychopath is quite a task. What do you think?"

Bobbie sat back holding the list in front of her. "Most seasoned… I wish I could go but Alex would spot me in a flash. Linda and Theresa work well together. Jo Burr and Hennessey aren't rookies anymore. Remember Jo is a nurse and could be useful."

Hearing her name, Jo Burr raised her hand. "I have an idea you might consider. I could apply to work at the hospital Edse works out of. If McGraw is going to have surgery, maybe I could get a job there."

Kitty dropped her head. "She does make sense. But we haven't time to organize."

Bobbie got up. "I'm going to check-in with the Chief. If anyone can push orders through, it will be O'Doul. Let's just assume Jo can go ahead and apply." She smiled, "After all we've got twenty four hours to get this done."

Carroll walked her to the door. "That's a great idea. I'll prepare Jo and document her credentials to work with Edse's needs."

Bobbie nodded. "The rest of us can begin canvassing the areas in this country starting back where Jane came from."

"Listen, I hope Dennis will understand he won't be seeing you much for the next …"

Bobbie put her hand on Carroll's shoulder. "Whatever it takes to find Jane alive and keep her safe…Later."

Chapter 8

Alex's shack in the woods. Thursday 6:00 am

Alex and Henry reached the end of the path at the street just as Michael arrived and pulled to a stop exactly at six am. Alex nodded as he opened the car door. "You are prompt." He looked down the street. *Hmm. No escort?*

They got in and Michael turned the light on in the car. "Neil called and met me at the office last night…"

He handed Alex three keys, a parking employee number and a page out of his notebook. "I need to go over this with you…He's drawn you a sketch of the men's room."

Michael held his pen light over the paper. "The airport bathroom has a locked storage room in the bathroom complex. A wall separates the storage room before you enter the men's room. There is surveillance in the bathroom but not in the short hallway."

Henry peered over the back seat. "What about a schedule for cleaning? Did he…"

Michael nodded. "I'm coming to that. Neil met up with the cleaning superintendent. He showed him his badge and asked about theft or lost items in the bathrooms. The boss told him the restrooms were cleaned after each take-off. All items found are put in the lost and found department. While they were talking, a security guard interrupted and told the boss that that particular men's room would be roped off in the morning for the eight o'clock flight, for only the passengers on this flight. Not to take any chances, Neil went back to the airport after he left my office. He had the schedule for the flights leaving from that gate. He said to tell you it's definitely doable. Knock on the door and he'll switch with you quickly. He'll have a cleaner's uniform in the push cart with your mask and whatever else he thinks you'll need. He checked and the light in the room doesn't show in the hallway. It will be tight but you should be able to change. As you can see, he has instructed that you wait there for at least a half hour after the flight takes off. He's left his car in the space marked on that ticket. You won't have to pay."

Alex grinned and leaned back. "Excellent."

Turning the key, Michael hesitated. "There's just one other thing. Where will you live while you're doing all this? Will you use Neil's car to go to the house in Shoreham? Neil said you could use his flat, but not for long. He's afraid people would ask questions."

Alex nodded. "Of course, I know I can't return to my house. Actually, I've left a few gifts for the Yard if they go back there." He grinned at his two partners. "On my way to Shoreham, I'm going to stop at Henry's to see if there's anything of Charlie's that would help me now. I'm quite sure the house Edse has will suit all my needs."

Before they got out of the car at the airport, Michael hesitated. "Alex, is there anything else? I don't think it's necessary for me to come in with you and Henry. You've got your passports…and I think it best you give me that paper back. I'm sure you've memorized Neil's notes. Wait, one other thing, how will I reach you? "

Henry leaned over the front seat. "Mom went through Charlie's stuff and found he forwarded all our calls coming in to a special number. He's got our phones rigged so line four is untraceable."

Michael frowned. *Son of a Bitch, what else isn't private.* "There's no number on that line. I never use it."

Henry laughed. "I don't either but all our calls coming in and going out use it."

Alex frowned and shook his head. "Not to worry, I've had your number ever since you started your practice. We better go."

Michael shut the trunk. Alex smiled and shook Michael's hand. "Good job. Both of you." He looked around and then turned his back. "There are surveillance cameras everywhere. Careful what you say now. Mike, there's an envelope under my seat in the car."

Alex grinned to the porter who offered to take his luggage. *I should ask him if he liked the pizza and beer.* "Henry, this is what is known as the elite express by Scotland Yard."

Henry pointed over the heads of passengers stumbling along with luggage. "Alex, there's the Johannesburg check-in."

Bobbie and Ross were at opposite ends of the security lines looking for Alex's arrival. She called from her two-way radio. "Dennis, it's like looking for a needle in haystack. I'm too short. I need a ladder to see way back."

"I've just spotted him. You can either work your way back by me or meet me at the gate."

"I'll go ahead. I want to make sure Kitty's girls have arrived and are set to go. Don't worry. I won't talk to any of them."

While they stood in line for the security check, Alex candidly surveyed the people on both sides of the walk-through detectors. *Interesting, I can't say I recognize all of the Yard agents. It's been a year, I'm sure they've brought in more recruits.*

Henry frowned. "I thought you never smiled. What's so wonderful?"

Alex gave a royal wave toward the walk-through he was about to enter. "Why, I would be deeply hurt if you weren't here to see me off!"

He extended his hand but Ross turned away to talk on his two way radio. "McGraw is through security. We'll escort him to the gate."

Alex turned to Henry. "Henry, are my rights being infringed upon?"

Ross glared at them. "No, we're making sure you have an uninterrupted departure."

They got to the gate for South African flights. Alex smiled again and nudged Ross. "I see you still have your girlfriend. Is she any better than Lizzy…or…Jane?" *Come on Ross be stupid and punch me so the world can see…* Alex laughed heartily seeing Bobbie stiffen at his remarks and walked toward her.

As she turned to confront Alex, Ross stepped in front of him. "I wouldn't go there if I were you." Fuming, he stared at Alex then blurted out. "That's if you still want to board this plane."

The eight o'clock boarding sign for the Johannesburg flight went on and the attendant announced for third class coach to come forward with their boarding passes. Almost a hundred shuffled to line up.

Alex saw the media standing idly behind his ex-partner and beamed. *Perfect timing.* "I'm a free man and you're threatening me! Why, that's police brutality. Isn't it?" He turned to the people who were already seated, raising his good arm. "Did anyone see this officer grab me?"

A lot of heads turned and many people left their seats hearing someone yell police brutality.

Two newspaper men saw a great story developing, grabbed their cameras, and quickly recorded the scene.

Facing Ross, Henry stepped in between them. "Inspector Ross, you need to step back. I'm Mr. McGraw's attorney. Here's my card. I will be filing a complaint with your superior."

Alex took hold of Henry's arm and whispered. "Let them take as many pictures as they want. This is great."

Henry turned his back to the camera's clicking. "Alex, I think you've made your point. Go sit down. Are you forgetting why you're here? How do you expect Neil to duplicate a black eye?"

"You strike when the iron's hot, my boy." Alex turned to face Ross. No one could see Alex wink at Ross, whose face was crimson. Ross made a step toward him when Alex leaned to put a kiss on Bobbie's backside.

Alex set him up again, calling out. "This officer is out to get me for no reason. I need protection."

Bobbie took a firm hold of Ross's arm and led him to the side of the gate to help cool the situation. With her back to the many passengers in the boarding gate area, she took his hand. "Dennis, he's not worth it. You know he's trying to get you out of his way! Getting fired over saving my *honor* isn't going to find or save Jane, is it?" She looked up at him with a loving smile. "Please don't take this in the wrong way, but I would appreciate the back up *after* I've had a chance to handle the situation, not before. You wouldn't have done that if I'd been a..."

Dennis glanced over her head to see his old partner watching him with a smug look on his face, and then looked back at Bobbie frowning. "I know, but..."

She squeezed his hand. "Dennis, there are no *buts,* I'm not a weakling. If that's what you want me to be, then you'll only push me away. I don't even think or care about gender." She looked out at the runway. "I just want to be my own person." *You won't let me be your equal.*

He squeezed her hand. "I understand."

The flight attendant announced the last rows in coach. As they watched some recognizable agents board, Bobbie nudged Ross and whispered. "Alex has spotted two of our agents and is pointing them out to his attorney."

Not wanting to turn around, Ross straightened and saw Alex's reflection in one of the big windows. Out of the corner of his eye, he saw the chosen four of the Dream Team go by and noted that Alex didn't bat an eye. Ross whispered. "Looks like Kitty's girls hooked up with one of the colleges going to the conference."

When the line dwindled to about fifteen people, Alex went to the counter. "Excuse me. I think my breakfast has gone through me. Do I have time to use the men's room?" He showed his ticket was for the business class.

She looked and nodded as she checked the showing of boarding passes going by.

He left his stuff with Henry and followed the yellow tape roping off the area.

Ross jerked a bit motioning to the agent by the door. The agent nodded as Alex walked by.

Alex hesitated. "Do your job, you want to come in and watch?"

The agent glared at him. "No one's in there. Just hurry up."

Alex knocked slightly on the closet door. As Alex exchanged places, he grabbed Neil's arm, whispering, "You've got a different tie on."

Neil's heart pounded as they switched. He grabbed Alex's tie off his neck and scooted to the urinal. Almost ten minutes later, the Yard agent came in. Neil was in front of the mirror adjusting his tie. Quickly he combed his hair with his left hand and smiled at the agent as he left. “Sorry, zipper trouble.” He raised his left hand and shrugged his shoulder. “Not left handed.”

Henry smiled, then frowned at Neil, handing him Alex’s stuff, he whispered. “How come you’re flushed? Did it go all right? It’s a perfect match. I wouldn’t …”

Neil looked at Ross and then whispered. “Tell you later. It’s me, now let’s go.”

They boarded and the attendant followed to shut the door.

Chapter 9

Heathrow Airport: Ten a.m.

Alex looked at his watch. It was already ten o'clock. *I should have worked harder at the therapy. I need to move more normally, but it's hard. The cleaning crew could show up anytime now.* He made some final adjustments and then opened the door gingerly. *No one's in here. Thank God for that.* He pushed the cart out and left it by the wall. *Maybe I won't need it. Can't see any of the yellow tape from here.* He peeked into the gate lobby. It was empty. *Until I get out of here, I better look the part.*

As he pushed his cart out of the men's room into the gate lobby, he came face to face with one of London's finest. Clearing his voice, "Good morning sir, hope you didn't miss your plane." He smiled and chuckled.

The bobby swung his baton. "Not on my pay. Just making my rounds." He stopped to watch some planes taxi slowly to the runway, and then he turned around. "Hey, Jake, were you here to watch the ex-Yard inspector get booted out?" The bobby frowned and walked over to Alex who was trying to look officially busy. "Jake!" He touched Alex's prosthesis with his stick. "Are you deaf man?"

Alex jumped. His first instinct would have been to either pull his gun or knife; instead he froze to listen. He saw his reflection in a shiny chromed mural on the wall for that brief few seconds. *Shit I've got a nametag on. I thought he was talking on his two-way. My name must be Jake. I've got gray hair. Look and act the part.*

The officer approached his cart. *My clothes are in the cart.* He turned slowly. "I'm sorry, I'm not hearing too good these days." He put his right hand in his pocket to hide his inability for a lot of motion and leaned back on his cart. "Did you ask me something?"

The bobby stared at him and looked around the lobby. He twirled his wand and pointed. "Yeah, there was a lot of commotion this morning at this gate. Our two-ways were buzzing. It was in the papers. You didn't see it? A year ago one of the Scotland Yard inspectors got convicted for killing his missus, and today he was escorted out of the country."

Alex shook his head. "This is my last gate to clean today. I would have been way on the other side of the terminal when that happened." He looked at his watch and smiled. "My shift ends at eleven. Sorry, I missed it. Did you see it?" *Now get the fuck out of here.*

The bobby shook his head. "No, I'm stuck at security. It's the end of my shift too." He swung his wand looking around. "Just thought you might have a story to tell. Have a good one."

Alex motioned back to the officer as he kept dusting with his mop until the area was clear. *That was too close. Time to go.*

He pushed the cart back into the storage room. He put on Neil's tie and jacket, then put the rest of his stuff in a bag he could carry. *Have to burn these clothes. There's enough sweat in this uniform to give plenty of DNA.*

Almost drenched with sweat, Alex unlocked the car and sat staring out the windshield. *I've been idle too long. This should be routine. Instead I feel like I've just committed my first job. My heart is pounding. Focus, what is the mission?*

He turned the key and shifted into reverse looking in the mirror. "Retrieve the logbook, get my money, kill the bitch and get even, no…get rid of…Dennis."

Nodding to the gate keeper he whispered to himself. "I wish Charlie was here. He'd love planning this one. Come to think of it, he never did like Jane. He said she was extra baggage."

Chapter 10

Scotland Yard. The Chief's office.

The Chief walked Ross, Bobbie and Inspector Carroll to the outer office. "So far your report is what I expected to hear. I agree something is amiss, but…" The Chief sternly looked at Ross. "I'm sorry Dennis. This is an order from the top. You must back off of this man. Aside from the reports I've just gotten from the inspectors at the security passenger check in and at the gate, I was told the media photographed you threatening McGraw! God knows what the papers will blast! Both security guards said you've got a mission rather than a case. Jesus, Dennis! Do you want to get fired?"

Bobbie stepped forward cringing. "Chief, Alex made a lewd remark towards me and…"

O'Doul grabbed his pipe. "Oh, I see." Crunching his mouth he glared up into Ross's face. "And you felt you had to be the big protector. Let me remind you that gender is not on the list of duties, responsibilities, or qualifications to be a member of Scotland Yard."

He stepped back flushed with anger. "Furthermore, until you can prove that Jane McGraw or whatever her name is alive, *proving her life is at risk*, I'm giving you a choice either to work with the Dream Team, under Inspector Carroll's supervision, or be relieved of duty without pay for six weeks."

Ross stiffened biting his lip. *Don't blow off now.* He felt Bobbie tug at his jacket. He nodded to the Chief. "I understand…it won't be easy, but…"

Ross turned back as he opened the outer office door. "I will prove to you that I'm right about this."

Chief O'Doul stared at Ross. *I hope you do my boy.* He then motioned to the women with his pipe. "Inspector Carroll, the plug hasn't been totally pulled out. You've got one month to work on this case."

The Chief hesitated at the door, raising his voice. "Ross, that means Carroll's in charge. You understand that?"

"Yes, sir."

The Chief shut the door behind the three inspectors and walked past his secretary mumbling. "Fat chance of that happening. This isn't good…I need a pill…Mrs. Gipson, where are my…"

"The first shelf in your closet behind the books."

The Chief hesitated at his office door. *How does she know where I hide my whiskey?* His face reddened as he gritted his teeth. *Nothing is sacred in this place.* His office door slammed shut. *You're fired...again!*

When the Chief was gone, Inspector Carroll spoke. "Ross, if you've got a few minutes I'd like to go over some ideas I have and get your input. I think you're right about running out of time."

Bobbie saw the condescending glance Ross gave Kitty. *This man needs your course on gender.* She looked at her watch. "It's almost lunch time. How about you get set up and Ross and I will go and get us some sandwiches and coffee." She stepped on his foot hard.

Inspector Carroll overlooked the grimace on his face. She winked at Bobbie. *She's got her hands full.* "That's a good idea. I don't always think about food when I 've got a problem to solve."

When the elevator door shut, Dennis pushed the button. "Why did you gouge my foot?"

"Because, Inspector Ross, I saw the condescending, contemptuous look you gave Kitty."

"Well, it's my case!"

Bobbie stared at him. *I don't get it. Is this a male thing?* The elevator door opened and Bobbie turned and glared at the two wanting to enter, "This elevator is occupied. Take another one." She pressed Closed and then Stop. "Your case! You've damn near gotten fired.

Kitty is doing everything she can to help you. She was notified, as was the Chief, this case would become an albatross to the Yard if it wasn't put to rest. To protect your job she went to the top and asked to have a chance to prove your suspicions about Jane as she agreed there's a case to be made."

Bobbie stood with her hands on her hips frowning. "So, before you get twisted up in your male ego, you might consider working alongside of her *...listening* for a change instead of looking for thc cracks."

She turned and pressed the elevator button. "Carroll's course on The Gender Gap, which I might add, wouldn't hurt you to take, dissolves issues like this. No one loses. Dennis, intelligence is for everyone! You don't have a monopoly on it!"

The elevator opened at the main floor. "Well, are we going for food or parting?"

Wide eyed he walked past her. "What do you think?"

When they returned to Carroll's office, Dennis blushed. He was the only male with ten women in the room. Inspector Carroll had put a folder on each seat in the room. "While you're eating your lunch, you might browse the materials in the folder."

Carroll scrunched the napkin into the lunch box and tossed the lot in the garbage can. "Okay, I think we can get started now. First, we have joining us our graduated recruits. They will monitor each team and coordinate activities as needed. Then, you all know Dennis Ross. He will be partnering with us in this case... That being said, we've got a lot to cover. Dennis has provided us with a few photos of Jane McGraw. Last week I had Ron in the art department do some sketching of these photos showing alterations in appearance, such as aging, disguises."

Dennis snapped his head up. *Excellent idea.*

"Ron pointed out that it is very hard to alter the structure of the face unless of course she had surgery. Normally, you don't study a person's features so the disguise works. Now your immediate assignment is to study and memorize each of these photos. Ron has put arrows pointing out the details you need to remember. One other item-different hair color and styles make recognition difficult. He suggested that body movement is another deception. She could walk hunched over, have a limp, have crutches, cane etc."

A hand went up. "Inspector Carroll, how do you know she's in the country? You have in this report that a lot of money was taken from her husband. Putting myself in those shoes, I'd sure get as far away as I could."

Carroll smiled. "You would think that." She opened another folder. "I contacted Immigration and there's not been any passport applied for by any of the names she's had and no photos were found remotely close to these in the last eight years. Unfortunately we don't have a fingerprint to corroborate this assumption."

Another hand went up. "Mum, could Inspector Ross tell us about her character or personality? Was she weak or strong physically and mentally?"

Ross looked around. *I like this group. Good ideas are emerging.*

He smiled and stood. "I can do that…It's been a few years… Initially when my wife, Lizzy, and I met Jane, she was quite shy. It was clear that she didn't come from much. She lacked the social skills. Underneath that, we felt she meant well. Lizzy liked her and said she had hidden layers. Alex and I worked long hours, as you well know. This allowed them to become good friends. Jane tried to emulate Lizzy. It was quite a transformation. They seemed to have fun."

Bobbie stopped taking notes. "Dennis, what did Alex think about all of this? For some reason I don't think this would sit well with him."

Dennis frowned for a moment. "I do recall Alex was agitated early one morning. I asked him about it. For a moment he looked angry saying something about Jane wanting a kid. He brushed it off and nothing else was said. Soon after that my wife became ill and it was downhill for me from that time on until she passed away. The four of us never got together after that. I will say this. Jane was a saint. She took care of Lizzy while I worked."

Bobbie looked up squinting. "Dennis, do you remember those two old guys we interviewed at Alex's old house. The one told us that Jane sat on the porch crying, grieving the loss of her best friend. After several weeks she disappeared."

Dennis turned to answer. *That day was the biggest shock of all. I had to sit down, I was so alarmed.* "We never did go back and question them further."

Carroll wrote on the board. Nursing homes, hospitals, mental facilities. " This is where we're going to start. Patti D, you'll be in charge of the recruits. I want all the information you can give on a fifty kilometer radius of Woking for the places on the board, no later than eight in the morning."

She bit her lip studying pictures and the few pages of information they had. *I can't send a rookie on this.* "Patti D., would you put a map on the screen. Thank you. Karen, can you make contact with the orphanage Jane came from in Scotland?"

Carroll found the name of the town in her notes and looked up. "It's called Bedrule."

Finding it, she drew a yellow circle around it. "Looks like it's on the border of England and Scotland. We can arrange a flight there to save time. I'm going to need you back ASAP."

Karen wrote everything down and nodded.

Kitty took her glasses off and stood before the women. "I want you to study this information, memorize it. You won't be able to have it with you. I may need some additional help so you new kids on the block, show me what you can do. Are there any questions?"

Karen raised her hand. "I have another question for Dennis. Can you think of anything about Jane that only you would know? Something from her childhood. Maybe she had a nickname."

Dennis studied the pictures he brought from home. Picking one up, he smiled at Kitty. "I haven't thought of this in years."

He handed the picture to Bobbie. "She had a nickname for me. She would leave me notes reviewing Lizzy's day. She'd start them off, *Ross-d.* Lizzy and Alex thought she was calling me Rossie. I don't think I ever corrected them, I thought of it as a shared secret. If you look hard, you can see a tiny dash and d after Ross in that photo. Lizzy said Jane was very quick to learn…" He pointed to it as he sat on the edge of the desk. "That's a sketch she did of Lizzy." He glowed at the picture and spoke softly. "I thought it was brilliant for a first time."

Inspector Carroll nodded at Karen. "This is good and will be helpful."

She looked around. "Before I end the meeting, I want to remind you that Alex McGraw is looking for her as well. Even though he has left the country doesn't mean you have all the time in the world to locate this woman. We don't, because the department has given us one month to solve this case and I wouldn't guess for a minute that McGraw has put this on hold until his return. Then I'll see you all in the morning at eight."

When the last team member left, Dennis stood. "Kitty, that really was a good meeting and…I would serve under you anytime."

Bobbie looked at him with mouth open and eyes wide. *Heart, be still!!*

Kitty smiled and sat on the edge of the desk. "That's very nice of you to say, Dennis. I have to make one correction. You'll never work for me, under me, whatever. We work here as a unit. I'm just the coordinator."

"Are you thinking of having men in the program?" He gathered up his folder and stood next to Bobbie's chair.

She folded her hands and was thoughtful. After a few moments she stood up observing him. "That's a big and difficult question. Of course I would want men in the program, but in order for that to work, two words would have to be obliterated from one's consciousness to allow combined teams to work one hundred percent efficiently." She raised her brow and wrote on the blackboard… ' Ego and Libido'.

Moving to the desk chair next to him, she pointed to the black board. "Because of those two words, many studies in law enforcement and military service show the negatives of men working with women outweigh the positives … That's why the entire task force training not only stresses fitness, physical and mental but the issues of gender are studied as well. I developed a course on gender and it lasts for the full two year term."

"What you saw here today is the result of six months of convoluted training. If you would ask anyone of those women what transpired here this afternoon, they could repeat verbatim the entire work session. We've about made robots out of them. The difference being, they think and reason quickly."

She stared at him and shook her head. “The Dream Team’s first class graduated five out of fifty applicants. This is our second graduation of six.”

Bobbie grinned. “Out of how many?”

Kitty put on her suit jacket shaking her head. “There were seventy applicants.”

Ross shook his head. “Not a good ratio is it?”

They walked to the door. Kitty turned off the lights. “If I’m asking them to put their lives on the line for God and country, then I have to make bloody well sure they’re prepared. My program would have a short life if we had lower standards, so I’m happy if even one makes it.”

Ross pushed the elevator button. “I guess you don’t need my help on any of this.”

“Yes we do, but in another way. Remember, Alex and friends know you and Bobbie. The team can’t be connected to you publically, but you can study the areas and give direction via our monitoring staff. Once the team goes into operation, my office will be open twenty-four seven. You can use any of my resources.”

Chapter 11

Alex goes to the Peckham home

The radio announcer started the three o'clock news as Alex parked Neil's car in front of Henry's house. He took his time looking around before going to the door. *This is a side of Charlie I would have never guessed. The immaculate grounds I get, but the flower boxes under each window, the bright and cheerful colors on the cottage and shutters. The fairy tale picket fence around the front yard. He can't have lived here. Not Charlie. I can't imagine what the back looks like.* He walked toward the cottage wide eyed, shaking his head.

Zilpha met him in the garden wearing a pair of light weight jeans and an apron that covered a short sleeved plaid blouse. No more than five foot six inches tall, her slightly graying brown hair was in a ponytail. From the car Alex found her a very ordinary woman. *Strange I don't see much of a resemblance to Charlie.*

She smiled radiantly pushing the gate open. "I was hoping you'd come."

Alex blushed as he shook her hand with his left. *Her face radiates happiness and her eyes are... are... beautiful.* "Really?"

She showed him each room. "In actual fact, there are two reasons why." She picked up a set of keys from the center desk drawer. "Well, first I wanted you to see how we lived and second..." He followed her to the cellar door. She unlocked the door and turned. "The ceiling is low. You'll have to mind your head."

"This must be Charlie's area…It's pretty cluttered. Or is it by design to put someone off?"

She moved a tall hutch that had hidden wheels under it away from a wall. She smiled. "You remember his love for deception." Unlocking a second door, she stopped and stood in front of the door. "Behind this door is my second reason…It is my wish as it was Charlie's that Henry would *never* follow in Charlie's footsteps. Henry has never been in this room and I pray he'll never need to be."

Alex stared at her. *Do uncles say that or parents?*

She opened the door and turned on the light, then handed him a small key. "This will open up each cabinet. You'll find a list of everything inside on every door. Would you like to stay for dinner? "

Alex stood looking with his mouth open. "I *can't believe this."* He waved his hand at the room. "No disrespect, but *this is a fuckin' arsenal."*

Zilpha pointed to a stairway. "If you want to use the computer, I'll turn it on for you. It's very sensitive."

"My God, a *second floor under the cellar!"*

At the foot of the steps was Charlie's big roll top desk and computer. Alex looked over the railing. "Not to worry, the screen is on."

He sat at the desk and the computer went off. Alex flinched and turned to Zilpha. "You said it's sensitive. Does it have butt recognition?" he said chuckling.

Zilpha motioned for him to switch places. "This is Mother Peckham. She's in charge of everything. So if your butt, voice, and prints aren't on the list, mother shuts down. Then the only way you can start her up is to have the code...And she only will give you a few minutes to put it in before she takes offensive action."

Alex rested his elbow on the top of the desk. "You're playing with me now." *I'll bet all our codes are in here identifying each job and the monies taken in… Should this be destroyed? I wonder if Zilpha knows any of this.*

She got up and motioned for him to sit. "Perhaps you'd like to find out."

Alex smiled. "Just put the code in. I know that grin. That is Charlie's 'don't piss me off look'.

She laughed heartily. “You’re right. Turn around so I can put the code in to make Mother Peckham happy. I’ll go up and prepare something while you look around.”

Alex put in some code words he and Charlie shared and sure enough the information came up. *He was beyond genius! This program plots all the information you give and then tells you what you need.* He swiveled in the chair reminiscing. He typed in a word or phrase over and over again trying to stump the Mother until his heart about bolted out of his chest. “Holy shit! I didn’t hear you come back.”

She laughed. “I used to do this to Charlie, but that’s not the comment I’d get. Dinner is ready.”

“That was fast.”

She smiled. “You’ve been down here over an hour. What is the expression, ‘time flies when you having fun’?”

Alex looked at his watch, and hesitated at the desk. Zilpha chuckled. “Mother will shut down now. She’s relieved you’re leaving.”

He leaned back putting his fork and knife down on his plate. “It’s been a long time since I had shepherd’s pie this good.” He stared at her. “You know, I’m spinning here with questions.”

Zilpha poured their tea nodding. She motioned if he’d like to sit out on the patio. They walked out and he sat next to her. “I get the strangest feeling Henry is Charlie’s son.”

Teary-eyed she looked off at the distant trees. “My childhood was anything but happy. However, I wouldn’t change it for the world. I was ten years old when I met Charlie. My dad married Charlie’s mother. “

Alex finished his tea and handed her his cup. “Then you could have married. You weren’t blood related. What was the big deal?”

“I was a very shy little girl. As you know, he was almost reclusive. Though we were ten years apart, I really think it was…I know it’s corny, but it was love at first sight.”

Alex frowned. “He had sex with a ten year old. That’s a bit much.”

She shook her head. ”No, no. You’re way off…” She dropped her head for a moment. “I’ve never told anyone this… In nineteen fifty three or four, Charlie had been to Korea for the end of the war." She looked over at Alex. "You met him there."

Alex grinned. "Yes, I told him we had a partnership given to us from the gods and I would get back to him." *It lasted over twenty years.*

"When he came home from Korea, his mom got him a job at the factory where she worked. My dad had a makeshift shop in the garage. He'd repair stuff for the people in the town we lived in. When I came home from school one day, my dad was drunk." She bit her lip and paused. "I'm sorry, it's still very vivid after all these years…Well, unexpectedly, Charlie came home from work early and saw me fighting off my dad's advances."

Alex chuckled. "I can just imagine what happened. Did he kill him?"

Zilpha shook her head. "I don't think so…My dad was huge compared to Charlie. Yet, Charlie became so enraged that you'd swear he had the strength of Samson. He yelled for me to hide in the corner. He just kept punching my dad in the face until he folded to the floor. Charlie was covered with blood. His mom came home after a bit. There was a lot of screaming between them. He came to me and said he was going to leave. Would I come with him? I just knew he would take care of me. Charlie packed up a case for both of us and we left. We lived in Ireland for a long time with some of his distant relatives. I went to school there. He never once made an advance toward me. When I was fifteen or sixteen, he came home from work one day all frightened and worried. One of his dart playing friends told him a bobby was asking questions about him."

Alex laughed. "I was trying to find him. I had gotten a job at Scotland Yard and put out feelers throughout the UK. I had a plan that I knew would be perfect for both of us. When I was given the address, you'd already left. Now I understand. He must have thought your dad had charges against him."

She nodded. "That's right. We moved back to England and came here to Crawley and you found him."

Alex shook his head. "No, he found me. Soon after that I got him a job at Interpol."

She smiled. "Soon after that, Henry was born. Charlie was a very proud father. It was several years before I knew what kind of work he was really doing. He never lied to me when I asked him about the additional monies he made. Charlie was brilliant and it was so obvious he was ecstatic solving problems for you. When your jobs got more dangerous, we decided it was best we didn't live together to protect Henry and me. So everyone thought he was my brother and that my husband was killed in Korea."

Alex chuckled and looked around. "He sure fooled me…I didn't have a clue. He mentioned once he had a sister he took care of. It sounded like you were some invalid." *Hardly that.*

Zilpha walked by the short garden wall and pointed. "When Henry was still little, Charlie bought up all the plots of land behind us. As you can see, he loved privacy…no, I think he really wanted secrecy. He planted the highest growing bushes, trees, anything that had height." She walked him beyond the patio. "This path goes to a road that's half a kilometer away. He used it when he didn't want to be seen coming or going."

She grinned. "That's when he had the idea of the cellar. To camouflage the digging in the cellar, he added on a room in the back of the cottage. The neighbors never questioned it. It's very private allowing us to be together more often without ever being seen." Alex stood behind her. She turned and stared warmly into his eyes. "I owe you a lot. You gave us many years of happiness. Now I want to help you where I can."

My friend, she is more than wonderful. No disrespect. Alex couldn't resist the warmth in her eyes and kissed her. She responded to his kiss and stepped back wiping her eyes.

"I'm sorry, I didn't mean to …"

Zilpha shook her head. "No need to apologize…" She gathered up the tea cups. "Charlie's the only one who has ever kissed me until now." She dropped her head. "I guess I'm just a one man gal."

She left Alex watching the sun lowering. *She's a treasure. I can't involve her in my problem. Charlie would never forgive me if…I feel I've broken his trust. Time to go.* He found her in the kitchen doing the dishes. "I think I better …"

Zilpha grinned and pointed. "No, grab a dish towel. We can talk while you dry."

He lifted his prosthesis looking sad at her.

She chuckled. "No, that's not a good enough reason. You can do it." She let him stumble, almost dropping a dish, but she let him work it out. "Have you a plan how to find Jane and get your money back?"

"Sort of. I was hoping I'd see something in Charlie's stuff to spark an idea, but my God there's far too much to go through. I have no idea what some of that is."

"Tell me what you want and..."

Alex put the towel down. "No Zilpha. I can't let you get involved. This is far beyond the scope."

She turned from the sink. "Who do you think catalogued all of that stuff down there? Who do you think plotted the ideas for all of your escapades for the last twenty years?"

She sat at the kitchen table. "Alex, Charlie was brilliant in coming up with ideas, but he taught, he encouraged and he loved the way I could put his ideas into a plan."

Alex laughed. " So, you're Mother Peckham …That sneak. All of this time I thought he had done it all himself."

"No and I'll tell you that I got so good at it, I charged him." She laughed with tears. "That was the fun part. I wouldn't give him his plan until he'd give me an amount. With all the research I had to do, I would sometimes up the ante."

He stared at her, nodding slowly. *Have I died and gone to paradise?* He looked at his watch. "I still have to drive to check out my new lodgings in Shoreham."

"You can stay here tonight if you like."

He smiled wide eyed. "That's a definite no!" *I'd forget my mission very quickly.*

She smiled shyly and left the room for a moment. She handed him a notebook. "Write down the address where you're staying and give me some idea of what your plan is to find Jane."

He grimaced touching his prosthesis. "I am learning to write left handed, but I'm not very fast yet."

"I suggest you start working at it. Your disguise will only work for so long. I would guess there aren't that many right arm prostheses in the country. If this Dennis Ross is as good as you say he is, word gets around you know, he's sure to put your fake trip together. I wouldn't be too casual about the length of time you think you have…How long will that mask hold up?"

Hearing Dennis's name caused the gears to change in his mind set. He rested his arms on the table and looked across at her. "You're right. Party time is over. To remove the mask requires a lot of chemicals. You could say this is the closest to having the surgery. I can shower or swim if necessary. I think only Ross or Jane would recognize me."

He looked at his watch. "Do you still have access to Interpol's records?"

She nodded. "Why?"

He handed her an envelope from his jacket. "Maybe this will help. There are some photos of Jane before and after her accident. Plus her history, names, places she lived."

Zilpha frowned looking at the pictures. "Pretty girl. That's quite a scar on her face."

Alex shrugged his shoulders. "Jane became so distraught over Ross's wife's death, I had to admit her to a mental hospital for a period of time and she evidently tried to hurt herself. " *Will she accept that? I've got to play this right.*

Zilpha thumbed through the pictures. *Hmm, interesting.*

After another hour of discussion, Zilpha walked Alex to the door. "You have the number here and at the law firm if you need to talk to Michael. Henry and Neil should be arriving in Johannesburg early tomorrow morning. Michael will let me know when they're settled. Call me in the morning. I should have some ideas ready for you."

He hesitated at the door. *I don't know how Charlie ever went to work.* He squeezed her hand and left.

He sat in the car, lost in thought, until a rap on the window startled him. He rolled down the window. "Son of bitch you scared me!"

Zilpha chuckled. *Just like Charlie he was daydreaming.* "Charlie couldn't multitask either. I just had an idea. Where does this Dennis Ross live?"

"Why do you ask? "

"Just tell me. I have to research it. I'll let you know tomorrow."

She stepped back with his scratch of paper smiling. "Be careful.

Roads are tricky from here to Shoreham." She waved and darted back to the house. *Now maybe I can get some of my own back for Charlie's death.* Zilpha grabbed the keys and zipped down to the cellar. *Don't have to worry about Henry coming home.* She still put on the security system. *Now to deal with Inspector Ross.*

She helped design this *Brainy-act* as she called it. While the computer systems were starting, she made some coffee in the kitchenette. She leaned against the sink looking around. *Alex was so stunned by all of this. Called it an arsenal!* She laughed as she poured. "Charlie called it the MP…Mother Peckham."

It had gone on ten o'clock as Zilpha poured another cup of coffee. She stretched her arms and twisted to crack her neck. She took her coffee to the other computer and spoke as if Charlie were in the room. "I'm sure we have a tracking device." Looking over at his work bench expecting an answer, she leaned back welling up with tears. *Charlie, tell me if I'm doing the right thing helping Alex.* She started to cry. "I know you saw him kiss me…Don't be angry…I'm just as at fault…I miss you so much… To be…"

The piercing sound of the private phone rang twice. She bolted out of the chair grabbing the phone. *No one there…* She frowned and went to a cabinet. The phone rang twice again and stopped. She grabbed it. "Henry! Charlie!" No one answered. *Could it be a sign?*

Off the main highway, Zilpha dropped the speed as well as turned off her headlights, leaving only the parking lights lit to see through the patches of fog. *I bet this is beautiful in daylight. The mist is something else tonight. I think I missed my turn.* Stopping short, she shifted into park and jumped out of the car with her flashlight. *Quicker this way. Hope a car doesn't come. Yeah, as if this is a main drag.* She flashed her light by a small handmade sign, GODSTONE. She got back into the car and continued slowly. The clock on the dashboard showed two o'clock in the morning when she rounded a last bend revealing the cemetery outside of the town chapel. *Not much of a drive north of Crawley, but forever on these back roads.* She didn't need a street map to find Coventry. *The village only has five main roads.* She pulled over to the side of the street, got out and removed the license plate. *Can't see the point of this this time, but a rule is a rule.*

She drove slowly turning onto Chapel Road looking for Ross's cottage. *Only one street light for this whole area and right at the corner. I'm surprised they have electric.*

The cottage was at the end of a cul-de-sac surrounded by trees and bushes. She parked her car under some low-lying branches and sat still for about ten minutes. Dressed in black, wearing night vision goggles, she checked out every house for any kind of movement. Very carefully she got out of her car holding a box of devices against her side. She put a small gun with silencer in her jacket pocket. *You can do this. How many times did you help Charlie when Alex couldn't break his cover? Charlie's here with you. He'd say, stand still and go over every step. No one can see you here. Get control before you move.*

She took a step and heard a cottage door open across the street. Stopping dead in her tracks, she heard someone talking. She shrank back and froze. Someone left a cottage across the road and was walking toward her. *Those steps are quick and close together, must be a woman. It's so quiet out I hope she can't hear my heart beating.* Zilpha heard her crying as she walked by. *She can't be more than twenty. What is a kid doing out at this hour. God if she gets in that car, she'll see me.* She watched until her back was visible and then Zilpha quickly moved to the front of her car and ducked, just as the girl opened the door. *That was too close. I never saw that car. Charlie would be so mad. Poor thing, crying like that.*

She waited another few minutes after the car left to make sure no one followed the girl. Zilpha walked in the shadows of the landscaping as long as she could. *Here's his car. Take the tape off the magnet.* She chuckled. *Charlie almost died laughing when I told him the device was bad because it wouldn't stick.* Removing the tape, she lay under the front of the car and felt the strong pull from the steel chassis. *That won't fall off.* She flicked the switch on it and carefully went back to a bush next to Ross's cottage.

She slipped on her goggles. *Don't push your luck. Should have asked Alex if Ross has a dog. Too late now...Where can I put this camera.* She looked at her watch. *Charlie said never more than ten minutes.* She eyed a tree that looked like it would do the trick.

Back in Crawley, she checked again the tracking device receiver showing the map pinpointing Ross's car. She parked and smiled with satisfaction as she strolled through the gate to her home. *Won't this be a surprise? That old bird nest worked well to camouflage the camera. Those batteries will only allow so many snaps.* She opened the door. *Doesn't matter, Charlie would be proud...*

Chapter 12

Johannesburg Airport

The seat belt sign went off and the passengers started exiting the plane. As the members of the Dream Team gathered their stuff, Neil and Henry walked past. Hennessy, being the shortest, was having trouble reaching her carry-on bag in the upper compartment. Henry stopped. "Need a little help?"

Hennessy was taken by his height and quipped. "They call you Shorty?"

Henry chuckled as he handed her the suitcase. "No, much worse."

Neil, posing as Alex McGraw, stood behind them. "High Pockets. You're holding up the line here."

Hennessy laughed as she moved out of the aisle. "High Pockets! That's a good one."

She turned and saw her teammates glaring at her and shrugged her shoulders.

Theresa shook her head and whispered to Linda. "Already she's cavorting with the enemy."

A couple of hours later they were settled in at the Twelve Decades Art Hotel. They had adjoining rooms on the first floor, 109 and 110, next to the exit door. Linda found the three others talking on the balcony overlooking a row of parking garages. "Beautiful sight, isn't it?"

They grinned. Hennessey snickered. "That's if you like looking at garbage cans lined up in a row."

Linda sat on the ledge. “It took forever to make connections, but I finally checked in at the Yard. Embassy said the satellite was acting up.”

Theresa questioned. “So what are our orders?”

“We’re supposed to attend some of the conference or be seen going in and out of the place. There are two cars in the parking lot for us. Keys are on the table in our room. I told them that Hennessy had made contact with the lawyer by accident. It was relayed that we aren’t to capitalize on that right now.”

Jo Burr stopped taking notes. “Are we to be solely watching McGraw and the attorney or Dr. Edse as well? Didn’t Kitty tell us an agent had been assigned to watch the doctor? Are we to make contact with the agent or agents?”

“Not yet. There are two agents watching. Two from Scotland Yard are acting as a decoy. McGraw will recognize them and act accordingly. An agent from the Embassy is watching Edse’s office and home. Once we lose sight of McGraw inside Edse’s hospital, we won’t be able to track him if he has the surgery.”

“I wonder when Jo can apply for a nurse’s position at the hospital. That would cover one of the bases.”

Theresa waved her hand. “Hey, how about if I make an appointment to have my boobs enlarged? If Jo gets the job, she can’t be alone in that hospital with Edse.”

They stared at her. “Enlarged?”

Hennessy bent over. “You can’t even run without a harness on them…ha, ha, ha, you mean have them deflated! Anymore fill they’ll burst. ” She stood up wiping her face from the tears pouring out from laughing. “I’m hungry, let’s go eat. There’s a restaurant off the main lobby.”

Jo glared at Hennessey. “No matter what the circumstance, this kid is always hungry. First thing tomorrow, I’m going to apply at Edse’s hospital. It wouldn’t hurt.”

Linda shook her head and rose from her perch on the balcony ledge. She watched a convertible pull in one of the car ports and motioned to the others to be quiet. “I think we better go inside. It looks like our assignment has just arrived and may live in this hotel as well.”

As the team went inside, they watched the two men carry their luggage.

Linda whispered. “I can’t report this news until later…For now we’re just going to act as natural as we can. I really don’t like the idea Jo would be alone in that hospital without a backup.”

Theresa waved her arm. “Hello, why do you think I suggested I go in for an exam?”

“That’s only if Jo gets the job.”

Jo Burr got her purse. “We’ve been told not to capitalize on Hennessy’s… accidental… bump in with McGraw’s attorney, so I think we should go out the back door until you find out if we should move to another hotel.”

With hands on her hips squinting at Jo. “Well, it was an accident. He was just *there!” And a very cute there, too.*

Theresa cringed staring at her young colleague and then argued. “However, we were here first…Besides wouldn’t this allow us to track them more easily?”

Later in the day the women returned to the hotel through the lobby. The clerk at the desk waved a paper. “Miss Severance!”

The four stopped chatting. Linda smiled. “That would be me.” She walked over to take the message. No one else was at the desk while they talked. “Linda, your mother has requested that you call her as soon as you can.” The desk clerk very carefully showed her a picture of Dr. Edse and whispered, “This man just arrived asking for the room number of McGraw and Peckham.”

Realizing the clerk had to be an agent from the Embassy, Linda motioned for Theresa to come to the desk.

Theresa turned to the girls. “You two watch while I’m at the desk. Laugh out loud or something if someone comes down that hall.”

The clerk showed her the picture. Theresa nodded. “They aren’t wasting any time, are they?”

Linda leaned on the counter. “Our mother has asked for us to call immediately but the Embassy can’t get me a line until tonight.” She stood back and frowned. “Say, we’re not far from the harbor are we?”

Theresa smiled. “Good idea, Morse code, ships… Or…Would the Embassy still have those capabilities?”

The clerk quickly called her boss at the Embassy. “Thank you, I’ll send her over right away.”

Linda put the message in her pocket. “I’ll take care of this…What room are they in?”

The clerk grinned. “Second floor above you. The room is bugged so you can monitor what’s going on. There’s a headset in your closet.”

Theresa shook her head. “I think you’vc fucked up by doing that, especially if Edse is up there. I’m sure he and McGraw are expecting a tail. They probably have found the bugs by now.” She stood back from the counter. “We can’t be seen talking to you. They’re going to know the hotel is involved somehow. Linda, tell the boss about this. We’ll go to the rooms until you get back.” She pointed at the desk clerk, “If I were you, I’d get those rooms debugged ASAP.”

Linda grabbed Theresa’s arm. “Wait up a sec.” They walked toward the front door. “Do you really think we should move to another hotel? Remember you did point out we were here before they came. Besides if they suspect they’re being bugged, why wouldn’t they move out or just go with Edse? I can’t see that we would be suspected just because we’re beneath them.”

Theresa nodded. “Yes, but, they could have booked the rooms in advance, thus the Embassy would have the heads up on them. Maybe I’m being overly cautious. They still should have told us or asked what we thought about it. I’ll have Jo and Hennessy sit across the street in one of the cars to watch whoever comes out with Edse. The clerk said Edse came in the front, assuming he walked.”

Linda looked at her watch. *It’ll be our dinner time soon.* “I’ll be back as soon as I can. I’m thinking Jo getting hired at Edse’s hospital will be our only chance to keep McGraw in sight… Remember not to discuss any of this on the balcony.”

Theresa threw up her hands. “Fuck it all, Linda, Jo’s not going in there alone.”

Theresa watched Linda go out the front entrance and then walked with the girls back to the room. She handed Jo Burr one of the car keys. “Because of this Embassy screw-up bugging McGraw’s rooms, we’re not sure what will happen now that Edse is here with them. My gut feeling is McGraw wants to change his identity as quickly as he can and will leave with Edse. So, until we know for sure, Linda and I think you should watch on the outside. Take one of the cars and park out front, somewhere you can see the front of the hotel and still not be conspicuous."

Jo left the room and Hennessey paused at the door. "Theresa, should we call in every half hour?"

"No, every ten minutes. I'll watch from the balcony. If they should take their car, I'll let you know. The clerk said she would call me if they should leave from the front before you can get set up."

Hennessy opened the door and stuck her head back into the room. "Will you be okay?"

Theresa frowned. "You're just playing with me… Get the…"

Chapter 13

Second floor of the hotel

"HP, I'm a bit indisposed, answer the door."

Henry opened the door. "Doctor Edse, come in. How does it feel to be officially free?"

Edse studied this man who towered over him. *I thought I could forget this young man's cheekiness from our last visit.* He grinned and walked past him. "Well, where is my masterpiece?"

Neil came out of the bathroom smiling. "You're the famous doctor who did all of this."

He shook Edse's hand and then posed for inspection. "It fooled everyone, Doc!"

Cringing, Edse stared at this creature impersonating his colleague Alex McGraw. *Doctor, you imbecile.* "The title is Doctor and my name is Edward. Not Doc or Eddie." He leaned against the balcony door, tightening his lips. "Do make this adjustment in your heads, gentlemen, as your stay may be extended and I do want us to get along, at least for your sakes."

Henry swallowed a bit hard as he looked at his best friend. *Are you reading my thoughts? Can we go home now? This man is as nuts as Alex.*

Edse looked around the room and wrote on a paper. "Have you debugged the place?"

As Henry opened his mouth, Neil put his hand over it and shook his head at Henry, wide eyed whispering, "He means a different bug!"

Henry nodded and shrugged his shoulders muttering to his friend. "I'm sorry I thought…"

Edse wrote for them to come with him and he would send his guy over to check.

They left the hotel and walked to a café down the street. Edse chose a table at the end of the patio, allowing more privacy. After they ordered, he took a notebook out of his pocket. "My job is to keep you alive and visible for at least two weeks. That should give Alex enough time to get back what belongs to him. He called me from the house I have in Shoreham and said he was confident the switch had worked. Alex is positive you're being followed, which is what he wants, and you two have to act as if you're free as birds. Neil, you must remember, out in public, your right arm is a prosthetic."

Neil smiled. "Edward, besides being very mindful of this role, I am ambidextrous. Plus HP's mother sewed a stiff collar stay in the right shoulder of my shirts as a reminder." He leaned forward pointing to it. "It would probably cut me if I went past the scope of what Alex could do."

Edse leaned back taking a deep breath. "That was innovative. Can we hire her?"

Henry laughed. "That's what Alex said! Did he tell you that she's Charlie's sister."

Edse nodded. *That must be Zilpha, Alex was talking about. So this kid is in the dark about his parents. Interesting. He's just a bit taller than Windsor.* "Ah, here's Alex's plan. When he's done straightening out his affairs, you will return to England. Your business associate, Michael, will pick you up and take you to Alex's house in Woking. Alex will arrive that afternoon and you will make the switch. Then Alex will fly back here for his surgery and we will start the second phase of our adventure."

When Henry was seated, his long legs almost lifted the table. He had to spread them apart, creating a problem for the waiter serving him. "I don't understand all the secrecy. The man is free. You're both free. Even if he finds his wife…"

Neil shut his eyes. "HP…Shush! I'll explain this to you later…"

The doctor sipped his chilled Chardonnay. "No, we need to be on the same page right now. I don't want you to fuck up this whole stratagem of ours." He leaned forward cutting his salad into bite sized pieces. "Alex needs to find Jane because she has, unknown to her, taken a formu…let's just say a vital document. He must get this back, no matter how."

Edse sat chewing, studying Neil. "Are you aware of this? Then tell him not to fuck up!"

Henry frowned. "How can I fuck up?"

Neil wiped his mouth. "Yes, I do know about this. Peter is…was my brother and he trained me especially after he got me into Interpol. I helped him and Charlie set up a lot of their jobs for Alex. Then Alex met you." Neil nodded at Edse.

Henry stared at his best friend with wide eyes. "Why didn't Uncle Charlie teach me? Neil, tell me! I'm smart, I'm big and…strong."

Neil sat back and drank his beer. Biting his lip, he stared at Edse. *Nice going, ass hole.* "HP, your mother made Charlie promise he'd never let you know about his outside activities. We, meaning Alex, your uncle, Peter and I, executed a…a lot of people for megabucks. His wife Jane found the list in a vault he had on his property. It also contained information about another direction they were planning with Edward."

Neil noticed a man sitting at a table within ear shot. *Hmm he looks familiar. He's in one of the pictures Alex showed me. Must be a* tail. He whispered, and rolled his eyes toward the next table. "Change the subject, *now!"*

Chapter 14

Several days have gone by. Ross's home in Godstone, Surrey

Dennis offered Bobbie a coffee refill. "I thought my mother was the only person who could make an English breakfast like that. Thank you…" He smiled putting the coffee pot back on the burner.

She sipped her coffee grinning. "Dennis, anyone can make that."

He shook his head. "Not so…I used to watch my mother and you baste the eggs and tomatoes with the bacon grease the same way."

"What about Lizzy, didn't she cook?"

He laughed, shrugging his shoulders. "This meal wouldn't ever be on Lizzy's menu…We lived a regimented life in this house. Health and fitness was the main topic. I think that's one of the reasons Jane became so close to Lizzy. Jane loved to walk. Lizzy was struck by how much Jane knew about nature."

Bobbie cleared the table. "Well, I'm a strong believer in moderation along with fitness, not all the counting out of calories and stuff." She picked up the tomatoes she hadn't used. "Dennis, put these in the cellar. They'll last longer."

He frowned. "We never used the cellar…"

Bobbie wheeled around from the sink. "What? Cellars are better than refrigerators."

He pointed to the cellar door. "This is a century home and then some. Lizzy loved this house. The cottage hadn't been upgraded at all. So when we moved in, we had to add electricity and plumbing.

Something about the cellar scared her. The headroom down there is so low, I couldn't stand up so I didn't bother with it. Lizzy wanted the door kept locked and it's been that way for many years."

He put his cup in the sink. "A lot of history in Godstone…Think I have a book on it somewhere. One of our neighbors told us one of the cottages has a tunnel that runs out to the road. An escape route for.." Ross glanced at the clock on the wall. "We better get a move on it. I'll finish getting ready. Leave the dishes. I'll do them later." He left the kitchen.

Bobbie took the tomatoes and tried the door. "*Interesting, it's not locked.*" She opened the door and put the tomatoes on a ledge a step down. *Strange, no cob webs. Maybe he has someone clean for him.*

She heard the telephone ringing. "Should I get that?" *He must be in the bathroom.*

Bobbie handed the phone to Ross as he appeared from his bedroom. "Kitty wants to go over some ideas with you."

"That was good timing, we were headed out. We're going over to Woking. While Alex is in Africa, I want to look around his property again. Have a gut feeling Jane isn't far from there." He turned toward the window to look out. "No, I don't…I was looking at the map and that creek has a path beside it. The creek borders on a park system…I'll chance it. Tell it to Bobbie."

He thrust the phone back to Bobbie scowling. "Don't be long."

Taken aback by his tone, Bobbie frowned. Then she heard Kitty. "Bobbie, take your camera and try not to cross too far onto the property. I heard Dennis tried to get a search warrant without success. His ego is going to mess him up…."

Bobbie turned to look out the window and spoke with tight lips. "He never mentioned a warrant…I've tried to get him to realize what he's doing, but he won't listen to me."

Kitty went on. "He knows only too well, the defense could and would find someone to testify they saw him on the property. Yet, he's determined to find anything he can, even at the risk of losing his job and the case. Trespassing without a warrant always helps a case in court."

Dennis, standing in the doorway, said impatiently, "Are you coming?"

Bobbie's stare at him was chilling. *Shit, it's about the warrant...*

Glaring, she shoved the phone in his hand. "You still don't get it, do you?"

He stood and listened to Kitty warning. "Oh, don't forget, Alex booby trapped that place once before. I wanted to tell Ross that our rookies have shown Jane's picture around a vast area and we are getting feedback. I'm surprised she's still using her name. One report came in that she's got quite a scar down the left side of her face. I've had another sketch drawn up to show that. Then, we had another report from a shopkeeper that's questionable."

Ross cleared his throat.. "I'm on the line again. What was questionable?"

"Oh, it's you, Dennis!" *Hmm, that warrant must have pushed her button.* "Okay...Let me read you this report...The shopkeeper said the profile was about the same, but, he said it was no girl but a man, unshaven at that. One more interesting fact, when we checked every sort of place she could live---we got nothing."

Dennis dropped his head. *Am I that chauvinistic? This is really great stuff.* He perked up. "That is strange. Are you plotting all of these sightings on a map? That would be interesting to look at. I'll tell Bobbie, if she'll even talk to me..."

Kitty bit her lip. "Dennis. If you could forget the gender and realize we all are able people. We're here to help you win your case."

He saw Bobbie walking toward her car. "She's leaving!"

"Dennis, let her go. She doesn't want to argue. We all need time and space to sort things out...Come to the office later and I'll show you these reports."

"Thanks, Kitty. I don't know if I'm too old to learn new ways of living."

"You'll do just fine...Desire is the key. See you later."

He walked out to his car. *I hope she's right... So far Jane's appearing and then disappearing is like part of a plan, but for what end. Does she want to be found? Hopefully Bobbie and I will be at Kitty's office this afternoon at three. Jane's acting like a ghost. She's got a game plan. The woman isn't stupid.*

Chapter 15

Johannesburg…one day shy of a week later

Linda walked into the apartment, looking like a college student, and dropped her back pack on the table. She waved to the girls to come in from the porch.

Hennessey took a banana out of the bowl. "Those two men are sun worshippers. All they do is lie out in the sun or play catch. That Alex is pretty good one handed. He must be embarrassed about his arm, he's always got a sleeve over it. He should be more creative and put different colors on."

Theresa laughed. "If this is so annoying, why do you watch them with binoculars? It's a wonder he's not dying with that cover on his arm. Go out and tell him to take the prosthesis off, we won't mind. If you ask me…"

Hennessey nudged her. "Which I'm not."

"Well, I hope you're not letting your female instincts get involved here. Good looks can kill you! Are you listening?"

Linda handed Jo Burr a folder, looking at Theresa and Hennessey. "Is there an issue here or are you two messing around?"

Hennessey threw the banana peel at Theresa. "I used the binoculars because I can read lips and I made the comment that the attorney is cute. Theresa has me going down the aisle."

Linda nodded. "In her odd sort of way she's concerned for your safety. Okay? Jo, I just came from the Embassy and we finally have a go ahead for you to apply at the surgery annex of the hospital. You've got a lot to memorize. You'll need one of the cars because you and Hennessey have a house to live in."

Theresa turned a chair around and straddled the seat. "How far away is this house? I don't like this idea. How are we supposed to back up or protect these two if they're ten or more minutes away?"

Jo looked up from reading. "You're not just kidding about all of this. I'm a resident of Johannesburg? Hennessey is my live-in lover?" *My husband will love this.*

They all started to laugh. Hennessey retorted. "Lover! You mean daughter."

Linda shook her head. "It really doesn't matter what the reason is. Okay! Can we get serious now? I don't know how this came about but an ad has appeared in the jobs section of the paper for a surgical nurse. Must be important. It's been listed on the internet too. You've got all the qualifications, Jo. The delay with your paperwork was the Embassy. They had to give you an established identity here. O'Doul and Carroll don't want the hospital or Edse to be able to trace you back to England. I suggest you go to your room and study. We can quiz you at dinner."

Jo took the folder. "When should I make the appointment?"

Linda grinned. "It's tomorrow at nine."

Jo smiled and waved the folder. "Here I thought I'd be under a lot of pressure!" She slammed the bedroom door.

Theresa leaned back her chair. "When do I go for an examination?"

Linda tossed each of them bottled water from the refrigerator. "Kitty said you're to do that only if we see Alex go to the hospital. So far, as you've seen, they haven't moved from that made up beach area out back. Since you can read lips, Hennessey, have you learned anything?"

Hennessey swallowed. "No! The attorney goes on about his mother. Have a feeling he's a mum's boy. He feels bad his Uncle Charlie never taught him how to fight like his Uncle Peter taught Neil, whoever, Neil is…As horrible as you say this Alex is, they sure have strange conversations. You'd think they would do some sightseeing." *He's still cute. I don't think he's a bad guy.*

Chapter 16

Alex and Zilpha collaborate

Zilpha met Alex as he drove up to her gate. "I see you're driving a different car. Did you take Neil's car back?"

He started to get out. Not giving him a chance to respond, she waved for him to stay in the car. "You can drive. I've been waiting. You are a minute late, you know. "

She returned carrying a brief case and a picnic basket. He reached across the seat and opened the door for her. "Are you always like this?"

She put the picnic basket in the back seat of the coupe and sat with her brief case on her lap. "I had an excellent teacher, who, I might add, learned from you to be early and prepared and ready to handle a change of plans at any time."

At the road, Alex, crossing his hands and pointing, looked at her with amusement. "I give up, which direction?" *Think Charlie has taught her too well.*

"You see, I have this clever box in my brief case and it says…turn left." She gave him a radiant smile. She stared at her box. "Get on the M25 north-west."

After a few moments Alex sensed, *we're heading to my house.* "Zilpha, we're headed toward Woking. Why?" He saw a dot moving on the screen she was holding and stopped the car on the marginal. "Okay, tell me what you've done. Obviously we're following someone."

She nodded. "Yes, we're following your buddy Dennis Ross... I'll tell you later how I did it, but we better go or we'll get out of range."

Alex pulled back onto the highway. "I know a short cut. We'll get off at the next exit. I have a back entrance to the property. It isn't as elaborate as Charlie made for you, but it'll work. This time of year we won't be seen."

Alex drove slowly until he found the path. *This stuff has grown since I went to prison. It's taller than the car.*

Zilpha chuckled. "I see what you mean. Perhaps I should have brought a machete to clear the way."

"We have to stop. I don't want to chance it any further. I can see the house now, but no Ross."

Zilpha reached in her basket for a camera and lens. "This zoom lens should help and I can document his moves." She scanned the area. "Well, he's arrived but his car is down by the creek."

Alex rested the lens on the steering wheel. "This isn't very light! Hmm. His girlfriend is with him." He managed to hand the camera back to her. "I can't operate this very well. I haven't the strength to lift it. Take it before I drop it."

Zilpha got out of the car. "I'm going to move behind the brush toward the creek to see what he's looking for. There's a pair of binoculars in the basket."

"Zilpha, if he crosses the creek, he's on my property. Make sure you get a picture if he does that." She nodded and left.

Ross parked at the end of the road. He touched her hand. "Bobbie, I really appreciate you coming with me."

She lifted the door handle. "We've a lot to do and I have another appointment today."

They walked to the creek without a word.

Bobbie set her case down at the water's edge and looked around. *He's not going to sway me this time.*

She took her camera and tripod out of her case, eyeing the area for a dry spot. Out of the corner of her eye, she saw him staring at a possible place he could cross the creek and warned, "I hope you're not considering rolling up your pants."

Ross retorted. "This creek is running pretty good. I didn't think

I'd need boots." *The rain must have been harder than I thought.* After a couple steps, Ross slipped. *She had to have seen that.* "Be careful, its muddy."

Ignoring his remark and his antics, she affixed a very large zoom lens on the camera and scanned the whole area slowly. "Alex must have had a party before he left. There's a big fire pit and a ton of beer cans all over the ground."

"Dennis, I think we have company." She snapped some pictures. "I see a car and one person near it. Let me scan ...There's another person behind a camera similar to mine about four hundred yards from us. I can only guess it's a woman because the brush is blocking the view...You realize we're sitting ducks here."

She saw Dennis on the ground turning his pant legs up. "Dennis, you're making a big mistake if you cross that creek."

"Maybe that's Jane!"

Bobbie snapped at him. "It isn't! Dammit, Ross. There's a car further back in the brush. I can't see much of it. There's too much foliage. It's like a jungle. I can see a man using binoculars looking at me."

Dennis jumped up to look through the lens. "It's a man but that's all I can see." *She's right. Jane wouldn't work with anyone else. What would be the point? Besides, she'd know it was me and wouldn't hide.*

Bobbie clicked several pictures in succession. "I wonder who they are. Wouldn't we know if the Yard has someone out here? And...for what reason?"

Ross stared in the direction of the mystery car. *This doesn't make sense.* He looked at his watch. "Whoever that is will be gone by the time we find that path over there. I wonder what they're looking for. Maybe Alex has someone watching his property. If so, that means he's hiding something." *Would it be Jane's body? First, he needs a new identity and then he'll get rid of the evidence. He won't need to with a new identity...*

Bobbie took hold of Ross's arm. "You're starting that again. I can tell when you're going past the mark. Just cool your jets and we'll go to the Yard. We've got a lot to sort out."

Zilpha took photos of Ross leaving the area and then made her way through the brush back to the car where Alex was waiting. "That was a work out." She put the camera back in her basket and then brushed herself down, pulling bits and pieces of brush out of her hair. "Do you think they'll come here?" She turned around. "Let me check the tracker!" She stared at him. "Alex, you're so quiet. What's wrong?"

Looking at the tracker she shook her head. "No they've gone east toward London."

Alex stood staring at the spot where Ross had left. *Two rifle shots and this would be over.*

"Do you hate him that much, Alex!"

He gritted his teeth and nodded slowly. "I didn't realize until now just how much I loathe this man. The sight of him infuriates me."

She stood next to him. "Then…get rid of him." She looked up at him frowning. "I don't see what the problem is."

Alex squinted, chuckling at the same time. "You sound like…"

Zilpha sat on the hood of the car. "Like Charlie! He was always saying get rid of it, or what's the problem? He would say, Zilpha, fire up MP. We need to find another solution. Well, do you want a solution? It would make perfect sense to waste them now while you're in Africa."

Alex stood rubbing his right arm, *Paybacks are hell aren't they?* Then he turned to face her, nodding. "Yeah, fire up the MP."

They got in the car. She turned her tracking box on. "Looks like they're headed northeast."

Alex turned the coupe around. "Knowing Ross, they're going back to the Yard to assess what has happened and stare at pictures. Everything is by the book with him. No innovation whatsoever."

Zilpha gripped his hand before he shifted gears. "Well, your opinion is wrong this time. They've just made a U-turn and are headed back to Woking."

Alex slammed on the brakes. "Are you fucking with me?"

She turned the tracking box. "See for yourself. That dot is moving northwest toward the city. You said that's his girlfriend. Maybe she wants to do some shopping. There's a huge street market in the old village."

He turned west out of the path. "We're five minutes from the old village. We'll make sure." *Dennis still has that piece of junk he's driving.* "We should see them come in."

As Ross pulled up to the entrance to the M-25 highway, Bobbie's cell phone rang. "Hi, yes, we're headed toward you now. Let me put you on speaker."

"I'm not at the office. I'll explain later how this happened, but I need for you to go into the old Woking Village to the farmers' market. We've made contact with Jane in a very unusual way. Dennis, you must do as I ask without fail."

Bobbie stared at him and he nodded. "He will, Kitty. I'll shoot him if he doesn't."

"How far away are you?"

Dennis cringed. "With this old car of mine, at least ten to twelve minutes away."

"Park your car by the fountain in the square. We'll see you and then give you your next step."

Ross downshifted and tried to go fast to make a U-turn in front of a huge semi, but his old car wasn't going to help. It jerked and sputtered a few times until he backed off on the gas pedal. The semi laid on the horn as it raced by in another lane. He saw Bobbie cringe and stare out the window. *Time for another car. I feel like I'm digging the hole deeper.*

"I'm not doing so wonderful, am I?"

She stared at him. "I truly hope all of this crazy behavior is from exhaustion and not a precursor to some sort of breakdown. Dennis, it is worrisome. Are you going to be all right?" *I don't know if I can control him anymore. I'm beginning to think the Chief should have ordered him to have counselling. That whole Braun case was more than he could endure.*

Gripping the steering wheel with both hands, he nodded without looking at her. "I'm okay. I promise." *I have to be all right. I wonder if I'll recognize Jane. Will she make contact with us?*

They passed a sign showing the sixteenth century village square was at the end of the road. He turned onto a cobblestone entrance and slowly made his way to a parking area near the fountain.

Bobbie pointed. “Follow that car. It looks like there’s enough room to park next to it. My goodness, it’s like going back in time. I’ve never been here before.” She gaped, “Even the people look old…I wonder if those are costumes they’re wearing.”

Dennis took off his sun glasses. “No. Those aren’t costumes. This life style has never changed. These are the real farmers. Lizzy and I would come here almost every Saturday to shop. She loved the atmosphere because everything was naturally grown. Poor souls can’t compete with the big farms that have all the big equipment, use the pesticides, and still make the big bucks.”

He glanced around. “I haven’t been back since her passing.” He smiled at Bobbie. “Everything looks the same. Nothing’s changed.”

Kitty interrupted them. “Okay we saw you pull in. Dennis, I can’t emphasize this enough. It could be a matter of life or death for Jane. We need you to go shopping. Don’t look around searching for her. Just be natural to one another. If Jane feels it’s safe, she’ll make contact with you, Dennis. Do you understand? Call me when you leave.”

Answering Kitty, Dennis peeked at Bobbie. “Thanks Kitty, I owe you. I’ve got my head on.”

Bobbie squeezed his hand. “Point being, we don’t know who else is out there. Remember we saw two at Alex’s. Kitty, we’ll tell you about it later. I’ve got pictures to show.”

They got out of the car. Ross opened the trunk and took out a small shopping basket. “I still have the same shopping basket.” *Hard to part with those happy memories.* “We’ll take it with us. You might see something you might like.”

Bobbie took the basket. “Yes, I need some veggies. Do you want to stay for dinner? Roast lamb?”

Dennis smiled warmly. “Now, you’re bribing me!”

She laughed heartily, looking around his shoulder at the car next to theirs, feeling she was being watched. *Those people are just sitting in the car. Strange.*

Feeling found out, Alex turned to Zilpha. “I know Bobbie’s looking over here. Why don’t you take your basket and go shopping. I’ll stay here.”

To play the part, Zilpha got her basket and kissed him as she got out.

As Dennis and Bobbie walked past the car, they heard Zilpha say. "Why don't you take a nap? I'll be back shortly."

The market area took up most of the village square. They walked past large displays of local produce. When the tower clock struck three, they approached a fruit stand. Ross grumbled. "Suppose we've missed our chance? It's too bad we can't use our two ways to talk with Kitty. I wonder where she is that she can see something we should know about."

Bobbie whispered as she smiled at him. "Kitty said if it's safe Jane would reach out. Enjoy the moment." She squeezed his hand and said out loud. "This really is wonderful. I love this place."

Several people arrived to look at the apples. Ross handed six apples to the vendor. "That'll be a pound twenty." Ross gave a ten pound note to the scrubby looking old lady. He scanned the people standing around while he waited for his change.

It seemed like several minutes passed. Ross mumbled, "Wonder what's taking her so long to make change. Man behind me is making rude remarks."

Bobbie noticed the old woman was having a hard time stretching back with the change. "Dennis, give her some help."

The old woman frowned at him. "Bloody hell, most people have the right change. You've taken all my ones!"

Dennis blushed. "I'm terribly sorry. I don't come to markets often." The old woman gave him the finger and went on to another.

Bobbie giggled. "These apples look luscious." She walked over to a bench. "We have time. Let's eat one."

While Dennis put his bills into his wallet, she reached in the bag and felt one wrapped. "On second thought, we can eat one on the way back to my house."

"What? We just..." He looked at her and saw a wide-eyed piercing stare. "Okay, sounds good to me."

She glanced back at the apple stand and noticed the same woman from the car parked next to them. She turned and whispered. "Don't look. I think we're being followed. It's the woman from the car parked next to us."

Dennis handed the basket to Bobbie and shut her door. He looked across the top of his car at the car parked next to them. *He's napping. Has to be coincidence.*

As soon as Dennis pulled away from the spot, Bobbie pulled out the wrapped apple. "This is why we had to leave!"

"Should I pull over? Is that a note?"

"Just keep driving. I'll call Kitty."

"Well, what does it say?"

Bobbie squinted. "Kitty, are you still at the market or have you left?"

Sitting on an apple crate in the bell tower, Kitty answered her two way radio. "You weren't very coy about leaving, so I'm having the team continue taking pictures to see who might be following you."

Bobbie pursed her lips. "I was that noticeable? I'm sorry. Putting my hand in the bag I felt a paper around the apple… "

Kitty chuckled. "You did fine for no training. What does the note say?"

She heard the phone make a thud and paper rattling.

"Kitty, still there?"

"Yes, go ahead. We're watching that woman you saw getting into her car. Hopefully one of our team can get a photo of the license."

"The note is scribbled. It says, 'Ross-d, I'm closer than you think. Don't try to find me. Alex must pay'." Bobbie paused and stared at Ross.

He glanced over at her. "Is that it?"

Bobbie shook her head. "No, she says… ' your friend is pretty…I was… once….Jane."

Bobbie leaned against the car door and waved the note at Ross. "Dennis, she had to be the shabby lady at the fruit stand. That's what took so long. She wrote this note."

Leaning back against the tower bell, Kitty checked her watch. "I want to get out of here before this bell makes me deaf as a post."

She heard Dennis in the background asking Bobbie for the radio. "Kitty, this note sounds to me like Jane is following a plan."

"I agree. All the more reason we need to meet. Has to be at the office in the morning. It will give my team time to sift through the photos they want to print. We've literally taken hundreds. How's eight in the morning. You bring the scones."

Bobbie grinned. "We'll see you eight sharp…"

He heard Kitty say, "Cheer up, I think we have a plan, too."

Ross stared at Bobbie. "Jane has a vendetta. Somehow we have to stop her." He shook his head. "He'll kill her. She doesn't have a chance against him!"

Chapter 17

The Village Market

Zilpha put her basket in the backseat and then shut her door. She smiled at Alex. "Well, I'm sure Jane made contact with Ross and his …"

Alex sat up and shifted the stick. "Her name is Bobbie and don't be fooled, very smart. How do you know they made contact?"

"Well, she may be smart but I can assure you, she's not at all discreet." Zilpha laughed. "I got to the fruit stand they'd just left and watched them. It looked like they were going to sit for a while and eat an apple. Her hand was in the bag all of a second, before she bolted off the bench and they left."

Alex turned the key. "The obvious question…What was in the bag? A note from Jane."

Zilpha grinned nodding. "That would be my guess. I studied as many faces as I could, without being noticed, and saw no one resembling the pictures you gave me. I left after the vendor at the fruit stand yelled at me that I was holding up the line."

Alex stared at her for a moment. "Let's say there is a note in the bag. What did the woman look like that yelled at you?"

Zilpha shook her head. "No, couldn't have been." *Or could it. She was about the same height, though a bit hunched over.* "You know, it could have been her. I was fooled by how dirty and shabby she looked." She opened her door. "I can go back and look around."

He patted her leg. "No, trust me, she's gone and won't be back there. I found her on the streets in London and took her in. While I was tracking down Charlie, I trained Jane to be a decoy. She was very quick to learn as if she was born that way. I must admit, we had fun executing a lot of people. If the caper suddenly took a turn, she was quick to improvise. She was astounded how much money people would pay to kill off someone. However, about the same time Charlie found me, Ross introduced Jane to his wife, Lizzy, and that was the beginning of the end of Jane's usefulness."

He drove to the road. "Which way are they headed?" Zilpha showed him the tracking box. He smiled. "They're done for today, and so are we. That dot is headed for, my guess, Bobbie's house."

Chapter 18

Progress in Johannesburg. Jo, the nurse, gets hired

Linda and Theresa walked down the hallway. “Is it the elevation, humidity or the fact we’re sitting on the Tropic of Capricorn that I feel so fucking lethargic? When is it going to rain? No wonder we pay for the fucking bottled water.”

Theresa took a swig of her bottled water as Linda inserted the key. “Seriously, the water is more expensive than a fucking bottle of beer!”

Linda opened their door chuckling. “I bet you can’t say a complete sentence without using that word.”

They were greeted by their other teammates stretched out on the couches asleep.

Theresa whistled. “We’re back.” With her hands on her hips, she pointed at Linda. “You lose. I just made a sentence…Three in fact. FOUR!”

Linda threw a pillow at Theresa. “Just shut up.”

Jo and Hennessey cringed. “Are you two having a spat?”

Theresa brought a tray of ice tea and put it on the coffee table. “No, it’s not a big fucking deal. She just lost a bet.”

Linda shook her head. “Okay…down to business. How’d your day go?”

Jo smiled and showed them her badge. “I’m now on the surgical staff at the Edse Memorial Hospital. Would you believe I was interviewed by Doctor Edse? He asked some difficult but interesting questions. I’ll write them done for you to give to the boss. Strange, he kept asking me if we had met before.”

Linda hesitated. "Have you met him? That could be a problem." She wrote the question down for her report.

Jo shook her head and shrugged her shoulders. "I've been a nurse for ten years and have been in a lot of situations and I can't say for sure that I have or haven't. Evidently he liked my answers enough to hire me. He did say that occasionally there are emergencies and I should be available. Of course, I was given the night shift, eight to five. In a way that might be good. I can't imagine they havc that many surgeries at those hours. I'll have more time to peruse the area."

Hennessey mimicked Jo. "Peruse? Well, I've been attending both Conferences at the Art Center. This afternoon when I was leaving, I ran into High Pockets! I almost asked him if the sun had disappeared for him to leave his chair in the back, but then I thought he'd know we're watching them."

Linda nodded. "You are quick with the retorts, Hennessey, so be careful you don't put your foot in your mouth." She looked out the balcony door. "We can sit out there if you want. Looks like Alex and the attorney are leaving."

Hennessey jumped up. "I'll be glad to follow them."

Theresa pulled on the back of her shirt. "Not so fast, Sunshine. I'm sure they're used to the agent who is following them. We don't want to blow our cover."

Linda took her tea and sat on the balcony wall. "Well, this is where we part. Jo, you have the keys to your new quarters. Theresa and I went over there today to check out the area. Actually, you could walk it or ride a bike if you wanted the exercise. It's less than a kilometer from the hospital. It appears to be well lit. Not exactly travelled by the rich and famous, but it didn't seem risky either. Hennessey, you'll need the car or you can take the bus to attend the conferences. We still need you to act as a student."

Hennessey stopped at the door. "We should eat out to celebrate Jo's job and that we've been here almost two weeks. Two boring weeks at that."

Jo grabbed her stuff. "Good idea, but I may have to beg off. I better take a nap. Not used to a night shift. Can't get fired the first night on the job."

Theresa stretched out on the couch. "That sounds like a good idea. Hennessey, we'll meet you here in the hotel restaurant around six. Not six thirty!"

Hennessey pushed Jo out the door. "Yeah, we'll see who's on time. Come on, Granny, I'll tuck you in."

The two of them waved to Linda as they drove by the balcony. "Why the frown?"

Linda looked at her watch. "We have time. I think I'm going to call Kitty. She may still be in her office. I'm concerned how flippant Hennessey has become. I get the feeling she's stepped out of the loop. That attorney she calls High Pockets really has struck her fancy. I saw her talking with him out by the garage, a couple of days ago. She brushed it off as if it was nothing."

Theresa grimaced grabbing their purses. "For all concerned, she needs to be replaced and quickly. I think I made a mistake vouching for her after the first time we all worked together saving the Admiral."

Linda stopped short. "Vouching? For what?"

Theresa held the door. "Do you remember when Hennessey came bursting out of that basement with her nun's outfit tied up looking like pants?"

Out in the hall, Linda locked the door. "Yes I do. None of us knew she was in there and I remember you cussed at her for being stupid."

Theresa raised her brow. "Fuckin' right. I drew my gun and almost shot the little shit. Though everyone laughed about her get-up, Kitty later asked me about it. She saw the horrible consequences that could have resulted and thought Hennessy should go back into training. I told her I thought Hennessy realized how dangerous her act of being funny was, after seeing a gun pointed at her. I don't think Kitty agreed entirely. Since then, I think Kitty upped the recruitment age to twenty-five."

They walked down the alley to the back of the Embassy. Linda stopped at the steps. "Wait here. This shouldn't take long."

Theresa sat on a ledge by the back door of the British Embassy until Linda came out. “We should have brought the car. I could have taken a nap.”

Linda shrugged her shoulders. “Sorry about that. The boss gave me a long update of their progress before I could give mine. Seems Ross and Bobbie have made contact with Jane in a strange way.”

“Why strange? They should be whooping it up.”

They walked to the main street through an alley. Linda put on her sunglasses. “Kitty wasn’t real explicit, but said, the problem is, Jane wants her own revenge and as much as has said for them to…”

Theresa laughed out loud. “The girl’s got balls. She probably told them to fuck off.”

Linda nodded. “For once you’re right. So that means our problem is minor. Kitty said until Alex leaves here, we have to deal with Hennessey. Her girls are already primed in their tasks. She doesn’t want to mess that up. They’re hoping to make contact with Jane another time before Alex returns, at least for her to accept some back-up.”

“Yeah, I can understand the frustration. Plus, the boss is running out of time to help Ross. Hey, don’t you think it’s strange that Alex hasn’t made an effort to even visit the hospital, yet Edse’s been wining and dining Alex and his attorney almost every day and...I was expecting him to be dashing over there for the surgery. Then back to England to find Jane.”

Linda peered over her sunglasses taking hold of Teresa’s arm. “Lord, we do have a problem. Look over at the café.”

Chapter 19

Inspector Carroll's office 8:00 a.m. sharp

Bobbie chuckled and motioned to Ross to look at their boss. "With that hair do, you'll win first prize for sure…" Bobbie saw the blanket folded sitting under the pillow. "Kitty, you weren't here all night?"

Kitty smiled and nodded. "It's far from being the first time and won't be the last. I just sent the rookies home for a few hours. You can mull over this report while I freshen up."

She handed Bobbie and Ross a folder and then went to her private office.

Ross gulped. "My God, this woman is efficient. These pictures are outstanding." He held a couple up. "Did you teach the team? They're already numbered and identified."

Bobbie squinted. "Maybe a few pointers."

Ross nodded. "I bet you taught a course for Kitty. According to this report, the woman you thought was following us, isn't in the system."

Bobbie pursed her lips. "Yes, but read further." She continued. "They were able to get the license number off the car as it left the village square and…"

They looked at each other stunned. "The owner of the car is Edward Edse!"

Ross blurted. “Holy shit! Then they had to be following us.” He almost fell into a chair.

Kitty appeared wearing a beige linen pant suit and looking all refreshed. “By the look on your faces you’ve read whose car it is.”

Kitty picked up her purse. “Well, it can’t be coincidence. Come on, we can talk at breakfast. My girls won’t be back until ten. We can chew over this at the Ministries’ restaurant. Where did you park?”

Ross opened the door. “To avoid the security check in the garage, I parked on the street.”

Kitty pointed at him. “That’ll save time. I’m in the garage. You get to drive.”

Bobbie cringed. “You’re in for a treat.”

Chapter 20

The cottage in Shoreham- by Sea

Zilpha arrived at eight thirty with scones. Alex made tea and they settled on the patio. Their breakfast was interrupted by a phone call. As Alex talked, he pulled the long cord so he could let her hear the conversation. He whispered, "It's Edward."

Cradling the phone under his chin, he took a sip of his tea. "I was right. Ross has made contact with Jane. She wouldn't have left that note in the vault threatening me had she not wanted retribution. She wants her pound of flesh."

Alex put the phone on speaker as Edse replied. "Alex, don't make a production out of this. You know fucking well this has nothing to do with Jane, but your damn *ego*! Get those account numbers and codes, and get the fuck out of there. If you get caught, then what? The money isn't that important anymore. Just remember, we're to meet with our new colleagues in New York in two months! My experiment is about finished. Everything on my end is going smoothly. Our plan is working perfectly. Please! Don't fuck it up with this obsession of catching *Jane!*"

Zilpha stared at Alex watching his eyes enlarge. *He's a doctor Jekyll. His eyes have gone black with hate. He's going to break that phone in half; he's squeezing it so...Not good.*

Alex gritted his teeth taking a deep breath, and leaned over the speaker. "Our Plan? Since when did *my* idea of utilizing nanotechnology on a massive scale, allowing you to develop *my* concept, organizing this meeting with *my* connections with the international crime syndicates, become Our Plan? Keep in mind, there are two other doctors presenting experiments such as yours! Besides, I know fucking well, she'll make a mistake." *Little does he know, those codes will give me the upper hand in this deal.*

Edward yelled. "Are you done? Let me remind you, you're the one who made the fucking mistake allowing her to come back at all. You knew how crazed she was over the loss of Ross's wife. You're the one who wants them dead."

Embarrassed, Alex took the phone off speaker and walked into the house. "Fuck you…I'm not going to get into a battle over errors made… Right now, Jane thinks I'm in Africa. At this point, she's not hiding from me. We're tracking Ross and I think he'll lead us to her. Yes, I want them dead, and Zilpha wants to help me do it. Two more weeks and we'll fly to Johannesburg. Now are you finished?"

Alex frowned and walked back out to the patio. "I'm going to put you on speaker again…Okay, repeat what you just said."

"Neil asked Henry last night at dinner who the girl was that he's been seeing."

Zilpha, startled, looked at Alex. "What? Henry? You must be mistaken."

Edse chuckled. "That's what I would have said too. He reminds me so much of Windsor…"

Alex cleared his throat in disgust. "No, Edward, he doesn't and he isn't." *No way would Henry ever fill the sick role Windsor played in Edse's life!*

The doctor heard Zilpha say she wanted Henry to call her.

"Zilpha, I'll have him call you tomorrow. He said it was nothing. Seems they've been meeting several times now. It's always in public. Henry told us he met her on the plane. She's a student attending the art conference. Right now I don't see a problem. I think he's bored with all of this free time. He wants to get back to his work in England… Ahh, you have trained him to handle a situation if needed?"

Alex saw Zilpha bite her lip. "No, Edward. He's an attorney, period. Zilpha doesn't want him exposed to this life at all. So if anything needs to be done, you and Neil will have to deal with it. I promised Zilpha Henry wouldn't be involved. We have a lot of planning to do. I'll touch base with you tonight."

Alex patted her shoulder. "Edse would say if there was a problem. Don't get yourself in a tizzy over this."

Not smiling, she stared at him. "Charlie saw Henry's potential and his love for the structure of the law. Henry and Michael would tell us the law was filled with mystery. That every word had a zillion ways of being used…"

They walked out to Zilpha's car. "Charlie felt Henry could work his way into the justice system. Perhaps even into the High Court. We kept telling Henry his record had to be blemish free." She closed her eyes. "Maybe I want him to sacrifice too much."

Alex held the door for her. *This is crazy. Fuck, I can't believe Charlie was this consumed in this parent stuff.* "Zilpha, talk to Henry first, before you draw any conclusions. I'm sure Edse is right. Henry's bored." *Not as bored as I am! Baby sitter, I'm not. Fuck this.*

She rolled down her window as he stepped back from the car. "Aren't you coming?"

Alex shook his head. "No, I have work I can get done here. I want to plot some maps. I think you need to clear your head first. Call me later after you've talked with Henry." *Such an eye-opener. One Jane is enough... Fuckin' kids…ruin everything... never ends. He's no fuckin' kid.* Not thinking, still fuming, Alex slammed the gate and kicked it hard in place.

Zilpha saw Alex in the rear view mirror. *Hope that gate was able to take that. He's got a temper. Makes me wonder if Jane really had an accident as he said.*

Chapter 21

Scotland Yard Dream Team meeting

Ross pulled into the Scotland Yard Garage. "I won't need lunch or dinner. That buffet was huge."

Bobbie grinned. "Guess you never heard of will power."

Suddenly they heard an alarm go off, lights started flashing everywhere and four guards surrounded the car. Ross gasped. "What is going on?"

Their doors opened. "Inspectors, get out of the car immediately. Stand over there!"

A guard hurriedly escorted them behind a wall. "No disrespect, sir and mum, but all vehicles pass over a screen, and there's something attached to the bottom of your engine. We're not sure. It could be a bomb. You'll be safe here."

They watched through an explosion - proof window as a huge transparent shroud lowered from the ceiling. Ross shook his head. "I'll bet that's one of Doctor Braun's inventions." His eyes big as saucers, he nudged Bobbie. "Remember when Mrs. Braun's limousine was inspected at the Yard's lab?"

Bobbie raised her brow recalling the experience and then told Kitty about the episode. "This all happened, before you were brought in on the Braun case. Have you seen the Yard's new lab?"

Kitty shrugged. "They have a new one?"

Ross piped up. "Why it's being kept a secret, I don't know. I didn't have a clue it existed, until the Chief sent me to investigate Braun's wife's death."

Bobbie grinned. “You really have to see it. I’ll go over with you. It’s mind boggling what the technicians can deduce from a speck of anything. When Mrs. Braun and her chauffer were found dead in a ravine, it was meant to look like a DUI, but that lab proved otherwise. They had been murdered and put in the car.”

Before she could finish, a man appeared from the bomb squad, looking like an astronaut in his bomb suit. He walked slowly around the car holding a detection device.

The three of them stared at one another, when another guard waved them over. “False alarm. We can’t be too careful with all the terrorists coming into England recently. I’ve sent for a technician to remove this.” He pointed to a monitor.

Ross frowning. “What the hell is it?”

The guard operating the monitor cringed. “It’s quite a sophisticated tracking device.”

Ross stared at Bobbie. “Alex’s house and…”

Bobbie nodded. “The market.”

Kitty saw the technician appear. “Wait a minute. Hold off removing that. For now, just park Inspector Ross’s car and we’ll get back to you.”

She waved for Ross and Bobbie to follow. “We need to discuss this first. I’ll meet you in my office. I want to talk to the technician.”

Kitty went back to Ross’s car. “Sergeant, could you provide me all the information available about this device? I’ll be in my office.”

The technician entered a bunch of letters and numbers into his keyboard. “If you have a minute, you can take it with you, mum.”

Before she could walk back to him, she heard the printer rattle away, and he handed her two pages. “This is all the information we have. It shows diagrams of the tracker and the receiver as well.”

She smiled. “What did we do before technology?”

Opening her office door, she found Ross and Bobbie sitting with her team forming a horseshoe in classroom chairs. She handed the papers to Patti D. “Run off a copy for each of us, please.” Leaving her jacket on, she went to the black board. Smiling, she looked at Ross. “I’m sure Ross and Bobbie filled you in about the garage.”

As she wrote ‘who and how’ in big letters, Patti D. handed out copies. “Place went into lock down, Boss, and we got to watch the incident on our monitors. It was great! Like watching a movie."

The others laughed.

Kitty shrugged her shoulders. "So far working with Inspector Ross hasn't given us many dull moments." She scratched her head. "That includes riding in the car with him."

Bobbie burst out laughing and patted his shoulder as he put on a sad face.

Patti D. looked at her colleagues. "Must be an inside joke…or a heads-up not to ride with him."

Kitty pointed to the board. "Anyone, what are your thoughts about this? Who could have done it? How was it done and how long has it been there?"

Ross stared off. "I haven't parked in the garage for at least a week, maybe even longer. The security checks take forever so I've been parking on the street. Alex certainly knows where I live, so anyone could have put that under my car at my home."

Bobbie touched his arm. "That would mean, Alex had in place two or more people to watch or follow you because…That was his plan all along."

Ross's eyes flashed. "He thinks Jane would come to me if she felt safe."

Kitty leaned against the chalk board. "Bobbie, you're deep in thought. What are you thinking?"

Bobbie put her hand on Patti D.'s shoulder. "Could you put on the screen the pictures from the airport, the day Alex left? I agree with Dennis…"

The lights went off in the room when the screen lit up the wall."Okay, what do we know about these two men other than they're Alex's lawyers? One of them went to Africa with him and the other is here. Are we watching the one who is here?"

Kitty studied the pictures and walked up to the screen with her pointer. "We have checked out both the men and they have no prior connection to Alex nor questionable backgrounds. They were hired to defend Alex at his trial. But, at this point in time, we could check a bit deeper."

Kitty glanced at Patti D., who hurried to the computer room. "I'm on it, Boss."

One of the new recruits raised her hand. "I think we need to find out more about the woman in the market pictures. My guess, she lives within the area. A couple of us could canvas the area with her picture."

Another recruit spoke out. "Yes, but wonder if we show it to someone who knows her and they'll tell her. That's chancy. I think we have to find her on our own."

Kitty shrugged. "Time is against us. For now, I think the tracker should stay on Ross's car to avoid alerting whoever is tailing him."

Up went a hand. "I have an idea, Kitty!"

They all laughed at the excitement of the recruit. "Okay, what is it?"

"Inspector Ross should give us his schedule for the day and we could be at each location prior to his arrival and be watching, taking pictures. Just for the heck of it, I would ask him to go back to the market where he first made contact."

Kitty nodded. "Good idea. What do you think, Dennis?"

"I agree. I can let Patti D. know where I'm going. I'm not quite sure Jane would go back to a place she had been so recently."

Dennis bit his lip. "I do have one question. How were you able to set up the meeting with Jane and can you do it again? The end of her note explains the reason for the vendetta. It also leads me to another question. Is she able to handle him physically? I think the scar on her face was the last straw. That being said, I certainly hope she's able to defend herself against him. If she isn't, it would be suicide for her to take him on." He stared at Kitty. "After all of this time, I can't imagine she's doing this to lose. She has to have a plan."

He then waved his hands. "Though, she certainly has been able to disguise her appearance and whereabouts for the long time she's been missing. Somehow, we have to alert her that we can give her support catching him."

Tapping her pencil on her desk, Bobbie frowned at him. "Dennis, I don't think Jane wants to catch him…She wants to kill him."

Kitty nodded. "I'm sure you're right. Still we have to try to catch them both if we can. Time is running out. Karen, tell us what you found out from the orphanage and how you arranged the meeting at the market. And, do you think you can set up another one?"

Karen put her notes on the desk. "When you sent me to Bedrule to get some background information on Jane, I met with a priest, Father James Turnbull. He started the orphanage and still runs it."

Karen scanned her notes as she talked. "At first, I thought I had been sent on a wild goose chase. He was very polite and eagerly recalled how smart she was as a child, leading me to believe that was all he knew. The priest really didn't leave any room for me to ask any other questions."

She looked up at them smiling. "As he tried to open the door, I stood in front of it and as a last resort showed him the photo copy of the sketch Jane drew of your wife. I pointed to the spelling of Ross-d. Father James stood in silence and then invited me to have a seat. He apologized for his abruptness because being a priest he didn't want to break his vows by lying to me. Jane had told him Ross-d was the only one she could trust. Father James told me Jane calls him when she can. It's usually once a week."

Ross grinned. "That was the sign. Very good. Then this Father James agreed to arrange it?

Karen cringed a little. "Not exactly…He told me he had no way of contacting her. The best he could do was relay our request the next time she called. He has my cell number, my home number, and the number to this office."

Patti D. poked her head out of the computer room. "Karen had a call here before she landed, but the man wouldn't leave a message."

Karen smiled. "I told him the lines for the Dream Team Office were secured. I called as soon as I walked in and he told me to have you go to the market place. She would contact you if she felt safe."

Kitty interrupted. "We didn't have much time to coordinate this operation. I knew you'd gone to Alex's, so we called you as soon as we got set up at the market. Truly, that was a feat in itself."

Bobbie shook her head. "You're unbelievable. This team is precision plus."

Dennis crossed his arms. "After all that, Jane tells us to stay away."

Kitty leaned back in her chair. "We can't be discouraged. Dennis, remember, you're the one Jane trusts. I think she's counting on Alex looking for her until he gets back what she has of his. She's very smart not to trust anyone other than you. Maybe she's trying to protect you from Alex. She did see Bobbie with you. Maybe she thinks you've remarried."

Karen tightened her bottom lip. "I can try again. I'll call the priest today and see what he says. I know he's not seen her in a couple of years but does know about the scar. I didn't have to tell him how treacherous Alex could be. Jane went to the priest after Alex beat her up so badly. He tried to get her to stay after she recovered, but she told him she had to fulfill a promise."

Ross frowned. "What promise? To whom?"

She studied her notes. "When I brought up the money she had taken from Alex, he called it blood money. He knew how it was gotten and that she had been involved for a while. She sent him some for the orphanage and wanted to send more, but his conscience wouldn't allow him to accept it. I asked him if he knew why she took the money. He got up and I knew our conversation was over. I started to ask the same question again, but he just smiled and said Jane had to give me the answer. He couldn't." She looked at Ross. "I assume she confessed and his vow of silence came into play."

Ross dropped his head. "There's more to this story than we figured. I have a feeling Lizzy brought out her better nature and Alex wasn't going to have it. We won't know unless this priest will help us get to her. I wish I could go see him, but we know that's out of the question."

Karen got up to leave. "I'll get on it right away. It's hard talking with him on the phone. He's very reluctant to say much. He acts like the phone is tapped."

Kitty held up her hand. "I'll call and get you on the next transport plane going to Edinburgh… When you see the priest, emphasize, we want to support Jane and protect her in every way we can. If we knew her plan, we could help. I'll also check if we can provide a secured line there. We may not have enough time to get that done."

Karen nodded and started to leave.

Ross got up. "If it's all the same with you, I'd like to go with Karen. Maybe I can shed more light on what the priest could say to convince Jane to let us help."

Kitty cringed. "I was hoping you'd give Patti D. your schedule for the next few days so we can get the team out looking for whoever is tracking you."

He thought for a moment, then addressed Karen. "Go ahead. Kitty's right."

Karen hesitated. "I'll call you on your cell if I have a question…Okay?"

Ross grabbed a cup of coffee and followed Patti D. into the control office.

Bobbie bit her lip. "I'm surprised he backed off as he did. I know how much he wants to handle finding her."

Kitty smiled raising her eyebrows. "His restraint showed willingness to be a team player, and that is really important at this time. We've got to find out who's following him and how many."

"In the meantime, you can help me target some areas for the rest of the team to canvas."

Chapter 22

Henry's dilemma

Holding the phone base in one hand, Henry paced from the balcony to the other end of the apartment talking. "Mom, it's nothing. I met her on the plane. She's funny and interesting. No, I haven't even held her hand. We're always in public."

Neil walked out of the bathroom with a towel wrapped around his waist. He whispered. "Do you want me to talk to her?"

Henry shook his head and mouthed, "No."

"Yes, I'm listening. I know what Uncle Charlie preached to me. Yes, I want that as well. I do miss my work and really want to come home."

Henry stopped, plumped on the bed, and stared at Neil. "What do you mean you're helping Alex? Mum! He's not the sort of person I would think you could be interested in. He's got…a… really bad temper!"

Neil chuckled as he heard Zilpha say, 'Not any more than your fa…uncle and we did just fine.'

Henry shrugged his shoulders and shook his head. "Okay, then do what you have to do so we can come home. Neil's going nuts too. Love you, goodbye." *I've heard her break off a word before when she gets flustered.* Henry stared out the balcony door. *She would have said father.*

Neil threw a pillow at Henry. "What's running around in that fat head of yours? You look like you're deep in thought."

Henry shook his head, tossing the pillow on the bed. "Nothing. It's a surprise that she sounds so invigorated. I really can't imagine how she's helping Alex." Henry put the phone back on the desk. "Maybe she's cooking up a storm and doing his laundry."

Neil got a razor out of his pack. "We still have another hour before the great doctor gets here. We can meet you in the bar if you like. Looks to me like you could use a beer. Something's bugging you…If you're not going to say, then go have a drink. That might loosen you up. I'll be down in twenty minutes."

Henry headed through the restaurant toward the bar and saw Hennessey sitting alone at a table. "Hey, did you get stood up?"

She smiled. "I'm waiting for some of my school friends. A couple of them live here."

He motioned. "Come on, we can watch from the bar. My treat." *She is so cute. I've never had so much fun with a girl before.*

Hennessey hesitated getting up, "As long as we can see over here. My friends always tease me about being late. So, I got here first." *It's hard to concentrate. His smile is captivating.*

Henry handed Hennessey a beer. "Here's mud in your eye." Holding his bottle up, he chortled. "I've always wanted to say that. Cheers."

Hennessey leaned back laughing. "I've always wanted to say, 'break a leg'." *Keep the small talk going. I really don't want to lie to you.* "HP, did you ever get ahold of your mother? You said the other day you hadn't talked to her since you got here."

Henry blushed. "Actually, I talked to her before I came here…" He frowned. "She's dating someone I don't approve of. I was upset about it until I saw you. Thanks for being here."

Hennessey shrugged her shoulders. "As our parents get older, it seems our roles get reversed."

He chuckled and raised his bottle to her. "Amen to that. Since my Uncle Charles was killed a year ago, she's become very quiet and less interested in going out. Then, I made the mistake of introducing her to one of my clients, and now I hear they're seeing one another."

Hennessey frowned. "Is he that bad?"

Henry swallowed hard and blurted. "Yes, he's disgusting...He should have been put to death, but my partner and I found a lot of technicalities in the case and were able to get him off with time served."

Hennessey stared at him. "Well, I can understand your concern." *Is he talking about McGraw? This sounds too familiar. But, McGraw is here. How is his mother...*

Henry leaned toward Hennessey and gazed into her eyes. He gulped the rest of his beer. "Your friends still haven't arrived. Would you like another beer?"

She squinted. "Not really, I'll keep you company."

He ordered one for himself, when Neil appeared. "Hi! Well, are you going to introduce me to your friend?"

Henry stood next to Hennessey with his arm around her shoulder. "Elizabeth, this is my client...Alex McGraw..."

Hennessey smiled and put her hand out. "It's nice to meet to you...You were on the news in England. HP told me how exciting your case was to win."

Neil frowned at Henry. *I sure hope you haven't said anything you shouldn't.*

Surmising what Neil was thinking, Henry quickly shook his head behind her.

Without thinking, Neil extended his right hand. *HP is right. She's a pretty girl with enchanting eyes.*

Holding his hand, Hennessey flinched. *I expected him to offer his left hand. My gosh, his hand is real.*

Both men saw a strange look in her eyes as she felt Neil's hand. They stared at one another. Just then their host, Dr. Edse, appeared. "Well, good evening all. I thought I might find you in the bar. This must be your new friend, Henry."

The doctor peered into her eyes, watching for recognition. *There would be only one way she would know my name.* He took her hand and felt it quiver. "My name is Doctor Edward Edse, my dear."

Hennessey smiled weakly, as her heart pumped wildly. *Where's Theresa...Why didn't I listen.* She swallowed hard. "It's nice to meet you, Doctor." She looked at Henry, "I really must be going. I have a feeling my friends may have forgotten or have overslept. They take naps in the afternoon…"

When she started to get off the bar chair, Edse pricked her arm with something. She stared at Edse and pulled her arm from the chair to her side. "Did you pinch me?"

Ignoring her, Edse looked at the men and whispered. "She can walk. Meet me at my hospital."

The bartender came to take the empties and saw Hennessey bleary-eyed. "Are you all right, Miss?" Hennessey tried to talk. Edse stood in front of her, handing the man a hundred dollar bill. "Will this cover the drinks?"

Wide-eyed, the bartender laughed. "This works…have fun guys." He grabbed the bottles and left.

As Edse took her arm, Henry stood in front of his girlfriend, staring Edse down, whispering. "I don't know why the big deal. She watches the news and reads the papers."

Hennessey leaned back to look around the doctor and saw Theresa. "My friends…" She stared at Henry. "What are you…"

Edse turned to see Hennessey's friends being seated.

Edse glared at Henry. "If you don't settle down and do as I say right now, I will give you the rest of this sedative, and there's enough here to put you out permanently. Do you understand, Henry?"

Henry and Neil stepped back to watch the doctor walk Hennessey toward the back door.

Theresa looked toward the bar when their waiter appeared. "What's the commotion over at the bar?"

The waiter tapped his pencil. "Too much to drink. It's always bad when it's a woman. You know, they get boisterous and…" Theresa glowered at him. "And men don't?"

Linda nudged Theresa and whispered, "Temper! Cool your jets. We don't need a scene."

She peered around the waiter at a reflection in the mirror behind the bar. "I'll have ice water and she'll have a gin and tonic…" As the bartender retreated to fill the order, Linda saw Henry and Edse helping someone.

She whispered and stood up. "Theresa, come on. I don't like what I just saw. Some female was taken out of the bar. My gut says it was Hennessey. "

They quickly went into the bar but saw no one. Theresa stared at Linda. "Are you sure?"

Linda nodded and wheeled around. "I'll ask the bartender. Check that door."

Theresa ran to the back door and came back. "A car drove away and I couldn't see anything." Linda motioned to Theresa to close the swinging bar doors. Theresa put the closed sign up.

Looking very anxious, Linda stood at the bar. "Tell me what that commotion was about!"

The man continued to wipe drinking glasses in silence.

Linda scowled at him. "I'm going to ask you once more, what just happened?"

The bartender snorted. "Yeah, and what the fuck do you dames think you're going to do to…"

Before he finished his smart remark back to her, Theresa moved quickly around the bar and grabbed his private parts. She whispered. "If you ever want to fuck someone again, you will tell us now what happened."

He grimaced in great pain and croaked. "Please let go."

"After I like what I hear."

He whispered to her all that happened. "Two of the hotel guests, the local doctor and a young girl. She might have been a…hooker? The doctor gave me a hundred bucks to look the other way."

Linda leaned over. "Did she have long dark hair? About my height?"

Theresa put pressure. He shut his eyes, stretching his back, taking a deep breath whispered. "Yes."

"What else did you hear?"

He winced. "The doctor got angry at the real tall guy for wanting her to be left alone. He told the doctor she recognized the other guy from the papers in England. The doctor threatened him and walked her out."

"Did the doctor say where he was taking her?"

Linda stared at him, and squeezed her hand at Theresa.

Seeing that, the bartender squealed. "He said to meet him at his hospital. That's all I know!"

Theresa let go and he fell to the floor. She knelt down and whispered. “You better hope that girl is still alive. If she isn’t, you’ll be looking at your balls in a jar. ”

Linda whispered as they ran to the back door. “We need to get to Jo before she goes to work.”

Chapter 23

Strategy or confusion?

Patti D. quietly entered the conference room carrying two large folders and a tray of coffee and tea. Right behind her was Karen Cogar. Inspectors Carroll and Bobbie Grantwood stood studying large maps on the table.

Not looking up, Kitty nodded. "I hope it's good news you're bringing."

Deep in thought, Bobbie was startled by Kitty's comment. She jumped seeing two people in the room with them. Blushing and wide-eyed, Bobbie took a step back. "My gosh, you scared me."

Patti D. chuckled. "Sorry, but we try to catch the boss with her guard down." She turned. "Excuse me. I hear the phone ringing in the control room."

Looking at Kitty, Bobbie questioned. "Do I need my hearing tested? I didn't hear them come in or that phone."

Kitty poured two cups. "Another part of training is to develop the senses, where you control your surroundings."

Bobbie sipped her tea. "I'm missing something. How do my senses gain control of my surroundings?"

Kitty sat on the corner of the conference table. "Good question… I incorporate the concept of multi-tasking in all of the training."

Kitty wrote on the black board as she explained. "We develop your five senses at the same time we develop your ability to think intently." She turned to Bobbie. "For example, you and I were studying the maps, writing down areas we want the team to survey. At the same time, I heard them come in the outer office. I glanced at the monitor to verify. Had it been an outsider, as we call them, I would have had time to effectively handle the situation, perhaps even saving a life."

Bobbie pursed her lips and shrugged. *There's so much to learn. I wonder if I'm too old.*

Kitty sensed her doubt. "You're on the list and the next term begins in September."

Bobbie squinted. "You read minds too?"

The conference room door opened. "Boss, we have a situation. Hennessey is missing!"

Kitty reeled around and stared at Patti D. frowning. *Shit...Linda tried to warn me.* The piece of chalk fell out of her hand to the floor, squeezed into many pieces. "Is Linda still on the phone?"

Chapter 24

Zilpha's patio and then Bedrule orphanage.

Alex pushed the doorbell. A rugged male voice answered. "Your name please."

He chuckled seeing the speaker in the corner of the porch. "Where are you?"

He heard, "On the patio" but it still wasn't Zilpha's voice. He cautiously walked around the outside of the cottage, finding her surrounded by papers on the table.

He stood and looked around. "Are you okay?"

She frowned at him. "Of course I'm okay. Put your gun away. Charlie fixed the intercom, so when I answered it would sound like a man's voice."

Alex relaxed, closing the little gate. "What are you studying? Looks like Interpol papers."

She glanced at him. "You didn't seem to know much about Jane, other than you took her off the streets of London, so I asked one of the men Charlie used for reference to run a history on her, giving the background you knew. I got back all of this. Did you know she was raised in an orphanage? In Scotland?"

Alex squinted and sat next to her shaking his head. "Zilpha, this isn't the first time I've heard this. Jane told me about the orphanage. In fact, after she made some real money working with me, she went to visit that old priest. She came back disillusioned and said she wouldn't be going back, and that was twenty years ago or more. She'll be fifty soon."

Zilpha handed him a picture of the orphanage with all the children and the staff. "If you'll notice, the priest is holding one of the younger ones. Look familiar?" She handed Alex a magnifying glass.

He handed the glass back to her. "He's holding her. So what's the big fuckin' deal? I told you she went there and…"

She pointed the picture at him. "That may be so, but, I bet she's got a copy of this picture. Alex, she was an orphan! She couldn't have been more than five years old in this picture. For a little girl, being held by him had to have been the happiest moment of her life."

Alex stared at her. "At five years old, I was a punching bag for my dad. So was my mother. He didn't need booze to get him started, either. He had an unfortunate accident when he took my mum and me to see the Cliffs of Dover. While she was setting up a picnic lunch, he went off to be the big deal climber, and he must have slipped." *I can see him sitting on a rock. He was already grizzling about something one of us had done to piss him off. I found a stone I could lift and got up behind him and...smashed his head. I heard my mum calling for us. He started to get up and staggered a bit and that's when I pushed him. He didn't make a sound. That was an act of genius for a five year old.*

Zilpha frowned seeing contentment rather than regret in the glow of his eyes. *I don't want to ask.*

She offered him a cup of tea. "I still say, she's not going to forget that if and when she needs help. Of all the people a scared person would turn to, it would be a priest. Why? For one reason, she values his vow of silence, and she feels kinship because he raised her."

She leaned against the cabinet holding her cup. "I think we should pay this man a visit."

Alex frowned. "What?" *What the fuck, she doesn't know Jane. Jane would go to Ross before a priest. He'll lead me to her. A trip to Scotland is a waste of precious time.* He got up and paced. "I think you're wrong. Jane isn't afraid of *anything*!"

He pulled a tattered note out of his wallet and slammed it down on the table. "Read this and then tell me she's scared. She had the balls to leave this in my vault after she emptied it."

Zilpha read it and stared at him, repeating it out loud. "This is for Lizzy! You killed the only real person in my life. Now, it's your turn to pay!" She handed him the note. "Is there no one that's not expendable to you?"

Alex stopped dead in his tracks. "You are. Charlie was." *Now's not the time to be tough. You need this woman. She knows I killed Lizzy.* "I'm sorry. Jane was all I had. But, she was cruel to me…She kept wanting more and more. Then she chose Ross's wife over me. Zilpha, I didn't kill Lizzy. She had cancer. Jane said this, because I resented her taking care of Lizzy rather than me."

Zilpha touched his shoulder as he sat with his head down. "I'm sorry. This note certainly accuses you, but, I can see it could have another meaning…" *Is he sincere? Or is he telling me what I want to hear?*

Grinning inwardly, Alex cringed, as he clenched his hands. "Thank you for understanding." *Now can we get back to the game plan?*

As he stood patiently watching the wind blow the high brush, he glanced to see if Zilpha had lost confidence in him. *At least she's still studying that picture and looking at a map. My ego and impatience will fuck this up. She is so smart and genuine. I've got to do something to save this.* "I'm sorry for shouting. Charlie was a lucky man to have you by his side." He put his hand on her shoulder. "You're right, we should meet this priest. Will you still go?"

She studied his face. "Yes, I think it's the right move. We could make it there in less than four hours."

Alex looked at his watch. "Okay, let's go."

Father James opened the big chapel back door. "Karen, come in. I got your message long after your departure. Please have a seat. Can I fix you a cup of tea?"

She glanced around his office and saw a transition being made. She smiled at him. "I see you have a computer and surveillance around the church and the grounds for the orphanage."

He nodded. "The money Jane sent me started all of this. I must admit it has proved to be a valuable tool." The old man chuckled. "I can't yell at them as I used to. Now I can watch who's doing what." His eyes sparkled at her. "I catch them in the act. Then I press that button over there and can tell them what penance it will cost them."

He saw her take out her notebook. "Well, I'm sure you didn't come all this way to hear about my children. What can I do for you? I have a feeling it's more about Jane."

Karen waited for him to sit and then sat in a parson's chair near the priest's desk. "Yes, you're right, and I'm sorry, Father James, for the intrusion, but my team thinks it is very important that you ask Jane to meet with Ross-d. Actually, we would like it if you could be there as well. "

The priest set two cups of tea on his desk as he sat. "No, I could never leave my children to do that. But why all the urgency?"

She then told him about the meeting at the Woking Market on the square and her note to Ross. "We are very concerned that she is taking on more than she realizes and …and…my boss feels Jane's intention is to kill Alex instead of bringing him to justice."

The priest dropped his head and clasped his hands. "I know about this and I've tried to reason with her. She truly believes Alex murdered Lizzy."

Karen's eyes bolted. "What are you saying? That's impossible, Father James. Mrs. Ross died of cancer."

He stared at her shaking his head. "No…no…Jane found in Alex's papers that he was drugging Mrs. Ross's food and drink with cancer cells. For some reason he felt she was a liability to him and…"

Karen sank against the straight back of the chair. *My God, my God. I can only tell this to Kitty and no one else. Inspector Ross will lose his mind if he hears this.* "That's why you said Jane had to tell us her reason for stealing Alex's money and documents."

A buzzer went off at the computer. The priest looked at the monitor. "That's strange, I know we are expecting a couple wanting to adopt but not until tomorrow."

Karen glanced at the screen and her eyes widened. "Father James, you can't go out there. I was about to tell you that at the market we noticed Ross and his partner, Inspector Grantwood, were being followed. Sir." Karen pointed to the screen. "That's the couple… For sure that's the woman."

She got up. "Let me go out and tell them you're indisposed at this time."

The priest shook his head. "No, my child. This is the house of the Almighty. I will be fine."

He got up and took his walking stick. "This shouldn't take long."

The priest took his time moving down the aisle of the chapel. "I'm Father James Turnbull. May I help you? Are you interested in adopting a child? Unfortunately our children are on a field trip. If you'd like to come back tomorrow."

He shook hands with Zilpha. Alex stood back further and bowed slightly to the priest, smirking. *Turnbull, that name's familiar. When I impersonated an officer to kidnap Admiral Benjamin, that was the name Charlie had on the name tag. Wonder if we're related.*

Zilpha smiled and handed him her Interpol badge with her picture and name embossed on it. "I'm Zilpha Peckham and this is Inspector James Gibbons. As you can see, we're with Interpol."

She handed him an old picture of him holding Jane "Yes, Father, hopefully you can help us." She handed him two more photos. She smiled. "These are more recent. The child you're holding in this photo, and who appears in these two more recent photos, has been identified as Jane Wainright. She's being investigated for embezzling. Finding out she's an orphan is making our job quite difficult. As you can see, Our Lady of Angels is stamped on the back with this address."

The priest frowned. "How do you think I can help you?"

Zilpha grinned. "You see, most criminals turn to family or friends for help, and we have nothing other than this picture."

Alex glared at the priest as the priest held the photo up close to his eyes. *He's not as feeble as he's trying to be.*

The priest handed it back to her. "My goodness, the date on the back is nineteen fifty. That's a long time ago, Miss Peckham. Most of the children who pass through here don't return or keep in touch with us. I have no record of a Jane Wainright being here."

Alex smirked stepping forward. "That's rich. You act like some senile feeble son of a bitch, and yet you know you have no record of a Jane Wainright. How about a Jane of any last name, old man."

Zilpha stood in front of the priest and faced Alex. "Intimidation doesn't always work, James! Show some respect."

The priest cleared his voice to be heard. "I can assure you, I want to help. When the children get back from their field trip, I can ask the sister who runs the office to do research for you. If you like, I can call you..."

Alex moved around Zilpha gritting his teeth. "How fuckin' stupid, do you think we are?" He raised his voice even louder. "Why don't we go to your office *now* and look at the files!" He grabbed the priest by the arm. "We wouldn't want you to forget to ask the sister to look this up. Now would we?"

Karen stared at the computer. She heard part of the conversation. Her eyes widened when the man walked toward the priest speaking harshly. *This doesn't look good. This equipment should have a volume control. This dial should help.*

A squeal shot through the sanctuary. Realizing she had turned on the microphone, she blurted out. "Father James, I've been looking for you. It's time for your medication. I'll send Sister Mary Karen with it."

She pressed the button again and it silenced. *What can I do? I think that man is going to harm the old priest.* She opened a closet door and found habits. She quickly put one on. On a hook she saw a cross on a chain and stuck it around her neck. She grabbed some pill bottles and the tray they were on. She glanced into the mirror. *Oh, shit, my lipstick.* She picked up her robe and wiped her face. *Hope I got it all.*

Zilpha was startled hearing the message. "Well, we've taken up enough of your time. Here's my card. If you think of something, reach me at this number."

Alex looked down at the old priest and whispered. "You know, Interpol hasn't any restrictions, so if we think you're lying, we have a number of methods to find out the truth. We don't give a fuck if you're wearing the cloth or not. Maybe I should give you a sample of what I mean." With his good arm he seized the priest's vestments and pushed him into a corner.

Karen scooted down the aisle trying not to trip on the habit covering her pant suit. She came to a screeching halt, puffing. "There you are, Father James."

Zilpha stared at Karen. *She's got street clothes on under that robe. I can see pants. Nuns don't wear make-up. Smeared at that.* She grabbed Alex's arm. "It's time to leave. Now."

Zilpha almost pushed Alex out the church door. She rushed to the car. "Hurry, I don't want them to get the license plate number. I'll drive. You walk in front of the plate as I turn around and then get in."

Alex frowned. "Zilpha, why are you so crazy about getting out of here? I could have gotten him to talk."

Opening the door, she snapped at him. "Alex, that nun had make-up on! She came to help the priest."

Alex jumped in and she sped down the drive to the road. Out of sight of the church property, Zilpha pulled over and hid the car inside a clump of trees.

Zilpha put her head against the steering wheel. *Think! Deep breaths!* She looked at Alex. "We can't leave until we handle this. Tell me what you're thinking. We need to talk this out."

Alex got out of the car. "I can think better standing."

She took out her notebook. "I have to look at my thoughts." *What a dreadful scene that was.*

He stared at her. "Nothing moves you, does it?"

"Alex, of course I get upset. Mistakes upset me. What's positive about all of this is…we know this priest is helping Jane. If he wasn't, then why the surveillance? The woman who came to his aid must have seen you approach him. What's more…she wasn't a nun. Who is she? Why did she need to disguise her appearance?" *She had a pant suit on, walking shoes.* "Could she be working for Scotland Yard?"

Alex stopped pacing. "If she is, I never met her. The Yard had only a few female inspectors. Most of the women I knew worked in the labs and offices. Whoever she is, she's fucking up our schedule." *Fuck. Zilpha's right. If the priest isn't involved, then why all the surveillance?*

As Zilpha put her notebook down, Alex rested his good arm on her car door. "I know what you're going to say. We have to get that surveillance tape and the priest. The woman we can get rid of if she's with him."

She stared up at him. "That's a given. More importantly, let me ask you. How long have we been parked here? What's happened, or should I say, what hasn't happened?"

He looked at his watch. "At least ten minutes." *I wonder what she's thinking?* He frowned at her and then suddenly grinned. "No police have come."

Grabbing the steering wheel, she turned the key. "That's right. Another reason I don't think she's from the orphanage or family services. If she were from either of those, the police would have been flying down that road, lickety split. Which would mean to me, she or they have contacted whoever is in charge to find out what to do. So, do we stay here and watch?"

Alex guided her turning around in the thicket.

Zilpha got out of the car with her binoculars. "Alex, check the map. The orphanage is right at the end of this road. Right? How big is this village?" She scanned the area. "I don't see anything in any direction except for the chapel at the orphanage."

Alex spread the map out over the hood of the car. He studied it. "This is called Dunhill Road, and it's the only road in and out of the place. There are no side streets or turn-offs. Nothing with a name." He looked around. "I wonder if all this land is owned by the orphanage. It's hardly been developed. Not a house to be seen. It's just a farm village. Are you thinking what I am?" He rolled up the map. "This town hasn't any law enforcement. It would have to come from a neighboring city."

Zilpha stood biting her lip. "We have to go back and find out what those two know. He did say the children are on a field trip. My guess is they'll be back before dark. That gives us a little more than an hour. I thought I saw a back entrance to the orphanage not far up this road. That might be a good way to return."

"Do you think she wants to get the priest out of here? Why don't we wait and follow them?"

She walked to the car. "Because, those kids could return from that field trip and then what? Shooting children isn't in my bag of tricks!"

Karen threw off her habit and knelt by the priest. "Can you get up or do you want to sit for a minute?"

The old priest dropped his head and closed his eyes. “We have to warn Jane. These people will show her no mercy.”

Karen wiped his brow. “Father James, I’ve got to call my boss. Sit here. I’ll be right back.”

He waved her off. “Go…I’ll be fine. Just need to catch my wits.”

She ran to get her cell phone. “Patti D. Need the boss. *Emergency!*” She replayed the surveillance tape while she waited. “Kitty, the two from the market were here at the church and had every intention of torturing Father James for information on Jane. Yes, I was able to stop it, but I’m sure they realized I’m not a nun. The surveillance tape shows them in the church, but the man blocked the license on the car when they left.”

She put the tape in her brief case. “Yes, I’ll bring him but I really think they will be back. Bedrule is such a small village. The police would have to come from the next town. The children are on a field trip with the sisters. They don’t carry cell phones. Yes, I’ve got my gun. Would you alert the crew at the airport and have them meet us? There’s an open field behind the town square almost to the orphanage. It’s big enough for the helicopter to land. The priest is hurt.”

She gathered up her stuff and pressed the monitor to look at the outdoor area. *Shit, there’s a car coming up the back of the orphanage. Oh fuck, it’s them.*

She ran out to the sanctuary. “Father James! We have to go. They’re coming back!”

She found him slouched in a pew. “My legs don’t want to move very quickly. You go and let me be.”

She shook her head and helped him stand. “That’s not an option. Where can we hide?”

He pointed to the confessional. “There’s a false wall in the priest’s part of the confessional.”

She put her arm around his back and pulled him. “We can save Jane if we stay alive.”

The priest closed the sliding door as Zilpha and Alex entered the sanctuary from the priest’s office. He whispered. “Hold onto my hand.” Karen took hold and in the dark, Father James led her hand to a protrusion in the wall. “You can watch out of this chute. They can’t see you.” Carefully Karen moved in front of him to look through the box like structure.

With that Alex opened the confessional door. "This is empty. That woman must have taken him out."

Zilpha screwed a silencer onto her gun. "We'd have seen them leave. They're here." She walked slowly pointing her gun down each row of pews. "Remember, the priest told us the children are on a field trip. He wasn't lying. A calendar in his office was marked field trip. At least it won't matter if we make a little noise. Too bad, we could have used one of his kids to draw him out. I don't think he'd like to see or hear one of them being shot!" She shouted. "Would you now, old priest?"

Karen could see the woman looking straight at her. *She's one mean son of a bitch. Hope she doesn't have any kids...God help them.*

Zilpha shot her gun off at a pew, then at the altar and podium. She stopped in front of the confessional. There was a noise. "Shush. Did you hear something?" She slowly walked around an archway and was startled by a couple of pigeons bathing in the holy water. They fluttered their wings and took off.

Alex drew his gun from his holster. "What did you hear?"

Zilpha shrugged pointing to the birds. "Them bathing."

Karen saw the pigeons fly toward a broken window. As Alex took aim, she shut her eyes, knowing the birds would be target practice.

After the shots, Zilpha looked at the bloody carcasses. "Not bad. You shot the heads off..." She motioned to Alex. "Let's check another building."

She walked past the confessional and stopped. She opened both doors. *Empty. The priest sits in the middle. How does he get in?* She studied it a minute. *There's a handle.* She turned and pulled on it. "I wonder when the last confession was given." Finally it opened.

Alex stood waiting. "I already looked there. I thought you said you wanted to check another building. I don't see any other place for them to hide. Come on. We're running out of time."

Zilpha pulled back from the cubical. She listened and stared at the relic. *This chapel is ancient. At least fourteenth century. The priests were the protectors.* "These archaic chapels were used as a haven for people who had respect for God, Pope and the like." Pointing the gun, she shot into the two sides and then aimed for the middle. "I'm not one of them."

Karen saw the gun. *My God, that's a nine mm military. Who are these people? That bullet may come through.* She held the priest tightly behind her.

Zilpha pulled the trigger. "I want to make sure we didn't miss anything." *Or anyone.* The priest felt Karen squeeze his arm and knew she had been hit. He braced himself against her to keep her from falling.

Father James heard the chapel door open and close. *Thank goodness she's short. I can barely hold her.* He gently moved her behind him to a bench jutting out from the wall. He held her against him and whispered. "You're a brave girl. Can you hear me?"

He felt her nod slightly. "Can you tell me where you're hit?"

She whispered. "I'll be all right. Don't open the door." She spoke in short breaths. "Can you see if they've gone?"

The priest looked out the chute. *No, they haven't left. I can see the man by the door.* He squeezed her hand and whispered. "They faked slamming the door. I can see them."

After a few more minutes, they heard a whirling sound outside. It got closer and hovered over the orphanage. The priest watched the man and woman race for the back door. He heard one say, "You were right. That bitch is from the government. That helicopter is for ops missions."

Karen felt her phone vibrate on her waist. "That must be the crew calling. We should have met them by now. Kitty probably ordered them to investigate." She took some deep breaths. "We'll be all right. They'll drop some guys down. Stay here until they come in."

The priest felt her slump against him. He cushioned her head, knowing she had blacked out.

Chapter 25

Speeding back to Crawley

Getting off the M-five, Alex looked at the clock on the dash. "Is that the right time? If it is then we flew. I'm starving. Let's go eat."

Zilpha glanced over and then at her watch. "It's correct." She went back to writing in her notebook. "That must be an all-time record. Four hundred kilometers in two and a half hours… I've just had a great idea. We're not far from my cottage. Take me home. We can eat later."

After pushing several buttons on two security systems, Zilpha motioned for Alex to follow her. He laughed. "What happens if someone breaches the system?"

Punching another code on a pad by the cellar door, she cocked her head. "The whole place goes up in smoke." She opened the door. "It vanishes, caput!"

Alex saw a dead look in her face. *I think I've met my match.* He followed her down the stairway to her inner sanctum. "I'm beginning to think this is really yours more than it was Charlie's."

She turned at the foot of the steps. "You're right. I didn't know any of the terminology so I would describe to Charlie what I wanted and he would find it. Being in Interpol, he had access to everything. When Henry's away, I practically live down here."

She brewed them some coffee. Alex followed her to her desk. She bent over her chair to punch in some more buttons and the whole room lit up. Machines turned on.

Alex shook his head. *MP has come alive.* "What ideas have you come up with?"

She stared at him a moment. She put her notebook down. Leaning against a post, she sipped her coffee. "Okay, what do we know?"

He started to talk but she ignored him. "First, we know that Jane in some way is… was… obsessed with Ross's wife and maybe even with him." She paused frowning at him. "Just how long did she take care of Lizzy?"

Raising his brow, Alex swallowed. "Well, Lizzy went through a lot of treatments for about six months. When that failed, she went downhill pretty fast. I'd say Jane was at Ross's daily for about five months. Toward the end she stayed around the clock. That lasted about a week."

Zilpha studied Alex's expressions. *His face tightens when he's angry. Even after all these years he relives his hatred. Charlie never let go what my dad did to me. Interesting…*

She blushed. "Sorry, your mannerism reminded me of something." She looked quickly at her notebook. "Next, she knew or suspected you had something to do with Lizzy's death. Then, you made two mistakes."

Alex glared at her. "Are you done with the questions? You're not making much sense. You're almost saying I deserve everything she's done to me."

She pointed her notebook at him. "Don't be stupid. Edse is right. You're letting emotion get involved and Jane knows it. Your first mistake, Alex, was you beat her up in that mental hospital so bad that you left her with a daily reminder…That scar!"

He put his cup down. "I told you about that. It was an accident. She tried…"

Shaking her head she laughed at him. "Commit suicide? You know as well as I do that's a load of bullshit. It's done. Let's not waste time arguing over it. So you fucked up. Get over it."

She sat to work on the computer, totally ignoring his anger. "Second, you didn't see she had baited you to take her back. She knew how to get back at you and stole everything that would put you in jeopardy. Now, she's determined to get her revenge." She turned and leaned on the desk raising her brow at him. "So much so, I think she wants to kill you."

Alex kneeled on the steps frowning. "I wish the bitch would try. She'd come out of hiding, if we kidnapped the priest."

Zilpha leaned back. "When she finds out the priest has been attacked and threatened, she will be very near breaking her cover. I think it's too risky to go back to the orphanage. It's a long shot, but I think we can bring Jane out to save Ross."

She saw his look of curiosity. "Okay, think about this. You said Jane was so wrapped up in Ross's wife that she left you high and dry to take care of her. I think we need to disable Ross… And here's how." She rotated the monitor. "Any of these debilitating drugs would work."

Alex peered over her shoulder. "I was going to use one of those to capture the Admiral, but Edse gave me a tiny capsule. Have no idea what it was. There was a needle at one end when you pushed it. There was no injection. I just pricked the Admiral in his leg and he was like putty in the hand. It really was amazing." *Edse did say he had developed this drug.*

He poured more coffee. "You must have a plan how you're going to do this. I can't do it. Dennis would recognize me…" He looked at his watch. "You have a secure line here? I need to call Edse."

She pointed. "There's a phone by the dark room…"

Zilpha turned on a recording device after he walked to the back of the room to make his call. She turned off her desk light and shut down her computer. "I'll be upstairs in the kitchen."

Alex nodded as he dialed. "Edward, we're closing in on Jane now. Another week…and…What!"

He looked around to make sure she had gone. "Shit! When did this happen? Are you sure, she flinched shaking his hand?"

Edse's voice bellowed out. "Damn good thing I was there to handle it. These two motherfuckers stared at one another and would have let her go. Alex, I've had it with these fucking yearlings. The girl is sedated in my hospital. Henry is determined to let her go. Now he's claiming he loves her. He said he'll take her back to England and she'll be fine. You know that can't and isn't going to happen. I'm not having a billion dollar arrangement destroyed by them or for that matter, you! Until you get your head out of your ass, here's the deal. I'm sending Neil back this Friday. The other two will be lost in the jungle…or I have a furnace for cremations, whatever. I'm fucking serious, you have until next week to return for this surgery to be done or else…the surgery is out until after the New York conference. Alex, this is not to make you a mask. This is major reconstructive surgery. The healing process is long. Am I getting through to you? Can you afford to be seen as Alex McGraw? Once they find Jane alive or dead…"

Alex bit his lip. "All right! I'll be there. Do what you have to do. End of story…"

Alex slammed the phone on its cradle. *I swear, after this damn surgery, he's history. He sounds like some old fish wife. I've got to get out of here. Why did they want their kid to be such a wuss?*

He found her in the kitchen. "Zilpha, I'm tired. Edse's got a problem and he's rattled my cage about it."

She walked him to the door. "Can I be of help?"

Alex shook his head. "No, he's unnerved about Jane… says I should drop finding her."

Zilpha watched him get in his car. *He's lying.* She set the security code and rushed to the cellar. Before Alex's conversation on the tape was over with Edse, she dialed her son's number. "Henry, pick up!" She dialed again. Then she dialed Neil's cell. *Still nothing. Where could they be?*

She shook her head and screamed. "This can't be happening! You promised!" She dialed Henry's number at the apartment.

Her hands were shaking. She gripped the phone and took a deep breath and dialed. "Alex, I've been trying to call Henry. He's not picking up on his cell. Would he be with Edse? Neil's not answering either." She shut her eyes and bit her lip listening.

"Zilpha, I'm sorry, I haven't a clue. Edse didn't mention them at all. He said everything was going fine."

She put the phone down. *My boy is dead…*

Chapter 26

Johannesburg turmoil.... Jo and Hennessey's cottage

Linda was still talking with their boss when Theresa and Jo came in from the kitchen. Jo set a tray of drinks and snacks on the table. She frowned at Theresa when they heard Linda raise her voice.

They both flinched when she slammed the phone on its cradle.

"Son of a bitch." *Kitty's right! Now I've got to make the decision.*

"Okay, Linda, let's have it. What's so upsetting?"

She dropped her head. "Making decisions is one thing, but when it's deciding who lives or dies, that's..."

Jo frowned. "That's bullshit. You're not making any decisions on your own. We're a team. So...Kitty's given us a choice. Either save Hennessey exposing our cover, or consider her dead and go about business as usual."

Linda nodded. "That's what she said. I know it sounds callous but dammit, she's right."

Theresa stood with hands on her hips. "You both know fucking well, we're going to get that kid back. How we're going to do it, is the question."

Linda looked at her watch. "We don't have much time. Jo, you've got to get moving or you'll be late for work."

Jo left the bedroom door open while she changed so she could hear the plans being made. Taking her slacks off, she hopped to the door. "I just remembered. I heard one of the nurses say the hospital has just replaced the cleaning company. They start tonight and come in the staff entrance."

Linda grabbed the newspaper. "I wonder if the cleaning company has an ad in the section for hire."

Theresa yelled to Jo. "What about the security?"

Jo stood by the door buttoning her blouse. "No. There's none. Not even in the emergency room. I found that strange. Actually, the hospital staff seems to be laid back too. More like a country town hospital than a big city…"

Linda rattled the paper. "Maybe this won't be so hard after all. It's called Quick Cleaning Services. They list hospitals under the commercial listings. It seems the only requirement is to be free of allergies." She lowered the paper. "Have you seen what they wear?"

Jo tucked her blouse into her slacks. "The hospital provides the uniforms. I'll see if I can find some extras hanging around. I'm pretty sure they arrive about nine and work until my shift ends. Have you seen my sweater? The air conditioning never shuts down."

Linda handed her one out of the closet. "What about badges or signing in."

Jo went to the door carrying her medical bag and a sweater. She shrugged. "I'm serious, there's none of that. You just walk in and say you're with the cleaning company and a staff member will point where to go. Okay, I'll see you at nine. I make my rounds soon after I get there, so if Hennessey is there, I should be able to tell you where. After you case the place, we should be able to make up a plan how to get her out."

Theresa sat on the arm of the couch. "You mean there are no security cameras, monitors, or guards anywhere. I find that hard to believe."

Linda cringed. "Jo, you make it sound too easy. Let's not forget we're dealing with Edse. The man is as nuts as McGraw."

Jo hesitated and stepped back leaning on the door jamb. "Trust me. I've yet to see a hidden camera anywhere. I'll double check." She saw the clock on the kitchen wall. "Hey, I've got to go! Don't forget to lock up."

Seeing Linda dial her cell phone, Theresa questioned. "Who can you call about this?"

Linda raised her hand to her. "Patti D., is the boss still there?" She whispered to Theresa. "I've got an idea and need Kitty's help."

"Sorry to bother. Could you arrange for Theresa and me to get a scanner from the Embassy? I know for a fact they've got an arsenal there and all the latest devices. For some reason, they don't jump through hoops for us as they do for you." Linda smiled. "Oh, is that who's the snake charmer. Well, could you ask him? Yes, ASAP. Jo's informed us the hospital hasn't any security to worry about. We find that unusual if not strange because of Edse owning the place. The scanner would do the trick. Thanks."

Theresa chuckled. "Let me guess, the snake charmer is Chief O'Doul."

Linda put her phone back in her pocket. "O'Doul's brother is head of the Embassy operations."

Jo began her routine when Head Nurse Jones met her in the hall. "Jo, we've got two emergency surgeries tonight. Dr. Edse would like you to assist me."

"Okay, but may I finish my rounds? I'm in the middle, and I need another half hour."

The head nurse agreed. "You do have two new cases. I'll take you to one of them now. It's just down the hall." Before entering the room, she smiled. "The surgeries aren't scheduled until eleven, so you'll have plenty of time to finish your regular duties."

A man was lying in the bed. Jo studied his chart and looked at him. Out of the corner of her eye she saw him shake his head to the Nurse Jones. *Why would he be signaling to her.* Her eyes widened. She tried to hide giggling. *The bartender.* She read muttering. "Bloody Hell!"

"What did you say?"

She looked at her boss, trying to remain calm. "I'm sorry. I just said, poor man. Is this one of the surgeries?"

"Yes, you saw one of his genitals needs to be removed. He's a bartender at the Artists Hotel and was attacked by two women." *So she thinks I had something to do with this?*

Jo frowned. "That's awful." *Theresa will be pleased to hear this.*

The head nurse looked at her watch. "One of the staff said you eat there a lot. We thought you may have heard something."

Jo stared at her. "Sorry, whoever said that is quite mistaken. I don't frequent bars, and I've eaten in that restaurant twice but not recently." *I wonder if WE mean Edse."*

"I have to check in with Dr. Edse. Why don't you finish your tour and meet me by the double doors on the second floor."

"Sure. That'll work for me." *Those doors are marked Do Not Enter.* The head nurse left and Jo continued down the corridor to her next patient. *Something is going on. I felt like she was watching me when we went in that patient's room. She has to be following Edse's orders. I wonder if they've tortured Hennessey and they know about us. I've got to warn the girls.*

At eight thirty, Linda pulled into the parking lot of the Edse Hospital and stopped behind Jo's car. Theresa set the scanner on the dash board. She plugged it into the cigarette lighter and turned it on.

The digital read-out came up with zeros across the screen. Theresa raised her brow. "I hope to fuck this isn't broken."

Linda observed. "From the front of the building, this hospital looks small, but from back here, it's huge. Look, there's an overhead walkway from the hospital, going over a back alley, joining up to another building. No wonder it looks so big. We have time. I'm going to drive to the end of the parking lot."

She backed out of her spot and drove slowly. Theresa's eyes widened. "Whoa! We've got some action."

Linda stopped. "Shit, that meter may explode, it's running so fast. There's a ton of something going on in the second building. I'm sure some of it is surveillance equipment. We need to relay this to Jo." The clock on the dash said almost nine. "No time, we can't take a chance. We need to get in there."

Linda pulled up to the back entrance. "I've got an idea. You go in. I'm going to check the outside area. That walkway looks interesting and might be useful. It's dark and I can snoop around. If they are as lax as Jo says, I'll slip in later. Keep your cell on vibrate."

Theresa frowned. "Makes you wonder if this hospital is a front for something…" She opened the door raising her eyebrows at Linda.

"Something, really fuckin' bad!"

Walking in the back door, Theresa was met by a tall man in a white spotless uniform. He directed her. "Get your uniform on and come back here." He pointed to the floor in front of him.

Theresa, reluctantly, did as she was told without comment. *I can't believe this moron even knows about cleaning.* In the locker room, she held up the pants. *These uniforms would fit a gorilla. Hmm. I wonder if Jack out there in the hall posed for this design...I better not ask.* She chuckled. She got her cart and, along with the other cleaners, followed his direction to the elevator. He placed a list of room numbers on each cart as it passed. Glaring at each cleaner, and in a monotone voice, he ordered, "When you finish the list, go home."

Walking down the hall, Jo stopped, hearing the elevator bell ring as it reached the second floor. The door opened and Theresa pushed her cart out, tripping on her baggy pants. "Fuck this cart! Fuck these pants!"

Jo took a deep breath to hold back a hearty laugh. "My goodness, you do have an interesting and loud vocabulary! May I remind you, miss, you're in a hospital! Now scoot!"

She quickly jotted a couple of notes in her notebook, tore out the page, squished it together and threw it into the trash bag on the cart. She continued her rounds, entering the next patient's room.

Another person had the same trouble getting off the elevator. A woman, much older than Theresa, missed out on getting the reprimand, but saw Theresa raise her middle finger mouthing 'Fuck you' to Jo's back.

The old woman leaned against her cart catching her breath. "What does One Size Fits All mean?" She pulled the waist band out. "Did you see the tag in your pants? See, it says that. One fits all!" She rolled the waist band about four times and tucked it. She took one step with her cart and her pants slipped down. "Bloody Hell."

Theresa laughed. "You go that way. I'll go this way. Meet you back here in a half hour." She tripped on her pants as she pushed the cart. "Fits all, my ass! Look for scissors and tape."

As soon as her co-worker was out of sight, Theresa found Jo's note. It warned her to stay clear of room fifty two, because the bartender would be sure to recognize her, and so far she hadn't seen Hennessey. *I need to relay this to Linda. Do I dare take a chance and call her.* She worked her way down the corridor, hastily cleaning each room. The last two rooms caught her attention. *Interesting. Name tags on the door. No curtain divider, only a desk and dresser.*

After she checked the hall, she hurriedly dialed Linda. "Have to whisper. Don't talk. The bartender is in room fifty two." She chuckled. "He's losing one of his balls. So far, Hennessey isn't here… Shush, someone's coming." She put her cell in her pocket and went on cleaning.

Two men walked past the room and one came back. "Excuse me, have you seen Dr. Edse?"

Theresa frowned, squinting her eyes at him. *Fuck it all! It's Hennessey's friend. High Pockets.* She went on cleaning with her back to him. "Sorry, don't know him. We're the new cleaning crew."

The young man paused. He shook his head. *She looks familiar.* "Sorry to bother."

Theresa waved, mopping the floor. The footsteps stopped. She checked the hall and pulled her cell out of her pocket. "Did you hear that? Yeah, that High Pockets kid. Hennessey's got to be here but where? Let me cross the hall. I think these last rooms are for staff members. They're empty but names are on the doors. Tell me if you see me. How close am I to the overhead walkway?"

Listening to Linda, she went through the motions of washing the window.

"Theresa, another four windows. A few minutes ago I saw Jo on the walkway. Now, I'm seeing two men on it. Must be that High Pockets and…it's Alex McGraw with him."

She pushed her cart down the hall and saw a set of double doors marked Keep Out. She went in the last room to clean. It was empty. She whispered. "Linda, I'm in the last room at the end of the hall. I can see the double doors. I hear footsteps, again. Someone's talking on a cell. Shush."

She started to clean quickly. She heard a man say, 'I don't fuckin' care anymore about your money. I can do this without you. I'm sending… Neil…'

Edse paused… "Wait a minute! I thought I heard something…

I'm sending him back in two days! I don't care if you need more time. This Henry kid, I can't be doing with him… What should I do about them? … You've got until the end of the week, and then I leave for another place where we'll be doing the processing of the drug." *There's that noise again.*

He stopped at the door. "Sorry, I heard a noise. I guess it was you." *Holy fuck, I wonder what this piece of low life heard?*

Theresa swished the mop quickly back and forth. *Better I don't hear him. I should sing. That'll rattle his cage. Dickass, motherfucker. Great lyrics! Hahaha!*

He rapped on the door. Theresa looked at him and frowned. "What?"

He stared at her, smirking. "I heard a noise. It must have been you."

She looked around and stared back at him. "Guess you're right." She leaned on her mop. "Hey! Are you that Dr. Edse?" She continued mopping. "If you are, two guys was askin if I'd seen you."

The doctor stood in the doorway, not at all amused by her lack of etiquette. "And, if I'm not."

Theresa recognized the sarcasm. She turned while mopping and grinned. "You're going in the right direction. Tell them yourself."

Edse glared at her. In the mirror, she saw him look at the number on her cart and leave. Theresa chuckled as she bolted to the door to watch him. *This is exactly why I turned down being rich.*

She whispered as she watched him go through the double doors. "Did you hear that? Edse is such a mother fu… Well, he is. Can you see him?"

Linda, with her binoculars, had moved back further in the parking lot to a higher elevation. "Yes, I can see him. Looks like he swiped a card after the door closed. It must be some kind of security, because the doors at the other end have opened. How are we going to get in there?"

Listening to Linda, Theresa scanned the room. Opening the closet door, she saw uniforms and on the door was an 'On Call Schedule'. In bold print, DO NOT LEAVE BUILDING WITH ANY BADGES OR SWIPES. "Wait a minute. I think we have our solution. The room I'm in is for a doctor and, according to this roster, our doctor is away and…" She went through the uniform pockets *Voila!* "He…read the bold print. We now have a swipe…."

With one arm in the jacket, she heard a wheel squeaking. *Oh fuck. That old lady is done. I don't want her down here…* She threw the jacket on a chair, grabbed her mop, broke the head off, and ran to the elevator. "I was almost done when my mop busted. How about a trade and give mine to that dickhead at the desk. I have two more rooms to do. I'll catch you later."

Theresa pushed the old woman's cart on the elevator. "Are you coming back tomorrow? You look bushed."

The old woman shook her head. "It's more work to keep these pants on than it is to clean the place. They can stick this job…See ya."

Theresa ran back to the room. She put on the doctor's jacket and looked again at the schedule. She frowned. "Linda, are you there…"

Linda drove without lights and parked under the walkway. "I'm here. Right under a trapdoor. My guess is it's an emergency exit if the doors fail to open. There's a short platform and then a ladder off to the side. We should be able to use this if I can get the door open. I can reach the ladder if I stand on the top of the car. Before you use that swipe, let me make sure the door unlatches."

While waiting, Theresa ran off to the other rooms to check the rosters for the other doctors. *I need a badge that has a woman's name.* She started to switch the tag. *No, she's Chinese.* She rushed to the other closet and grinned. *Finally! Rachel Brown should work.*

She stared at the roster. "What is this? Rachel is a chemical engineer?" *Did she get lost? Why would a hospital need a chemical engineer?* She went back to the other closet. *Wonder what Miss China does? Doctor of Prosthetic Neuronal Memory? What's going on in this place?*

"Theresa! The door is unlatched. I think we're good to go." Linda had night vision goggles on and scanned the area. "No one is around."

"Linda, wait a minute! Why on earth would a hospital, here of all places, need doctors in fields other than medicine?"

Linda frowned. "Theresa, we don't have time for this now. We've got a small window of opportunity, and I'm sure we won't get another chance at this. I'm worried. We haven't seen Jo come back."

Jo and her boss walked into a patient's room. The curtain was drawn. Jo frowned. "This is marked a quarantined area. Shouldn't we have protective gear on?"

Head Nurse Jones shook her head. "No, it really isn't. Dr. wants to keep the others out. It's a special case and he wanted you to handle it." She pulled the curtain. "He thought you might be able to give some pertinent information."

Jo saw Hennessey lying in the bed with an oxygen mask on, and some kind of IV in her arm. *The color of that fluid in the IV bag doesn't look like nutrients.* She stared at her boss. "Why are you asking me? How can I…"

Nurse Jones pulled the curtain full circle and revealed Henry and Neil. "According to this girl's boyfriend, you know her pretty well."

Jo frowned. "I met this kid on my return flight from England. She's a student attending the art conference."

Hennessey heard Jo's voice and opened her eyes. Jo took hold of Hennessey's wrist looking at her watch. "What's wrong with her, and why are you interested in my knowing her?"

Henry stared at Jo. "I tried to tell them what you just said and Dr. Edse is…sure…she's…"

Neil poked Henry in the back and whispered. "Shut-up!"

Jo leaned forward to look into Hennessey's eyes with a little flashlight. "She's heavily sedated. You still haven't told me what is wrong with her?" Jo looked up at Neil and then at Hennessey. She felt Hennessey grab her hand and pull. Jo bent over Hennessey as if listening to her heart with her stethoscope. Her eyes wide staring at Jo, she mumbled. "Not…not…him…" She pulled Jo to her face and whispered. "Not him, Alex."

Jo squeezed Hennessey's hand. "You have to relax…"

Hennessey held on to Jo, staring. She rolled her eyes toward Henry and Neil. Fighting to stay conscious, she muttered. "Has arm."

Jo smiled and mouthed "okay, I got it". Hennessey relaxed. She knew Jo understood.

The head nurse saw the girl's effort to communicate and pulled out a gun. "I think we've seen enough. Doctor Edse will be here shortly and can dispense with you."

Just as she backed up motioning for Jo to move away from the bed, Theresa rushed up behind Nurse Jones and cracked her head with the butt-end of her gun. "Fuck you, babe!" She held the gun on Neil and Henry. "What about these two?"

The nurse fell to the floor. As Jo pulled off the oxygen mask and removed the needle from Hennessey's arm, she motioned to Theresa to watch Henry and Neil. "Hennessey is in this mess because she found out this man isn't Alex."

Henry stepped forward. "Let me help! I'll carry her wherever you want."

Neil shook his head. "You know Edse will kill us both."

Henry pleaded. "I can't let him kill her. I truly love her."

Theresa waved her gun at Neil. "Okay, do I shoot you or are you going to help?"

Neil went to the door. "Okay, I'll find Edse and keep him busy. Get her out of here."

Henry scooped up Hennessey's limp body and motioned for Theresa and Jo to go. "How are you going to get her out of here? Edse will sound the alarm, and you won't get past those doors on the other side."

Theresa pulled the nurse's body out of the way and took her gun. "We found a way out. Come on."

They followed her to the double doors. She peeked and saw two nurses walking toward them. "Go back to the room!"

Henry and Jo scurried back. Jo pointed for Henry to take Hennessey to the other side of the room. It was dark there.

The head nurse had come to and tried to stand. Jo turned her around and socked her in the throat. Nurse Jones slumped and Jo pushed her onto the bed. *That will be permanent.* She quickly pulled the curtain around the track, hiding the body. After putting a blanket and oxygen mask on the body, Jo stood still to listen.

They heard conversation in the hall, and Jo shook her head. *That's Theresa and those nurses. We don't have time to socialize!*

The curtain opened a bit. Jo was ready to execute a blow when Theresa peeked in. "It's clear."

Henry stepped into the light, trying to balance Hennessey's sudden jerking actions. "What's causing her to thrash like this? I'm afraid of hurting her."

Jo took off her nurse's jacket. "Theresa, hold her legs while I tie my jacket around them. That drug is causing her to hallucinate." *Poor thing. We've got to keep our cool.*

They got through the double doors. Theresa pulled out her cell. "Linda, we're here!"

Theresa and Jo helped lift the trap door open, and then dropped down to thc platform. Henry lowered Hennessey into their arms.

Henry heard shouting behind the double doors. "Hurry! I can hear Edse. The man is crazy. He's coming. I'm sure he's sounded the alarm."

As the double doors opened, Henry lowered himself to the platform. Edse ran to the trap door shooting. "You motherfucker! You're both going to die." He kept firing down the opening.

Neil came chasing after him. "Edward, don't be stupid. You've got to get out of here."

Neil pushed Edse backwards. "It's no use. Let them go. Take your experiments and get out. You've got a helicopter. Get out while you can."

Edse pointed the gun at Neil. "You knew about this!" He shot at Neil, hitting him in the arm.

Neil fell. "You fool. I can fly the bird for you."

Edse pulled him up. "That's a flesh wound. Get up! You'll fly or you're dead."

At the bottom of the ladder, a dozen police vehicles appeared with spotlights aimed at the walkway. Jo saw Linda get on the platform. "She's hard to handle, the drugs in her system are causing her to jerk and squirm. Take her shoulders. The three of us can carry her."

Jo handed off Hennessey's shoulders to Linda, cradling the kid's torso as Theresa held her legs. "When did you call for the back-up?"

"Kitty must have alerted the Embassy after I didn't call back when she said to. Two men are on the top of my car. They'll be able to take her."

Jo heard a thump. "Theresa, Henry's been shot."

They handed Hennessey to the policemen standing on Linda's car. As Hennessey's body was lifted over the rail, her eyes opened just as Henry's bloody body fell to the platform.

Jo rushed back to him. "Hold on, Henry...We'll get you to the hospital." His clothing was full of blood. Jo looked at Theresa and Linda as they laid his shoulders on Jo's lap, and she shook her head.

Theresa, teary eyed, took his hand. "Henry, you're tough. You can do this. You saved Hennessey's life. She'll need you."

The spotlights from the cars almost blinded them. Theresa waved to shut some off.

He grabbed her hand. "I don't think I'm going anywhere..." He gasped. "Tell my mom, I didn't mean to disa..."

Jo felt his neck and shook her head to Theresa. "He's gone."

Linda stood up for the paramedic to get by. "You'll need a body bag."

He turned to go back. "That makes two. The girl didn't make it before we could give her CPR."

Hearing that, the three inspectors shrank in disbelief.

Linda heard her name being called from below. She leaned over the side of the platform. "Up here. I'm Linda."

The policeman held a phone. "Inspector Carroll is calling."

Linda scrambled down the ladder and jumped the rest of the way to the top of her car. He handed her a cell phone. "Kitty!.. No, dammit..." She watched the officers put Hennessey's body in a body bag. Tears rolling down her face, Linda cleared her throat, and wiped her eyes. "She didn't make it, but the kid held on long enough to tell Jo that Alex never left England. This man is an impostor! You've got to warn Ross."

Looking up, she heard a noise coming overhead. "A helicopter has just taken off. I would bet that's Edse getting away. We want to find out what makes this second building so important. I'll call as soon as we're done."

Turning away from the others and from the glaring lights, with a swallowed sob, she whispered. "Oh, Kitty, I feel so responsible. They're just kids."

Chapter 27

Scotland Yard – The Chief's office

Standing at the conference table, Chief O'Doul puffed several times on his pipe, staring at his three colleagues. Mrs. Gipson handed him four newspapers and left his office. He nodded to her and waited for the door to shut. Dropping three of the papers in the center of the table, he shook a copy at Ross, Carroll and Grantwood. "Great headline, don't you think? British female secret agent and lover murdered in Johannesburg, South Africa!" He tossed the paper on the table and shouted. "Have you read the articles? "

Ross held up the paper. "None of these stories are true, sir."

Pacing, the Chief glared at Ross, bellowing. "Of course they're not. Do you think that will make a difference to the parents of these two and to the defense minister? What's more, too many names are reappearing in these stories. Alex McGraw and now Doctor Edward Edse's hospital was mentioned." Two deep puffs as he continued to visualize the departments mess he blurted. "And, to further this catastrophe, you can be sure the media will note my presence meeting the plane and will want a news conference."

O'Doul slammed his hand on the table. "A month ago when you three were here, I told you then, the K Code couldn't be exposed! If some brainy reporter goes digging, and finds a relationship existed between McGraw, Edse and Windsor Braun, there's no telling what this will unravel. How many times do you think I can use the brainless comment ' it is under investigation'?"

Kitty raised her hand. "Sir, at the risk of being fired, I would like to point out these stories, though they appear to make fun of the Yard," she frowned, "haven't really compromised our case."

The Chief puffed several times on his pipe. *This I've got to hear.* "How in God's name is the murder of a twenty-one year old girl, still wet behind the ears, spying for Scotland Yard, having an affair with Alex McGraw's attorney, whom she was assigned to spy on, not a revelation?" He sank back in his chair. "How was her association with the Yard even known?"

"Well sir, the only way it could be known is through the Embassy in Johannesburg. My team was shocked at the blasé attitude of their agents. They're not discreet about whom they're following. Perhaps you could have a word with them and find out. My team never carries any identification other than what is needed for the job. In this paper the only names given in the article are Hennessey and the attorney, Henry Peckham."

Bobbie patted Kitty's arm. "The London Tabloid article indicates Peckham was attorney for Alex McGraw, and the incident took place at the Edse hospital."

Kitty cringed. "Still, according to my team captain, Jo and Theresa are the only ones who saw the man posing as McGraw in the hospital. Plus, there's no association made between Hennessey and the rest of my team."

The Chief puffed more on his pipe. Kitty knew that meant he was going to interrupt.

She sat up very straight and blurted. "What we do know is McGraw never left England, and the man impersonating him fled the hospital with Edse. My team reported they heard Peckham call him Neil. Two of my team, who were in the hospital room, gathered the two men were either close friends or they've known one another for a long time. They also suspect that Neil fled under duress from Edse, because Neil did help them escape by detaining Edse."

Ross lifted the paper. "I agree with Kitty. We were there for the conference call, and this incident has also exposed some highly questionable activity in the building where Hennessey was held. We have to investigate it…"

The Chief grizzled. "The *Embassy* will handle that. Carroll, bring your team home. You've got one dead and one in the hospital. That is an order… By the way, how is she doing?"

"Thank you for asking. She's doing fine and may be released soon. The surveillance camera tape got some good pictures of the man and woman, and they're the same people from the market. It's just a matter of time before we identify them."

Bobbie put her hand on Kitty's shoulder. "It just occurred to me, the man who showed up at the orphanage when Karen was shot could have been Alex in disguise."

Ross brushed his hands through his hair. "My God, that would make sense…That had to have been Alex in the yard behind his house. But, who is that woman? How does she fit in?"

Ross leaned forward. "Chief, this is coming together. We need …"

The Chief stood and stared at Ross, pointing his pipe at his inspectors. "The answer is no! No more extra time, Dennis. You have one more week and this case is closed. Where's the evidence that I can use to argue on your behalf? You've only got conjecture."

Ross stood with his brief case. "What about Alex's impersonator? The airport? The priest business in Scotland? Karen getting shot? If something awful wasn't going on in that hospital, we wouldn't be getting two bodies shipped back to England. Why would Edse kill two people? Money or power is behind all of this, and I know Edse and McGraw are involved."

O'Doul raised his hands. "Sure, maybe all of this will lead to something… Maybe it will! What you have now would or could put Alex in jail for six months at best. Did anyone see Edse shoot the gun? To avoid the risk of reviving the K Code and the Braun family's association, I've been ordered to put a halt to this. I was given that directive this morning! I hate to say this, but, if you ignore my warnings and orders, it will mean your termination."

He paused opening his office door. "You realize that means all of you. You've got one more week, from today."

Not a word had been spoken when the three inspectors stopped outside Kitty's office door. Kitty opened the door. Ross turned to leave looking very sad. "I want to thank you both for…"

Kitty frowned, giving a waving gesture. "Dennis, are you quitting or just leaving to go to your home, your office, or the men's room?"

He and Bobbie raised their brows. She grinned. "Since I'm the team leader, I'm saying we still have a case to solve." She paused at the door. "We will work around stepping on Dr. Braun's toes and causing an international incident." She walked in muttering, "I can't promise anything, but we'll try."

As she opened the inner office door, Patti D. handed her a phone. "Kitty, Linda's been calling. It's very important."

Kitty put the call on speaker. "We're all here, Linda. What did you find?"

They could hear pages turning. "First off, we found blood on the floor outside the double doors leading into the second building. We're almost positive Edse shot Neil, Alex's impostor. One of the staff here saw two men get into the helicopter, so we're assuming Neil is a pilot and if Edse did shoot him, it must have been a flesh wound."

They heard another couple of pages turn. "Next, the Embassy let us go through the building with them."

Kitty interrupted. "I was just going to ask what they found out. How'd you manage that? Chief O'Doul made it clear you were to stay out of it and I'm to order your return."

Linda chuckled. "What would I do without Theresa? When she manages to get us inside the impossible situations, I've learned not to ask how she did it. So, I don't ask. Actually it worked out well. The Embassy personnel are more like agents than inspectors, and were grateful for a different kind of eyes. That being said, we uncovered an elaborate testing laboratory. Behind a waste basket, Jo found some notes that didn't make the shredder. Seems Dr. Edse was making a serum that would attack the brain cells. Right now, we should assume he was successful and has escaped with his findings."

Taking notes, Ross asked, "I can't imagine Edse doing anything for the good of humanity. Has Jo any understanding of what you found?"

"I've put the phone on speaker so we can all talk." They heard

Linda ask Jo to report her findings.

Jo read off some of the chemicals in the formula. "I know this is all foreign to you but maybe I can explain it this way. A serum is made up of the virus itself, mixed with either animal fluids or plant milk. It's an antitoxin and usually used to attack the existing virus in the body, for example hepatitis. We found a few drops on the counter. My guess is Edse was in such a rush he must have transferred the product into a vial and spilled some. The paper I found gave some of his findings, and it appears this serum will be used to create a malfunction of the brain… like being a zombie, brain dead…but still functioning. The strange part about this is, it isn't being used for inoculation, but in another form."

Kitty frowned at Ross and Bobbie. "So, you're thinking Edse is masterminding something intentional?"

Jo blurted out. "I'm sure McGraw is involved as well. That's my fear. If the Embassy will let me, I could run some tests on the serum and prove my assumptions."

Linda cut in. "I've just thought of something. Theresa, when you accosted that bartender, didn't he say that Hennessey walked out with Edse?"

Kitty quipped. "Accosted? Should I know more about this?"

Theresa answered quickly. "No Boss, we did everything by the book. To answer Linda's question, he said she looked bleary-eyed but could walk."

Kitty cut in. "We'll find out soon enough. O'Doul's brother runs the operations at the Embassy and all the red tape was omitted. The bodies should be arriving back here soon. I'd rather the autopsy be done here, anyway."

There was silence for a moment. Linda cleared her throat. "We know. We made the identifications. It wasn't easy, considering all that happened."

Sensing their emotions, Kitty spoke sternly. "Most importantly, you've got to impress on the Embassy that this operation can't be discussed with the press. We've just come from the Chief's office and it wasn't pleasant what he had to say." *This has got to be a shock to their systems. They'll have to go through counseling when they get back.*

Theresa could be heard in the background. "Tell them about the calendar."

Linda rattled some pages. "Theresa's just handed me a big calendar we found in the lab. The days were being crossed off. We're in August and we found written in bold letters, Edse's and McGraw's initials across the whole first week of November. Conference in New York is written at the end of that week."

Bobbie cut in. "That's a bit over two months away. Is there more information like what kind of Conference?"

Linda continued. "No, we looked but couldn't find anything. Personally, I think it's something private or limited to a few interested in Dr. Edse."

Ross cleared his throat. "Linda, do you find Alex's name anywhere else?"

"Yes, back in May, June and July, are entries of 'AM, facials.' Gives the arrival of the attorney, Henry Peckham, his departure, and the arrival of Peckham and Neil Ghent…Now we have the last name for the man Edse took with him."

Kitty put her pen down. "Sounds like you've covered all the bases. It's awful it had to end this way. I think you better wrap it up now and come home. Jo, see if you can bring that sample with you. I'm sure our lab will be interested in it. I have a feeling the drug will be found in Hennessey's body. Okay, well done. Wrap it up now."

"Boss…"

Kitty paused pushing the speaker button. "What is it, Theresa?"

"If you should meet Henry's mother, tell her Henry's dying words were he was sorry to have disappointed her. He really proved to be a good guy. He tried so hard to save Hennessey…and the rest of us as well. He wouldn't follow us until we were all safely down the escape opening."

They heard her clear her throat and go silent.

Kitty cut in. "Fly safe. We'll see you in a couple of days."

Two days later, Ross and Bobbie entered the office with the coffee and scones.

Patti D. peeked out of the control room. "The boss should be back soon. She and the Chief are at Heathrow meeting Hennessey's parents. Her coffin is being flown in this morning."

Not even a half-hour later Kitty arrived looking drawn. As she walked toward her office, she motioned. "Give me a few minutes."

They both nodded. Bobbie gritted her teeth. "That really has torn her up."

Ross nudged her. "Maybe you should give her a shoulder."

"I wouldn't know what to say… Sometimes it's best not to say anything."

Patti D. paused outside Kitty's office door, and then knocked. "Boss! Sorry to interrupt, Karen's calling from the hospital." She pointed to one of the wall screens. "I've put it out here for you. It's the Week's News program. Karen's on line two if you want to put her on speaker."

Kitty pressed the button. "Hope you haven't popped a stitch. What's up? Yes, we're watching. I just now got in from the airport. Chief O'Doul and I met with Hennessey's parents after they met the plane." She snapped her fingers to Patti D. "I didn't meet the plane. The Chief walked out with them…"

They all watched two caskets being lowered from a cargo plane and several people walking up. They heard the commentator give the names Hennessey and Peckham.

Kitty wheeled around to Patti D. "Are you taping this? "

With hands on her hips, "Of course. I tape everything."

Bobbie gasped. "That's got to be the woman from the market. My gosh, she's the attorney's mother?"

Karen blurted out. "Oh, she's a mother all right! I almost fell out of bed when I saw this earlier. I wasn't sure the first time I saw it as it's a side view of her but, I'm sure now. That's the woman who shot me!"

Kitty cut in. "Okay, let's cool it. Karen, we've seen enough. You get yourself back to …"

"Oh…I'm dressed and ready to leave this place. I'll be back to work…"

Kitty cleared her throat. "As I was saying, you'll be back to work when the Team fitness trainer says so…" They heard some under the breath comments before the speaker went off. She chuckled a little putting the receiver down.

The meeting seemed to be over. As Dennis walked up to the screen on the wall to study the rerun of the news, Kitty whispered to Bobbie. “I need to talk you, privately.”

Bobbie frowned. “With or without Dennis?”

Dennis pointed to the wall. “Patti D. Can you play it back and freeze this profile and the next one…The mother and son pictures.” He turned. “Bobbie and Kitty, where have we seen these two before? Not recently either. This kid is well over six feet closer to seven feet tall. Patti, can you call the news and find out where they got this picture of the mother and son? I know we’ve seen them together. You don’t forget a picture like this.”

Kitty whispered. “Without.”

Bobbie continued to frown. *This sounds serious.* Sitting with her chin resting on her palm, she stared at Ross’s pointing. She glanced over at Kitty. “I think he’s right. Where have we seen them?”

Patti D. peeked out of the control room. “BBC had it in their obituary files from last year. Mrs. Peckham’s brother, Charles Donnohue, worked for Interpol and was killed in a crime shootout.”

Dennis chuckled. “Oh, that’s how it was worded.” He looked at Bobbie. “We attended the service to make sure there were no mishaps or any statements given to the press. It was a grave site funeral. Only a few attended. Do you remember?”

Kitty dropped her head. “Damn, I hope the Chief hasn’t seen this. Dennis, you could go and find out. God, I pray some news editor doesn’t think there’s a story here to resurrect!”

Bobbie stood by the door. “Now we know there’s even more of a relationship between Alex and this woman.”

She looked at Kitty and pointed to the screen. “That Charles Donnohue was part of the effort to take Kimberly Braun hostage. He posed as one of the lighting technicians the day of the robbery. You can’t imagine what it was like being in a secret room observing a diabolical situation evolving, and we couldn’t do anything to save you or Arthur…”

She stared at Ross’s slight limp as he walked toward them. “Braun’s right hand man Arthur was brutally tortured. Alex shot you, and then Braun’s dog mauled Alex to protect the niece… It was horrible. I will never forget it."

Ross picked up his brief case, staring at the screen. *I live through it every night.* "You know I'll hear the wrath of O'Doul, if he has seen it. Hopefully, he'll be having his afternoon nap. I will tip toe past his office on the way to mine."

While Ross made later arrangements with Bobbie, Kitty went into the control booth. "Patti D., I'll be in my office. Would you patch in a call to Karen?" She motioned to Bobbie to go to her private office.

Bobbie frowning, took, a seat next to the desk. "What's with all the mystery? Hope I haven't given you any grief?"

Kitty shut the door. "No, you haven't, but I need to share something with you."

Bobbie stared at her friend. *She's fighting back tears. No matter how strong you are, it still cuts deep.* "What's the matter? I can tell this is especially hard on you."

Kitty sat with her hands folded. "I waited with Hennessey's parents as the coffins were lowered from the plane. It was heart wrenching to find out this was the mother's only child. Hennessey's stepdad handled most of the meeting. When I had to ask her to sign the form for an autopsy, she reacted quite harshly." Kitty threw her pencil across the desk. "You know, I can't blame her one bit. I feel a lot of anger for this loss and I can't imagine what a parent would feel. It was too soon and too hard to watch it on the news." Teary eyed, looking down, she took a deep breath. "It made me wonder."

Bobbie shrank. "I saw you turn away when the coffin was lowered." *Kitty, wonder about?* Suddenly, she sensed the answer and grasped Kitty's hand. "Don't even go there. You are not going to end this unit or training program! Look at me! Sad things happen when rules are broken. It's hard I know, but…"

The phone rang once. Kitty raised her brow. "The ugliness of this case is about to go from bad to worse."

She pressed the speaker button. "Karen, I'm here with Bobbie. Repeat for her what Father James told you about Ross's wife."

Bobbie leaned forward frowning. "Ross's wife?"

"Karen, what happened before you had to hide?"

"Before that couple arrived, who we now know is Peckham's

mother and Alex in disguise, Father James told me this whole situation, stealing Alex's stuff, was to take revenge against him for killing Lizzy."

Bobbie interrupted. "Karen, that can't be. She died of…"

"That's what I told the priest, but he said Jane had proof Alex had Lizzy ingest cancer cells."

Bobbie stared off breathing hard. Moments passed as she struggled with this news. "How could anyone be so…so… there's no word for it."

Kitty touched Bobbie's arm. "Do you agree? We can't let Dennis know about this atrocity?"

Bobbie dropped her head. "My God! Dennis would lose it."

She heard Karen explain. "I'm so sorry to tell you this, but I had to report it and Kitty said it had to be kept totally quiet."

Kitty ended the call by reiterating to Karen that this wasn't to be told to anyone else. "You understand? Not to anyone."

"Yes, mum, I'm clear on that."

Bobbie sat bewildered. "I've seen a lot over the years but I've never felt so sick in my stomach as I do now." She shut her eyes. "How am I going to keep this from him? He's already told me my eyes can't keep a secret."

Kitty stared off and quietly said. "Because you have to. And you will." Swallowing some tea, she put the cup down and leaned toward her friend. "I need to be frank with you. A few minutes ago you were all upset thinking I would end my program because of Hennessey's death. Right?"

Seeing Bobbie's attention changing from dwelling on Ross, Kitty firmly said, "You're wrong. We all know, crime is changing. It's no longer the stick-em up, take the money and run away. My God, the end result of a robbery is a useless killing. No witnesses."

She shrugged her shoulders. "I'm sure you've noticed the crime scene photos you're taking are no longer the gunshot to the head or heart, the same with the knife, but now our departments are seeing more and more brutal and disgusting causes of death. These murderers have no conscience. Sure, I'm deeply upset over the loss of Hennessey, but, I'm more upset knowing I could have saved her, had I trained them up to the next level."

"Why didn't you?"

Kitty shook her head biting her lip. "Because, the next level is equal to the training the navy seals go through. They don't and they can't think twice, and it's a permanent mind set. I know only too well what the tradeoff is. I'm sorry, but I can't steal that away from my girls."

"I can understand how heart wrenching this is for you." *Something horrible must have happened to her. I better not ask.* "Thanks for helping me see the bigger picture."

Kitty stood by the door. "I can't stop wondering why Alex set up such an elaborate scheme. Why didn't he go to Johannesburg, have his surgery and then on to New York? Obviously, the intent was to make Ross think either Jane was dead or it was no longer a big deal that he find her. Or…" She squinted at Bobbie, mulling over the sequence, and in unison, they said, "He was thinking Ross would lead him to her."

Bobbie sat up straight. "However, we don't know if the killings of Hennessey and Peckham have made him feel exposed."

"According to Linda, Jo and Theresa never saw Edse. They did talk with Peckham and McGraw's impersonator, Neil Ghent. When Peckham wanted to help them escape with Hennessey, he pleaded with Neil to help. What's important is that neither man knew anything about our team."

Bobbie leaned on the desk. "Do you think the autopsy will show a correlation with the serum they found in Edse's lab?"

Kitty shrugged into her jacket. "I do, and I also think those calendar dates for a conference in New York put pressure on Alex to find Jane. It doesn't make sense that Alex would attend a medical conference in New York, so this has to be for something else, certainly not for any humanitarian reason. Jane may have stolen a lot more than money. Unfortunately, it took this tragedy to expose the evil. What Jane has could lead to another type of human suffering. The fact remains, Edse escaped with whatever he's developed. We still have a deadline, and Alex is still on the loose."

Bobbie squeezed Kitty's hand. "Then we've got to save Jane."

Chapter 28

The cottage at Shoreham by the sea

As Alex finished reading the paper, the phone rang. The caller id said 'unknown caller'. *Can't take a chance.* Then he heard Edse's voice. "Alex, pick up!"

Alex grabbed the phone. "Where the fuck are you? You realize your name is in the article. I see your dad covered for you, saying you were on a trip out of the country. And you said I fu.."

Edse screamed at him. "You're right! I fucked up so we're even. Are you satisfied? In the shed you'll find a briefcase."

The phone went dead. "Edward!" He slammed the phone on the cradle. *That mother hung up.* Alex looked at all the keys on the rack by the back door. "Damn you, Eddie, why play hide –and- seek for the fuckin' key… Jesus, I don't have time for your crap!" He found the key behind another one. The tags had twisted.

He tried to open the back door with his prosthetic and got more pissed. *Alex, cool off. No one's here to blame or beat up.* He stood at the door until focused.

In the shed, he found a box with Edse's handwriting on it. "Anthony Taylor?" *Must be my new name.* He read. "Contingency Plan: Use this cell phone to call the number on the back."

When his call was answered, he heard bird calls in the background. "Sounds like you're in a fuckin' zoo."

"We're at one of my parents' houses in the jungle. You need to get out of there as soon as you can."

Alex shook his head. "Not going to happen. My picture is on the surveillance at the orphanage, and I'm sure the Yard has a bulletin out for me. I don't think anyone has seen me here in Shoreham, but I can't be sure. You said we. Who's with you?"

"Neil's with me. Lucky for him, I'm a horrible shot and just grazed him. We were able to escape in my helicopter. Listen, your best bet is to go to New York. I know people and can do the surgery there. I made another mask in the event something like this might happen. The paper work for your new identity is in the brief case. You'll find the chemicals you need and the mask in the bottom of a chest in the shed. Whatever you do, come alone. We can't afford any more mistakes."

As he listened, he pulled out the papers in the various sleeves of the case. He bit his lip and shouted. "Edward, this fuckin' passport has expired."

Edse snapped back. "Hey, shit happens. You're the one with all the answers. Lest you forget, you wanted more time to find Jane. Well, you've got it. I'm going to be adapting the serum into a powdered substance this week. I could use that formula you had! But, if you don't catch her, I'm sure I'll figure it out."

Alex groaned in frustration. He heard water splashing in the background. "Edward, let me talk to Neil." He shut his eyes straining to hear. *Sounds like splashing in a pool.*

"Neil, who can I call to handle this passport shit? Damnit, are you there? What's all that splashing going on?"

"Alex, right now, all you have is Zilpha. No one else I know will get involved."

Alex slumped on a crate. "I was afraid you'd say that. I promised her Henry wouldn't get mixed up in any of this and then …that maniac kills him."

"Tell her that! If I could, I'd settle the score for her right now, but I can't. He's very…Have to go now. Good luck. See you in New York."

Alex waited for Edse to return. *At least Neil doesn't know I approved Edse's actions.* He heard Edse make a sexual remark. *I get it. Neil's saving his ass. Or is loyalty only for the moment?*

He could see his reflection in a dusty dresser mirror on the floor leaning against its mate. He got up yelling to release his anger and hatred. "Edward!" He then kicked the mirror until it was only shards on the floor.

"Sorry, Neil should have told you to call when you're ready to leave. We won't need to be out of here until the end of October. When you're able to stick to a schedule, come to Africa or New York. My family keeps a suite of rooms at the Ritz… I really must get back to changing his bandages."

Their connection went dead. Alex, gritting his teeth, stood drained. *When you can stick to a schedule!* He stared out the shed window and saw a woman walking with her child hand in hand down a path. *Remember when dad beat up on mom? What did I do?* He shut his eyes and smiled. *Remember what trouble Lizzy was. She took Jane away! I got rid of her. Remember when Charlie was attacked and murdered. Who caused that?* Opening his eyes, he grabbed a hammer from the shed tool bench and threw it, shouting, "Had Windsor and Edse not been so fuckin' eager to traumatize the Brauns, we would have gotten the code." *Now you are leaving me out! Who the fuck do you think organized this conference? You need me more than I need you!* He found a hatchet and smashed everything in sight until he fell to his knees. Breathing hard, he got to his feet. *Those formulas are mine. It was my creation and now you want to take the credit? I think not, you fuckin' parasite.*

Three days passed before Alex had totally removed the mask. He had to wait another two days before he could apply the new one. The phone rang. He cringed when he heard Zilpha's voice.

He forced himself to speak quietly and calmly. "How are you doing? I saw the paper and it's been on the news. I thought you needed time. I just don't know what to say. Something went wrong. I haven't been able to find out what happened until today. I thought it best to wait to tell you what Edse reported …"

It was silent and then Zilpha asked. "I'm okay, tell me."

"Edse said the police came in shooting. He grabbed his experiments and ran. As far as he knew, Henry and Neil were behind him. When he got to his helicopter, Neil was the only one there. Neil told him the police killed Henry. None of that was printed in the paper."

She held the phone against her chest, wiped her eyes and nose. "I met the plane two days ago. I had Henry cremated. His ashes are here with Charlie."

Alex's shoulders stiffened. *What do I say? I need the fuckin' passport....* "Zilpha, had I been there, this whole nightmare wouldn't have happened. I hope you're telling me you can't help me anymore. ...In fact, I've decided to cut my losses and leave the country. I still have plenty of money. Why don't you...come with me?" *She won't leave those urns.*

He heard a muffled cry and then her voice cleared. "Alex, we should continue as planned. I've worked out some areas where Jane could be hiding. I still think that if we drug Ross, making it a news headline, she'll come to care for him. When can you come to my cottage?"

Alex hesitated. "I had to get rid of the mask because of the surveillance cameras in Scotland. I found another mask out in Edse's shed. It doesn't look damaged. I'm going to use it." *This will tell if she'll help me.*

Zilpha quickly asked. "Is there a name on the box or any records inside like the others he's made? You'll need some identification."

Alex grinned shutting his eyes. *Thank you! Thank you!* "There's just a name and nothing else. Not to worry. I'll call some..."

"What's the name? I'll run a history on it and make up at least a driver's license. You'll need that for now."

He gave her the name. "Call me when you want me to come over. You take care of yourself first. There's no rush." Smiling, he hung up. *How long before I can ask for the passport.*

Zilpha laid the phone down and ran the recording another time of Alex's conversation with Edse of the week before, approving her son's demise. She played it again and again, staring at Henry's graduation picture with Charlie and her. "We were so proud of you, son." Tears streaming, she took the picture and held it tightly to her breast. "I feel so responsible. Had I…" She cried herself to sleep in her chair holding the picture.

An hour passed and with a jerk she sat up and looked around. "Charlie!" *He was right here. He talked to me.* She rubbed her arm and then her cheek. *You touched me and kissed my face. You told me I have to make this right.*

Chapter 29

Ross's cottage in Godstone

As Ross and Bobbie drove down his road, a flash of lightning lit up the sky and boomeranged as far as they could see. It started to pour. Dennis laughed. "How's that for timing? Another two minutes and we would have been inside. Now we have to run for it."

Bobbie opened her door. "This came up awful sudden. I didn't see it on the news. That blast must have hit a power station. The street light is out. I don't see any lights on in the other cottages. Hope you have candles." She ran behind Ross.

Inside his little house he struck a match. "I keep a candle on the table for these occasions. We lose power a lot around here. They need to upgrade our…holy shit!"

He lit the candle and saw out of the corner of his eye a woman sitting in his hallway holding a gun. Bobbie wheeled around, starting to draw her weapon, but stopped. "What's the…Oh, my God, it's…"

Zilpha motioned for them to sit. "I'm Zilpha Peckham… Henry Peckham's mother. I know you're looking for me, and I will surrender, but first, I can help you catch Alex and find Jane."

Dennis questioned defensively. "How did you get in here? There are special locks on the doors! What makes you think you can find Jane?" *What made her turn against Alex?* "Is this part of Alex's plan?"

Zilpha tossed a large envelope to Bobbie. "Just sit and look at these."

Studying them by the candle light, Bobbie squinted at Zilpha. "Are these of Jane? She's drinking something in the first picture, drying her hair in another, and walking out of a tunnel in this last one dressed in a soldier's outfit. Where and how did you get these?"

Zilpha shoved another envelope across the table. "When I put the tracking device under your car, Inspector Ross, I stuck some cameras in your trees aimed at the windows of your house and then a few elsewhere. You see, I'm what you would call an information getter. Godstone has quite a history."

Dennis replied slowly staring at her. *How did this woman get in here?* "I know. I recently told the inspector I had a book on Godstone. Its history attracted my wife and me to move here."

Zilpha crossed her legs, propping the gun over her knee. "I read the book, and my gut feeling is Jane did too, maybe when she took care of your wife. The second group of pictures should tell you where one of Jane's hiding places has been for the last few years."

They leaned over the pictures. Dennis grabbed his jaw as it opened. His eyes bulging, he blurted. "Here? Are you kidding? Here?"

"The times are about the same. Those pictures are dated and she arrives between two and three in the morning. At least once a week for sure and it's not always the same day."

Bobbie stared at the last picture showing the tunnel. "Dennis said a tunnel existed but didn't know which cottage it led to. You obviously found it came here. Did you go in?"

Zilpha shook her head. "I was afraid to in case she might be in the cellar. Putting myself in her shoes, I would run if someone tried to communicate with me other than the priest. I was tempted to leave her a note, but again, feared she'd panic thinking she was found out."

Bobbie studied Zilpha a moment. "A few days ago after breakfast, I asked Dennis to put some veggies in the cellar. He said his wife was afraid to use it and they never went down. Well, I found the door was unlocked and opened it. I thought it strange there weren't any cob webs but dismissed it thinking he had a housekeeper. This makes sense. Jane must have investigated and found the tunnel entrance. So, she's keeping it web- free knowing Dennis wouldn't go down to the cellar. Dennis, remember Jane's note said she is closer than you think."

Dennis rubbed his forehead. "This is…unbelievable. All this time, she's been around. Then, why are you here?"

A sudden crack of lightning shook the cottage, causing a window to open and blowing out the candle. Zilpha shined her flash light squarely on both of them. "It's not that I don't trust you, Inspector Ross. Light your candle." She motioned for Bobbie to shut the window.

When they were seated again, Bobbie saw Dennis' calculating expression and nudged him. "Dennis! I think Mrs. Peckham is warning us not to scare Jane off. We can't exactly sound the all clear horn and expect Jane to appear."

Zilpha fastened her eyes on Dennis. "If she's aware that you know her location, she'll disappear, Inspector. She's survived this long because her mind is geared for defensive action. I can speak from experience. It will take a while for her to work her way out of that mind set as it did me. My guess is, she wants to protect those she cares about, you and the priest, from Alex."

Zilpha turned to Bobbie. "I'm sure she's aware of the mess we caused at the orphanage. She's probably ready to make her move. That's where I can help by encouraging it to happen."

Ross stared at her. "Mrs. Peckham. How do we know you're not setting me up for…"

"Call me Zilpha. You don't have anything but my word. Alex told me he's changed his mind and is going to leave the country in the next two weeks, whether or not he's found Jane. If that should happen, he'll get away with…" She stopped and faced them. "I can't let that happen."

Bobbie frowned. "What do you have in mind?" *This woman is hurting. Her face is almost lifeless.*

"I think the only way Jane will surface is to put Inspector Ross in jeopardy. I've already told Alex I could cause you to have what would appear to be a stroke."

Bobbie put the pictures on the table. "Is that why you're here?" In the candle light, she saw Zilpha gritting her teeth.

"Yes, for reasons you don't need to know, situations can change. I'm offering to help save Jane and catch the man who murdered your wife!" *As he did my son.*

Ross gasped. "What are you saying? How could he have murdered Lizzy? She died from..." His eyes glazed, he looked at Bobbie. "You don't even look surprised! Bobbie, did you know this?"

Feeling his shock, she looked at him teary eyed. Biting her lip, she dropped her head. "We just found out about it and thought you were torn up enough with Jane's disappearance."

Zilpha raised her voice. "Inspector, I'm sorry, but it's true. Jane left Alex a threatening note that he carries in his wallet. She found out what he had done. Right now, I can't go into it any further. This is your chance to make all of this right." *Don't do anything stupid.*

Bobbie took a deep breath. "I agree with her. The newspapers would eat it up. After that airport scene with McGraw that made the front page, people would still remember you."

She squeezed Dennis's hand. "Then you think Jane would see the news and want to care for him."

Zilpha nodded. "Most definitely. These pictures show she has access to the house. She certainly knows your routine."

She looked at her watch. "You haven't much time to give me an answer before I take matters into my own hands."

Bobbie sensed Zilpha's determination. *A week ago her son was alive. I wonder if she blames Alex for his death.* "If we agree, what would you have us do?"

Concealing a tiny dart shooting syringe, Zilpha rose holding her gun on them. She gathered her pictures. She got within two feet of Ross and pulled a little trigger emitting a dart that hit Ross in the neck. "I'm sorry. You really haven't much choice in the matter. I wanted you to know because this is the one way I can bring an end to Alex, and at the same time to assure you what appears to be a stroke will wear off in about a week."

Ross grabbed his throat, tried to stand and fell to the floor. Bobbie's heart pounded as she cradled Ross. Looking at Zilpha wide eyed, she shouted. "What have you done?"

Zilpha put her hand on Bobbie's shoulder. "The more he stays relaxed, the less he will hurt. This has to look real. It's up to you. Will you trust me?"

Bobbie rolled Dennis's shoulders onto her lap. Dennis tried to speak, staring at Zilpha, but made only guttural sounds.

"Inspector, don't try to talk. Take deep breaths. Relax. You'll be fine. I need your trust now to make this work. Can I count on your help? Blink your eyes."

Bobbie squeezed his shoulders whispering, "Dennis, we have to end this nightmare. I want to trust her."

Dennis blinked and passed out.

Bobbie felt his body sink. "Zilpha! He's not moving!"

Zilpha took his pulse. "This is a normal reaction. Don't panic. Call for an ambulance as soon as I leave. The news media will pick it up by tomorrow. You won't see me until the end, but I promise to turn myself in. Tomorrow I'll show these pictures to Alex. Ross will be out of the hospital, in two days at most. They will say he's had a mild stroke requiring some in-home therapy. He shouldn't need around the clock nurses. Certainly not at night. Expect Alex to appear soon after Ross is brought home. He will want to kill Ross and Jane."

"How will you know Jane is here?"

She took one of the envelopes. "I'm leaving you the envelope with the tunnel photos so you can plot where it is. The pictures have the info on the back. I put a silent alarm at the tunnel entrance. It can be monitored a good thousand feet away. Alex will either be alone monitoring the device or with me. I can't give you any other information. All I can say is, be prepared for the worst."

Bobbie nodded. "Thank you, I feel this is very hard for you as well.."

Ignoring Bobbie's comment, Zilpha handed the phone to Bobbie. "The hatred that's involved is beyond comprehension, and I wouldn't count on a plan being followed. Just expect violence. It will happen…Are you good with this?"

With a clenched mouth Bobbie shrank. "I'm praying Ross won't remember you told him Alex murdered…What's worse is I knew about it. The priest told one of our agents."

Zilpha dropped her head. "I'm really sorry about shooting her… Is she…?"

"She's fine."

Zilpha turned toward Ross's bedroom.

Bobbie reached up and took her hand. "How did you get in here? The tunnel? The cellar door is locked."

Zilpha pulled her hand away. “The bookcase in the hall. I must leave. I don’t want to scare Jane or this will all end in vain.”

“Zilpha…your son, Henry” Zilpha stopped and turned.

Bobbie whispered through her emotions. “He saved our team from being killed. Before he died, he wanted us to tell you he was sorry he disappointed you.”

She stood with her head bowed, listening.

Bobbie squeezed the phone. “He could have escaped with the others. You should be very proud. He chose to be on the right side of the law.”

“Make the call for an ambulance.” Zilpha rushed down the hall. From the burst of lightning, Bobbie saw the hall bookcase open and Zilpha disappear.

Chapter 30

Zilpha's home

Closing the ammunition cabinet, Zilpha heard the doorbell. She looked at the monitor to see Alex huddled at the front door. Lightning flashed behind him. *That storm just doesn't want to give up.* She answered, pressing some additional buttons. "Door is open. I'm in the office."

He headed for the cellar and stopped before two closed doors. "Which one? I don't want to set off any alarms."

"You won't as long as I'm by the computer. Voice recognition identifies the person, and then I decide if they are welcome. The door on the left. The new mask makes you look a lot older."

He saw the camera in the corner tucked behind a flowering plant and grinned. "I hope that's a compliment."

"The whiter hair and more lines in the face suggest…not wiser, maybe more distinguished."

He sat next to her desk. *She's trying to hold it together. My story of Edse's account of the police shooting spree has done the trick. At least she trusts me.* Putting his hand on hers, "Are you sure you're up to this? Don't you think you should back out now?"

She slid her hand from under his. "Alex, everyone handles grief in their own way. I have to keep busy. Have you seen this morning's news?"

"No, I was destroying any evidence of my being in that cottage. I'm almost done. It will be sterile."

She turned on the wall monitor. "I taped this at six this morning. Watch." *I was afraid of this. He is going to make a run for it.*

Seeing Ross being carried on a stretcher from an ambulance into the hospital, Alex rose and listened intently to Bobbie tell the media how Ross keeled over in his house. He wheeled around staring at her. His eyes radiated satisfaction. "You did this, didn't you? How did you fuckin' do it?"

She leaned back. *Thank God I taped this. He'll stay.* "I've been following him with the tracker box. Last night, he and his partner were nearby at a grocery. I got over there as they were leaving. As I passed him, I shot a dissolving dart in his leg. By the time they got to his place, she would have been calling for an ambulance."

Alex sat clapping his hands. "You are one brilliant lady. I could…" *I see the fuckin' urns. She'll never understand I've given her a fresh start, getting rid of her kid. She'd be such an asset to the New York project.*

She handed him the photos of Jane. "I think you're going to be surprised. You might have a second thought about leaving."

He sat shaking his head. "I don't believe it. All this time… You found a tunnel?"

She handed him the little book on Godstone. "It pays off being a history buff. I've been there twice. First to find it, and then to set up a hidden motion detector documenting time and dates she goes in. That's where I got that picture you're holding. I haven't been in it for fear of being seen or meeting up with Jane. I don't want to scare her off."

Finally, I can get rid of that bitch…to watch them both suffer will make the loss of my arm worth it. He glanced through the pages and read the underlined passages. "You're right! I can't pass up this opportunity. I can get them both… Zilpha, you're my hero!"

Zilpha crossed her hands in her lap. "Question is, how are we going to get in, get them both, and get out? We can monitor the tunnel and know when Jane is there. Do we want to block it so she can't leave or do we need it for an escape? Then who do you want to kill first? I'm assuming you want to do them both?"

She filled a tea pot with boiling water and clipped the tea hanger from the handle. *I've got to get Alex really into this so he doesn't want to leave until this is done...* "I need all your thoughts about this. Alex, this is *not* a piece of cake to plan. We've little time because Ross will be released from the hospital in a day or two. Keep in mind he will have some movement, at least to shoot a gun."

Alex smirked and showed his right arm. "You mean we will be on the same playing field."

She frowned. "I think you'll have the advantage." *I hope his partner is working something out with her department.. His eyes tell me he'll settle for nothing less than death...for both Ross and Jane.*

Chapter 31

Dream Team office at Scotland Yard

Bobbie entered carrying two bags of scones. "These are fresh out of the oven. I hope the tea is ready." She smiled at the sudden appearance of many faces. "Hey, when did you get back?"

Linda, Theresa, and Jo, all tan, gave her hugs as they helped her with the bags. Theresa waved a scone. "When no one knew what a scone was in Johannesburg, I knew it was time to get the…" Everyone suddenly cleared their throats.

Kitty appeared holding her cup. "Did I hear the magic word?" She grinned at Bobbie. "It's good having the troops back, isn't it?" She looked around. "I thought I saw someone who should still be in bed."

Patti D. stood aside from her door. "She's hiding, boss."

Karen walked out. "I am ready to go." She put her hands on her hips. "I passed the physical."

She curtsied when they all applauded.

Bobbie pulled a chair out for Karen to sit and looked at Kitty. "Have you heard how the priest is doing? You said he's up in his years."

Karen sat chuckling. "He is that but very resilient. I was told he called every day I was in recovery. Fact is I talked to him yesterday just before I checked out of the hospital. He sounded great and was happy I could go home."

Karen saw the frown on Kitty's face. "Boss, cross my heart. I'm not fibbing. You can check with that grouchy fitness director. She tested me."

Kitty grinned. "I'm truly overwhelmed with your dedication, but I've lost one and almost a second. Hennessey's funeral was heart wrenching. I can't go through that again. Perhaps you'll understand why we keep training. I know you get irritated drilling the many skills, but, a mistake kills. Emotions create unpredictable situations and usually end in disaster." She raised her voice more than usual. "Don't ever think this job is routine!"

Linda pointed to the others. "Theresa and I can attest to what you're saying. Your training kept us alive. Hennessey…" She dropped her head.

Theresa put her hand on Linda's shoulder. "Pure and simple, the kid's emotions fucked her up and that young man too. I have to say, that Henry kid came through. No one knew Edse's hospital was a cover for his experimentation. Without Henry's help, we'd be lying next to Hennessey. That maniac came running shooting his gun. That kid was riddled with bullets."

Jo handed Kitty a folder. "I just got this from our lab. The autopsy showed Hennessey was injected with a small dose of the same serum we found in Edse's laboratory. That stuff literally creates zombies out of anyone and there's no antidote at this time. The doctors at the lab said Hennessey couldn't survive even that small dose. My question is, what was this created for?"

As Jo slumped back in her chair, Theresa leaned over and whispered. "After what you reported…"

Kitty frowned and handed the folder back to Jo. "Theresa, do you want to add something to Jo's report?"

Embarrassed, Theresa explained. "I was just saying to Jo that after her report about how deadly the serum is, I really applaud Hennessey's efforts to stay connected enough to let us know about McGraw's impostor. I just wanted to share a good thing."

Kitty leaned on the chalk board and motioned for Theresa. "While I have a meeting with Bobbie, I want you, Jo and Linda to go to Counseling and arrange for some PTSD time."

Theresa backed off. "No, we're fine."

Kitty put her arm around her and motioned for the other two. "I'm not laying you off, but I will if you don't cooperate. I just want you to take the morning and talk with them."

She opened the door for them. "God knows, I need you for this case. You're my building blocks." She smiled as they left. "See you at lunch."

Closing the door behind her, Bobbie handed Zilpha's photos to Kitty. "Jane's note wasn't far from the truth! Look at these. "

Just then Kitty's door opened, and at the same time her phone rang. Chief Inspector O'Doul pointed to the phone. "Someone's telling you I've ignored protocol."

Bobbie swallowed her bite of scone and jumped to attention. "I guess you have, sir."

Kitty stood in front of the desk and glared at Bobbie. *The pictures!* "Chief! You're right! This is an unexpected visit…Actually, you've never been here. Ah, can we offer you a scone, tea?"

Bobbie caught on and scooted the photos behind her as she moved in front of the desk. "Maybe you'd feel more comfortable out in the conference area."

The Chief smiled. "No, ladies, I'm on my way to the hospital to see Ross and thought I would first get all the details from you." He tilted his head and tightened his lips. "You know, I get the feeling that something's running amok! Wouldn't be you three have ignored my orders, would it?"

He stared at both of them. "You know the week has run out. The case is officially ended?"

Kitty shrugged her shoulders. "Yes, we are totally aware of that and have started on other projects…Haven't we, *Bobbie*?"

Bobbie nodded. "I'm sure Dennis will be happy to see you. He's coming along very well and should be home tomorrow."

The Chief hesitated at the door. "I see, and does it require you and the Dream Team to facilitate his rehab? I found it interesting all ten of you signed out for a two day leave of absence…"

Bobbie cleared her throat. "Sir, I know this looks…"

O'Doul straightened his shoulders and turned the knob. "You will call if you need back-up." and left.

Kitty sank in her chair. "I think we're on his watch list."

Bobbie chuckled. "Poor man, I hope we haven't pushed our luck out the door. I think he's really under a lot of pressure from the powers that be."

Kitty picked up the photos. "Let's just hope this woman is telling us the truth and not setting us up for a huge embarrassment."

Bobbie frowned. "I swear that woman is hurting. At one point, I saw tears. They were genuine, all right. Her son is dead and she wants revenge, and in some way, she thinks Alex is responsible and wants him to pay. It has to be that. Why else would she come to us?"

She handed Kitty the photos of the tunnel. "Peckham said Alex has a time table. He told her he's attending a meeting in New York that's more important than finding Jane. She happened upon the tunnel reading a history of Godstone. Wondering if it really existed, or still exists, Peckham plotted it on a local map and traced it back to Ross's cottage. These photos are the icing on the cake. She's monitoring that tunnel and as soon as Jane enters it, she's sure Alex will want to go for it."

Kitty studied the pictures. "So, we've got to have our girls in place before Ross gets home."

Bobbie shook her head. "I don't think so...His house is a one bedroom, one floor cottage. Literally one of everything..." *I can't imagine two people living there.*

Kitty pulled a map out of the file cabinet and spread it on her work table. "Then we've got a problem. We can't evacuate the street. How close are the houses?"

Bobbie drew a narrow u-shaped circle on the chalk board. "The X marks are the houses. The length of the road is about the size of a soccer field. Right at the end of the circle is Ross's cottage. The road slopes down from the main road. At the top of the slope is the village chapel."

"So what you're saying is, we've got nowhere to hide. What do we know about the tunnel?"

Bobbie shrugged her shoulders. "All Zilpha Peckham told me was she found where the tunnel ended away from the village. According to Dennis, the church was a sanctuary from the king. We have to assume there's a tunnel from the chapel to Ross and then away." She drew a circle around the area of the map. "These are the coordinates on the back of one of the pictures in Zilpha's envelope. We don't know if Jane is using both ends of the tunnel. Come to think of it, we don't know if she is going in or coming out in that photo. Time is running short. We can't investigate both, can we?"

Kitty frowned. "You know you've raised a good question. I wonder if Jane or Zilpha have considered there are two openings?"

Before she donned her suit jacket, Kitty put on her shoulder holster. She opened her desk drawer and pulled out her gun. "You're right. Time is not on our side. When are you picking Ross up?"

"He's waiting for the doctor to make his rounds. That's usually around seven." She looked at her watch. "It's nearing lunch time so we've still got six hours. It won't hurt him to wait a bit either."

They went into the conference room with the other team members. Kitty stood before them. "Here's the plan we've come with. Patti D., put the Godstone map on the screen, please."

She gave them a moment to study the area. "This isn't a very big area. The village goes back to the sixteen hundreds and as you can see, everything revolves around the chapel. Bobbie tells me Ross's cottage has just one of everything, no extra space. So we can't do much there other than put listening devices. We also have to be discreet and not make a show of our presence."

Some hands went up. Kitty pointed. "Linda, you have a question?"

Linda stood. "Why don't we borrow some trucks from companies that would fit the scene? Ross is coming home. We could get a truck from a medical equipment place or ride with the delivery people." She looked at Bobbie. "He will be getting a special bed for a while, won't he?"

Bobbie nodded. "The neighbors would expect it, and we can carry on with our installations. Good idea."

Kitty smiled. "Then, perhaps the water department should pay the chapel an unexpected visit." She opened the control room door. "Patti D., order lunch for the team. We'll eat here and then we'll be gone the rest of today. See if you can find out who the priest is at the Godstone chapel, and if he's there, set up a meeting with me later this afternoon."

Kitty and Bobbie rode with three of the team members in a van from the Thames Valley water department. Kitty looked at Bobbie. "If this truck were any bigger, we wouldn't make these bends in the road!"

Bobbie chuckled. "Ross can drive this blind-folded, and that's after a few beers."

Theresa whispered to Karen. "He fuckin' needs something."

Kitty saw the driver hold back a gut wrenching laugh, and shook her head. *No point in saying anything. Theresa is ...Theresa. Can't live with her and can't live without her.*

Linda opened her door with a sigh of relief. "Finally we're here. I was beginning to wonder if we should have walked."

The driver, a big husky fellow, opened Karen's door for her. "You get used to it. Actually, my crew and I have had some worse climbs than this in the winter." He got some wrenches out of the outside equipment boxes. "Inspector Carroll, are you wanting the water shut off?"

Kitty shook her head. She saw his name tag on his jacket. "John, do you have a map of the underground stuff for this area?"

He opened his driver's side of the truck and reached into a side compartment in the door. "Yes, mum." He spread the sheet out on the hood of the truck. "It's pretty detailed. There haven't been any upgrades in over twenty years. Another five and it will be on the list."

"Good to know. There wouldn't be a tunnel marked on that map…?" She looked at her team and cringed. "I hope it wasn't made a part of the sewers."

The driver studied the map and bit his lip. "Is this what you're talking about? There's a dashed line from the chapel down to that cottage at the end of the road." He pointed right to Ross's place. "It's in blue with VH after it. That means vetted historical. But, yes, we can't use the area."

Kitty nodded. "Are there any markings where the tunnel begins inside the chapel?"

He shook his head. "No. There aren't any notations on the map from previous foremen…Are you wanting to find the tunnel?"

Bobbie raised her brow. "We need to find out if it's usable."

Kitty stood at the chapel door. "For now, wait at the truck. We'll go in and talk to the priest and see what he has to say."

The women were met by a nun. "I'm Sister Mary Francis. You're from Scotland Yard?"

Kitty showed her badge. "Yes, we're supposed to see a Father Logan."

The nun showed her age, squinting and turning her head to hear better. "I'm sorry, Father Logan passed away last month. I'm running the church until his replacement is chosen."

When Kitty showed the nun a picture of Jane, Karen saw the nun's eyes enlarge. *This woman knows something.*

When asked about the tunnel, the nun frowned. "I've only been here a short time. Father Logan was from this area. He never mentioned a tunnel to me. You can look around if you like…I must get back to my work."

As the sister walked away, Karen blurted out. "Sister Mary Francis!" Karen turned to Kitty, "I have an idea."

Kitty waved her on. "Let's hear it. We're running out of time."

Karen raised her voice at the nun. "Do you have a phone, Sister?"

The nun frowned and nodded.

Karen handed her a number. "Would you call this person?"

The nun stared at the number and then at Karen. They followed the nun to the office. In the doorway she stopped. "Would you wait here please?"

She went to the priest's desk and dialed. Turning her back to them she whispered, "Jamie! There are women from Scotland Yard here! What do I tell them? I'm afraid. They want to know about Jane and the tunnel. Yes, one of them is called Karen and she has reddish hair. She gave me your private number."

After a minute, Sister Mary Francis turned handing Karen the phone. "Father Turnbull would like to talk with you."

Karen grinned. "Father James. Have you recovered from our last meeting? Have you heard from Jane? Hmm. We thought as much. Yes, we think it will be soon. We're doing all we can to save them both…Thank you."

She handed the phone back to the nun. "He wants a final word with you."

After a few moments, Sister Mary Francis hung up the phone. "Please, follow me." She hoisted her floor length garb and moved quickly, causing eye brows to rise.

Karen walked beside her. "Did you and Father Logan know Father James well? With that Scottish brogue, I thought I'd take a chance and give you the number. I was hoping you might be from the same clan or area."

"You guessed right. He's my uncle. He asked me to come to this parish because of Jane. She needed someone she knew close by."

Walking behind, Kitty asked. "Did you work at the orphanage too?"

The nun stopped to answer. "Oh, yes, I started to work there just before Jane left our little family." She dropped her head. "She was never adopted. This bothered her a lot..." She sort of smiled at the inspectors. "Uncle Jamie saw it as an omen of things wonderful to come. He wanted her to stay on and be the art teacher. I think she felt she had failed and needed to find her place in the world." She grinned at them. "She's so gifted in art. . ."

Kitty nodded. "Yes, we saw her sketch of Ross-d's wife."

The nun smiled warmly. "You should see the others she's done. My uncle showed them at the art fair Bedrule has each year. Many people asked for her card. Much of the money made for the orphanage has come from Jane's pieces."

Bobbie nudged Karen. "Good job. What did Father James tell you? Has he heard from Jane?"

"Yes, she called him right after she saw on the news about Ross. She told him she had to see Ross was all right and would stay close. She's afraid Alex will try to hurt him, and considers it a last chance to finish Alex off."

Bobbie nudged Kitty. "Doesn't sound like she's afraid or backing off."

The nun picked up her gown again. "If you'll follow me."

Theresa laughed. "We were nuns once and it works well to pull the dress through your legs and tie it to that hanging rope you have around you."

Kitty shook her head. "She's the real thing. Show a little respect...I'm sorry, Sister Mary..."

Sister Mary Francis stopped, leaned over, and pulled her dress through. "Like this?"

They all laughed. Theresa giggled. "Now you have it."

She took them inside the chapel to the confessional.

Karen remembered her earlier experience. "I wondered if that's where the entrance would be."

The nun opened the center door where the priest would sit. As she pushed on the back of the priest's chair, they heard the panel creak as it slid back revealing an entrance to the tunnel. She turned. "Be careful, the steps are steep." There were a box of matches and oil lanterns along the ledge of the stairway. She lit them and handed one to each member of the team. She made the sign of the cross. "Follow me."

At the bottom of the steep stairway was a bicycle. She pointed to it. "If the bike is here, she left using this opening. If the bike is gone, she's at the cottage or left the tunnel at the other end. Mostly she does that as it's closer to the outside of the village."

Kitty chuckled. "No bends in the road. She doesn't drive. How does she get around?"

The nun lifted her lantern. "She rides her dirt bikes. She has them all over the area. No one would be able to catch her. She knows every trail. I want to show you how to move through the tunnel. I won't be going with you."

They watched and listened. "If you're going to come back to the chapel, there're hooks in the ceiling every ten meters. You should make it with five lanterns. The oil will burn for hours."

Linda waved her flashlight. "We have lights too."

As the nun put her lantern on the first hook, Bobbie held hers high to look further along the tunnel. "Sister Mary Francis…ah are there any other openings for …intruders? Like rodents."

Theresa put her silencer on her gun. "Two legs or four? Rats come in all shapes and sizes…"

Sister Mary Francis smiled shaking her head. "I don't like them either. There's rat poison along both sides of the tunnel. We haven't seen any signs of them. At the end of the tunnel, there's a small cabinet type door. Only one person can get through at a time. It's not something you can walk through. You'll see."

Kitty checked her watch. "It's going on four o'clock. Thank you. We can take it from here. Theresa, go up to the truck and bring two listening devices and a reel of wire. We should put one in the chapel office for the Sister in case we need her to call for back up. The other one can go just inside Ross's cellar. Linda, maybe you should give Theresa a hand." She looked at Bobbie. "Should you go with the driver? I think we'll have to set up and then sit and wait. Once you bring Ross, anything can happen."

Bobbie looked at her watch and cringed. "I was hoping to see how the door works in the event I need to go to the cellar."

Kitty nodded. "Why don't you bring Jane's bike along and then you can ride back."

Bobbie held back so she could get used to the bike. *Jane's legs must be like steel. A conventional bike would never handle this ground.* "Kitty, this tunnel should be a training spot for the team."

In less than ten minutes they came to the door the nun described. Kitty put her hand up. "Shush. Noise!" They froze watching and listening. Karen pointed to the strange looking door half way up the wall. She mimed opening it to her boss. Kitty signed back to wait. The door opened slowly. Out of the pitch black darkness a pair of night vision goggles came at her.

"Jo! Dammit, you damn near got axed."

Jo dropped the goggles. "Sorry, I saw the light from the lanterns."

Kitty frowned. "It's a damn good thing that happened. I don't relish the idea of having to sit in the dark."

Linda stuck her head through the door and flashed her light. "Any rags or papers around we could use to stuff the cracks."

Jo answered. "Ross has a lot of newspapers on the coffee table. I'll have one of the team bring them down."

Bobbie and Kitty climbed over the opening into the cellar. Kitty shined her flashlight up to see Jo. "Did they get the bed in place for Ross?"

Jo nodded. "Good idea Patti D. rode in the truck with me. Some wind kicked up as they brought in the main frame and it took the five of us to get in safely." She cringed. "This place is way too small. To hide in the closet we'd have to empty it."

Bobbie frowned. "I was afraid of that. Were you able to put any listening devices in so you can monitor Ross?"

"One in his bed and the other in the sitting room. They're power operated too. We should be able to get better reception...But, if the power should go out. We're SOL. The Yard is sending out alerts about this storm on my cell phone. Quite a storm brewing over the North Sea. Damn thing won't move on."

Kitty raised her light above her shoulder to illuminate an open area of the cellar. "Is this where Jane's been hiding?"

Jo directed her torch to the left side back corner. "There's a made up area in that corner. It's very creative. She's got a bed, made a closet and shelving. Definitely Jane lives there. All sorts of items are neatly arranged. Clothing, papers, books. Her makeup mirror is quite interesting. Several artists' books show ways to disguise the flesh with make-up. She's got a cooler with dry ice in it. A shelf on top of the ice has various foods and beverages. Well planned. No electricity in this area, so we're limited on the equipment we can use. Don't want to take a chance and run a lot of wires. I'm sure she knows every nook and cranny down here."

Bobbie frowned. "So you're saying you can't put a monitor in Ross's bedroom for us to watch when Alex comes."

Jo nodded. "We can put a battery operated listening device, but...you're not going to hear much unless someone talks... If this storm gets any worse, you won't hear anything even if they talk right over the mike."

Kitty opened a notebook. "Jo, you and Patti D. make up a sketch of the cellar. Put as much detail as you can."

Suddenly, they felt the walls and floor rumble. Some dirt fell from the cracks from the floor above. Theresa climbed through the tunnel opening. "Mother fucker, what was that?"

Linda emerged behind her. "Another wave of that storm is coming through. I saw lightning flash through the chapel windows when I was coming back from the truck. I think John is getting a little bored up there and would like to leave. His dispatcher has been calling him too."

Kitty went with Bobbie to the opening. "Do you think it's a good idea, bringing Ross back to this? We could have one of the team do a switch in the ambulance."

"I know where you're going with this and the answer is no. Now that Dennis knows Alex murdered Lizzy, he would rather die than let Alex get to Jane. Besides, Alex would kill anyone posing as Ross immediately and then leave, knowing it was a set up. No, Zilpha said he can respond if he stays relaxed. I know he's working with that. His speech isn't back yet, but he can walk with effort and he's got some of his strength back. The doctors have been told not to report his progress to the media. We want Alex to feel he has the upper hand."

Bobbie climbed over the opening ledge. "Per usual, what starts out to be a good idea, always gives us challenges." She got on the bike and rode about fifty feet and stopped. She called Kitty on the cell phone.

Kitty looked down the tunnel. "We have reception. That's interesting. It might be because of the storm. Air waves are closer. Call me when you get to the house with Ross. I'll keep my phone on vibrate. Oh and thank the driver for being so patient."

Chapter 32

Zilpha challenges Alex's plan

"Alex, it's only eight o'clock. Why do you want to go to Ross's now? It won't be dark for another hour. Plus, it's pouring out. Jane never gets there before two in the morning." She handed him a cup of tea and sat at her desk, shaking her head. "This doesn't make sense to me. You're going to screw this whole thing up." *Talk about Jekyll and Hyde...I've no way of warning Ross and his partner.*

Alex put the cup down. "Do you have any beer? I need something stronger than this. I want to be in full swing for this momentous occasion."

She shook her head. "We'll celebrate afterwards. I don't drink it and I don't serve it." Zilpha sipped her tea. "Okay, tell me what your plan is."

Alex put his feet up on the side of her desk, and pulled out a paper from his pocket. "First, I've a question. Do you have any of those small explosives with the ten minute timers on them? Once, Charlie and I used them for a job. Can't remember what he called them. The weather report said this storm will be an all-nighter. So it would be to our advantage to kill the power. No one would think it strange."

She went into the inventory list on the computer. "Those are called igniters. I've only got twelve on the shelf, and there are twelve houses plus the chapel. Why not take out the transformer?"

Alex shrugged his shoulders. “We can check it out, but, if it’s underground, we’ll never find it. The chapel is at the top of the hill. It’s hard to see from Ross’s, so it doesn’t matter if we don’t kill its power. Besides, who’d be there at night anyway? As long as the houses around him are out, he’ll think the power has blown.”

He put his feet down. “Do you have a map of the area?”

Zilpha pointed toward the kitchenette. “There’s one in the first file cabinet over on that back wall. Look under ‘G’.”

He smirked. “Very funny.” *That’s a good sign.*

She spread one out on the work table. Alex pointed to the road where the tunnel opening was. “I drove out there after you showed me the pictures. Took a while, but I found the opening. I saw where you hid the motion detector and where we can hide the car behind some huge bushes.”

He sat down again. “I’m thinking I need to make my move on Ross first. Depending on how able he is, I want him in the cellar to watch Jane’s execution.”

“What about his partner? She’s a good officer.”

Alex raised his brow. “Yeah, she is.” He chuckled as he glowed. “I’ll be a gentleman and give her the choice of dying first or helping Ross to the cellar.”

“How will you get in?”

He stared at her. “Obviously, we have two ways. Which one, though? The power being out gives us an advantage. At first, I thought I’d shoot Bobbie from a window. But, the odds are I’d be seen. He rubbed his chin and stared off. “Strange, all the cases Ross and I investigated, there was *always* some fuckhead that saw something. Then I thought she’d be helpful getting Ross into the cellar, so killing her is out.”

Zilpha folded the map. “So you want to go through the tunnel. I’ll wait for Jane and close off the opening as I follow her in.”

“That’s about it. After all, they don’t know about Jane’s living there. No one else has any pictures. If they did, we’d know by foot prints. The Yard wouldn’t be able to keep that a secret. The media would be all over it. It should be easy going through the cellar and up to the kitchen. The noise of the storm will help if I have to force the lock.”

"Have you been in the cellar?"

"Soon after we were made partners, Ross asked me to help him lock the outside entrance to the cellar. Since he was too tall to walk down there, I bolted it from the inside. Lizzy was frightened of the cellar and wanted all the doors locked."

He jumped up. "We better get going. We've got lots to do. Do you have a box for the igniters?"

Zilpha hesitated. "Have you considered his doctor may have a nurse there or perhaps some Yard people?" *I've got to make sure he thinks he's making all the calls on this plan.*

Alex stared at her. "Zilpha, they still think I'm in South Africa. One of the newspaper articles said a hospital orderly saw McGraw and Edse board a helicopter."

She turned as she felt the tears well up. "That's right it did. I forgot." *They omitted Edse shot my son eleven times with an automatic.* She took the tea cups to the sink for a minute to recoup.

Alex frowned. "Are you okay?" *She doesn't seem too eager. It's that fuckin' kid of hers. I shouldn't have mentioned the article.* He put his hand on her shoulder. "I can't do this without you. You mean everything to me."

She stared into his eyes. "I've changed my mind and want to go with you to New York. I need to start my life over again."

He leaned forward to kiss her but she shook her head. "Not yet, I still need time."

He stood back as she went to get her things.

"Do you need any ammunition?"

Chapter 33

Ross comes home from the hospital

A flash of lightning struck as Bobbie turned onto Chapel Road. She looked over at the church and saw lights burning. "Do you think we should stop and see if the team has heard anything?"

Ross patted her hand and pointed to his house. He tried to speak.

"Don't strain yourself, Dennis. I'll call Kitty when we get in." *I don't know if he's up to this. I could take him to the Chapel and let Sister Mary Francis sit with him, but it would be a damned if I do and damned if I don't situation. ... This has to end and soon!*

Opening his door, she saw him hyperventilating, staring at the cottage. *Come on Ross, don't do this to me. No telling what he's reliving. He needs counseling so badly.*

In the pouring rain, she shook his arm and raised her voice to rouse him from his trance. "Dennis, look at me! We aren't going one step until you calm down. Remember what Zilpha said? Relax. Ross, dammit! If you black out, I won't be able to hold you. The only help we have is the team and then they will be exposed. Maybe I should take you to the Chapel."

He sat back in the seat and took a deep breath. He saw the worry in her face. He took hold of her hand. "I'm...sorry...I want to..." He took more controlled breaths. "To help you."

Bobbie smiled teary eyed. "I know you do. Come on now. Here's your cane. You start walking and I'll get the door open. Can you do that?"

Standing next to the car, he held onto the door and balanced with his cane as the wind gusted. After a few mean lightning flashes, she opened the front door and then scooted back to walk beside him into the house. "You're doing fine. I'll get some towels to dry us off."

The grandfather clock in the hallway started to chime. Coming out of Ross's bedroom with two towels, she stopped and looked at the bookcase next to the phone. *That's how Jane comes in. So that water Ross saw...He was so upset that the roof was leaking. Will Zilpha tell Alex how to...* Leaning against the hall table, she saw Dennis try to get his coat off and rushed to help him. "Let me help. It's just going on nine o'clock. I'll make us some tea." She handed him a towel. "You can do your hair, hands and face. Can you manage to get to the sitting room?"

As the kettle was heating, Bobbie dialed Kitty's cell phone. A series of lightning flashes occurred and the cottage went dark. She heard crackling sounds as the land line died. She flipped open her cell. "I hope the cell towers can hold on. That's all we need if they go out."

Dennis lit the candle in the hall, and then slowly made his way to the settee.

Bobbie couldn't hear anything. The static got louder. She held the phone in front of her mouth. "If you can hear me, the power has gone out."

She strained to listen. "Dennis, I can barely hear Kitty. It's all broken up. But I'm sure she said the power is on."

Bobbie went to the front windows and looked up the road. "There's not a light to be seen."

While the tea brewed, she made them some marmite and cucumber sandwiches. *This should keep him busy. He loves this combination.*

With the big old clock ticking in the hall, and thunder shaking the cottage, they didn't hear the cellar door burst open. Alex saw the little domestic scene from the candle light in Ross's sitting room.

Alex loomed in the doorway. "Well, isn't this cozy." A large flashlight hooked onto to his prosthesis focused on their faces making them flinch. "I'm sure you know it's me."

Bobbie reached for her holster. "You can't disguise those

wretched eyes."

Alex chuckled. "I must say, Ross, you do pick them…Don't be stupid, Bobbie. I do have a gun in my left hand. But, don't let me interrupt your meal, we've got time before our little party starts. You go right ahead and finish up your snack. My associate is waiting for our last invited guest."

Bobbie squeezed Ross's hand. *Dennis, just relax and breathe easy.* She saw he looked like he understood her gesture. She turned to Alex.

Alex stared at them. "Can he walk? Zilpha told me she got you good at the market." He smirked at Bobbie. "She said his speech would be the last to come back. For once I don't have to hear you give me a dissertation on what the situation appears to be."

Ross glared at him. Bobbie could feel his hand tighten. She squeezed his hand. "Dennis, he wants you to have a reaction."

"That's right, Dennis, I do want you to have a reaction, but not just yet. Help him up! We need to go to the cellar. That's where the party will be."

He moved backwards. "Oh, I almost forgot…You won't need your gear. You both are off duty now. I know he's carrying so put two on the table."

Bobbie slowly put her gun on the table and then Ross handed her his. She started to give Ross his cane.

Alex shook his head and barked at her. "You're his cane."

Bobbie stopped at the kitchen door to the cellar. "I need more light. The step to the landing isn't going to be easy for him. The landing is too small for both of us."

Bobbie stood on the landing. "Dennis, your shoe is too big. You'll have to turn sideways to step safely."

Standing behind Ross, Alex grunted with disgust. "Jesus, Ross, can't you go any faster than this? Shit, you're not blind," and pushed him through the door.

Missing the step down, Ross grabbed for something to break his fall to the landing. Bobbie pushed him back from falling down the cellar steps. He landed on one foot and then his knee.

She lashed out. "That was real smart. He could have broken his leg, you idiot! If he passes out, then what is your great plan?"

Alex glared at her. “You’ll find out who’s the idiot.” He pointed his gun at Ross’s head. “Should I shoot him now? Then you can take his place at the festivities.”

She helped Dennis up, staring at Alex. “We need more light!”

He tossed her a flashlight. “Now, get the fuck down there with him, or I’ll be losing it.”

She gave Dennis directions. “Dennis, there’re ten steps. Sit down on the landing and, on your seat, take each one at a time.” At the bottom, the head room was too short for Dennis. She put her arm around his back to help him walk bent over. “Take it slow so you don’t trip. We’re almost there. Just relax.”

Alex pointed his flashlight to some stacked crates. “Put him on that first set.” He shined his light on a box near her. “Use that duct tape to tie his wrists and his ankles.”

She blurted out. “For god’s sakes, he can’t move now.”

Alex set his lantern on a box and moved to strike her. When she heard Ross gasp and struggle toward Alex, she yelled. “Okay. I’ll do it.”

Alex stepped back. “Please don’t do anything heroic, because I’m in the mood for lots of blood.”

Bobbie wrapped Ross’s ankles and hands. *With the power outage, I wonder if Kitty is hearing any of this. We shouldn’t be too far from that cabinet. I’ll wait until Zilpha gets here.* She spoke quietly to Ross. “Are you okay?”

He nodded and squeezed her hands.

Alex checked his watch. “Our party should be starting very soon…”

He walked up to a wooden pole support. “Now, it’s your turn. Put this handcuff on your one hand and stand up to this post, putting your hands behind you around it.”

Bobbie hesitated. She saw Ross shake his head.

Pointing his gun at Bobbie, Alex patted Ross on the shoulder with his prosthesis. “As you know, killing people isn’t new to me. And my friend, you may have won the prize for pissing me off. Now you’ve already watched poor Lizzy die, then you’ll watch Jane and then Bobbie, but, I can always change the order, if you want to continue to fuck with me.”

Ross nodded to Bobbie to put the cuff on.

Alex grabbed her chin and kissed her. "Now that's what I call being smart."

Sensing her outrage, Alex stepped back quickly just as Bobbie lifted her knee and snarled. "You're as sick as your buddy Edse and that Windsor Braun freak."

Alex pulled out a knife and waved it in her face. "I think you may have won the prize of watching lover boy die after Jane."

He used his teeth to unroll a bit of tape. Holding the roll with his prosthesis, he managed to cut off a piece and stuck it across her mouth. "You're such a bitch!" He stood back and eyed her. "I think the only way to tame you is …" He wiped his chin and stared at Ross. "Ross, I'll be doing you a favor. Besides, you're too old to handle this bitch on your own."

He checked his watch again. "Aren't you the lucky one." He kissed her on the neck. "Don't worry. Before the night is over, you'll feel my ecstasy oozing all over you. It's time to be quiet and wait." He sat on a crate and turned off the flashlight.

Chapter 34

Sister Mary Francis in the Chapel Office

Sitting on her legs in the priest's office chair, all bundled in her coat, Sister Mary Francis was glued to the intercom and the phone device the Dream Team had set up for her.

She heard Kitty call. "Sister, did you just hear Bobbie's call? Did she say the power was off?

All excited, Sister nodded to the unit. Then, she shook her head at her foolishness and pressed the button. "I did hear that. We don't have heat but we have power!" She paused shivering. "My voice goes different at night. It's so cold."

She adjusted her position in the chair. "Inspector, I can ride my bike down to Ross's cottage."

Quickly Kitty responded. "No, no. I need you to stay where you are. I'll send one of my team up." *My God, that's all I need. Another victim.*

After twenty minutes, Patti D. returned to the chapel. She ran down the church aisle squishing in her tennis shoes. She shot past the office and down the steep steps before Sister Mary Francis could jump up to ask her what she had seen.

Patti D. used Jane's bike to get to the end of the tunnel. She got off the bike and bent down to her knees taking deep breaths. "Boss..." She blew out of her mouth whispering. "The window shutters are closed, and all I could see was a flashlight moving and candles flickering. The houses in the area are out of power. I ran to the back of Ross's cottage and found the meter was okay, but the load side of the cable blown apart. I went to look at his neighbors and it was the same way. I can't believe that's from lightning."

Kitty heard something on the device. She snapped her fingers twice and whispered. "Leave four lanterns going and turn everything else off. There's so much static from the storm."

Theresa touched Kitty's arm. "Can you open the cabinet door a little? Maybe you can see something."

"Good idea. Can you angle your light enough to find the lever? Okay, all lights out now." Kitty slowly lowered the catch. When it was pitch black, Kitty barely opened the door past a crack. She couldn't see anything but shadows. Alex had Bobbie and Ross more in front of the cabinet. She put her ear to the opening. Two minutes passed and she lifted the latch in place.

"Lights." She motioned for them to back away from the cabinet door. "Patti D., do we have a stethoscope with us?"

Patti D. rummaged through the tool box and held one up.

Kitty pointed to the cabinet. "While I talk with the team, see if you can hear any more from the door frame."

Kitty and the team walked back to the first hanging lantern left burning. "Sounds like Alex is in control of Bobbie and Ross. We expected that. Ross is tied up and Alex has cuffed Bobbie to a pole. The last words I heard were 'the party will start soon'."

Linda questioned. "Should we call for back up?"

Kitty shook her head. "I don't think we have time. Besides, what will they do that we aren't doing already? It'll create chaos."

She looked at her watch. "It's near midnight. For some reason Alex thinks Jane will be arriving sooner than her normal time."

Karen whispered. "Maybe she knows this is the showdown and would want to be there waiting for him?"

Kitty nodded. "That's what I'm thinking too, except, Alex beat her to it. So how can we avoid this blood bath?"

Jo raised her flashlight under her chin. "It would help if we knew what Henry's mother was planning, and if she really meant she would help save Jane from Alex."

Kitty frowned. "I questioned Bobbie about that and she swore Mrs. Peckham had come to Ross's cottage to prepare them for this situation. It's up to us now to create and execute a plan of least resistance."

Theresa whispered. "Except, we already have two strikes against us. No power and a fuckin' door only one can go through at a time."

A flash of light crossed Kitty's jacket. They turned to see Patti D. motion for them to come back. She met them half way. "Boss, I think Zilpha is there. I heard Alex tell someone to 'grab her as soon as she came in.' Assuming he meant Jane."

Kitty nodded. "Jo, Karen, and Linda, go to the cottage and see if you can get to the cellar using the kitchen or you may have to go all the way to the other entrance of the tunnel to get in."

Karen objected. "We haven't got time to go back to that tunnel entrance."

Jo took hold of Karen's arm. "Boss, I've got an idea. Bobbie told us about that bookcase in the cottage. When we were setting up Ross's bed with the men, I did some snooping and I think we could get down to the cellar that way. It's further away from where Ross and Bobbie are tied up. If we take Theresa, I think she could sneak around." She reached into her pocket. "I still have the keys to the cottage."

Theresa dropped her mouth. "You're smaller than me! ... You're afraid you might see a rat or mouse....You big fu..."

Kitty touched Theresa's arm. "Enough. That's a good idea. Maybe you could release Bobbie. From what I could see, she's tied to a post near the cellar steps." She quickly sketched the area she saw.

"That leaves me with only Patti D."

Out of the shadows of the tunnel they heard, "And me!"

They turned to see Sister Mary Francis dressed in the priest's pants and a Notre Dame sweatshirt. "I can help." She smiled as she marched up to them. "I'm strong and can handle myself. Uncle Jamie taught me boxing. He called a few minutes ago from his car. He's on his way and told me to help you."

Kitty shook her head. "Okay. I can't argue. Sister, you come with me. The rest of you better scat. Time is an issue." She bit her lip. "Just be safe. I can't..."

Theresa hugged her whispering. "I'll take good care of them. We'll stop this mother fucker."

Chapter 35

The Cellar

The four women ran in the rain as fast as they could through the mounting puddles accumulating at the bottom of the slope.

The frequent blasts of thunder allowed them to get inside Ross's cottage without being heard. Jo motioned with her flash light the direction they needed to go. As they passed the hall table, she paused whispering, "Let me diagram where we are." She found a pencil next to the candle. No paper in sight.

Linda snapped her fingers. "Draw on the wall."

They hurried to the opposite wall of the bookcase. "Here's where we are." She drew a square on the wall. "This is the book case. This is the bottom of the kitchen entrance to the cellar. A few more feet and you'll see Bobbie tied or handcuffed to the post. Ross will be about ten more feet from her…Theresa, from this bookcase there's a short ladder of three steps. There are tons of boxes and crates down there. Looks to me like Jane may have moved them to create her boundaries. So the area you have to drop down should be walled up pretty good. You can't use a flashlight but still you should be able to move without being noticed."

Theresa took off her jacket, her shoulder holster and shoes. She unclasped the buckles on the holster and it became a holster she could strap to her ankle. "My pants are soaked. I'm afraid I'll make noise. See if Ross has some shorts." *As tall as he is, they'll be like pants.*

Karen flashed her light into the bedroom. "Wait a minute." She ran in and found a pair of jogging shorts.

"Here, these should fit."

Theresa glared. "Thanks! Where's the belt. No pockets."

"Pull the ties."

Theresa put her hand out to Linda and whispered. "Let me use your pocket knife. I know how sharp you keep it. I have my handcuff keys."

As Linda handed her the pocket knife, Theresa dropped the handcuff keys in her bra. "I know what you're thinking…It'll fit."

Jo turned off her flashlight and slowly opened the bookcase. She whispered into Theresa's ear. "Be careful…We can listen in Ross's room."

Theresa stood on the first step and waited for a crash of thunder. When it came, it was so strong it shook the cottage. Down she went. *That blast felt more like we're under attack. Fuck, it's cold down here. Keep shouting ass hole. Bastard!* She crawled slowly until she could see Bobbie silhouetted on the back wall.

Theresa reached for her gun and peeked through the boxes. *Fuck you! I don't have a clear shot. That bastard keeps moving around.* She felt something furry run over her leg. Like a flash she captured the intruder and squeezed until the wiggling stopped. She threw the rat away from her and wiped her hands in the mud and then on her shorts. Drawing some deep breaths, she bit her lips tight. *Damn, son of a bitch,* Fuck *the world! I don't want to do that again. Fuck...Fuck! I can't look! Maybe it was a mole. Jane couldn't live around rats, surely!* She suddenly thought if that had happened to Jo. *Jesus God. She'd be running back to London.* That picture amused her so, she had to hold her side to keep from bursting out laughing.

Her focus snapped back hearing Alex in a loud voice, revealing to Ross why he had to get rid of Ross's wife. "Dennis, surely you can understand." He started pacing again. "She was messing up Jane's head…"

He stopped in front of Ross and slapped his face hard, knocking him back. "Son of a bitch, Dennis, Jane stopped paying attention! To me! To making money! You know why!" He grabbed Ross by his hair and pulled him forward. "Because, your fuckin' wife got Jane wanting to have kids!" He slapped him again and again. "That's why I did it…Lizzy crossed the fuckin' line. Jane wanted to be like her."

He slapped Ross again and let him fall back against a crate. Alex backed off waving his arm. "It was too late…Jane went nuts over Lizzy's death. Now can you get the picture here? You're to blame, you mother fucker." He started to hit him with his prostheses, when he heard Bobbie scream through the tape on her face.

Showing his knife, he ripped the duct tape off Ross's face. "Tell her to shut-up before I cut her bad."

Barely able to move, Dennis motions to Bobbie he's okay.

Alex stood in front of his ex-partner smirking with a raised brow. "You should have accepted my offer at Crowley. I tried to give you a break that we were all square…Remember? From what I've told you now, you certainly can understand, we are far from being even and it's not in your favor, Dennis." Glaring at him, he slapped him across the face with the back of his hand, knocking him backward. "This time I won't miss!"

Alex flinched seeing Zilpha standing by the tunnel entrance. The look in her eyes was daunting. She glanced at her watch nervously. "You've made your point. I thought you wanted Ross to watch Jane go down…"

"Why aren't you sticking to our plan?"

Ignoring his question, Zilpha found a rag and wiped the blood off of Ross's face. He opened his eyes. She mouthed to him, "Are you okay?" He blinked his eyes with a short nod.

She turned and stared at Alex. "Can you settle down? You won't be able to blame anyone if Jane hears you…"

She stood quietly and looked away. "That last flash of lightning hit a tree. It fell, missing the car by a foot. A little close for my comfort."

Nearing the cellar steps, Theresa found a couple of pebbles. *Poor Ross. Alex's anger is helping me but not Dennis.* At the end of the stack of boxes she peeked around and saw Bobbie with her head down. Theresa tossed a pebble at Bobbie's leg. *That's it. Look this way.* She tossed another one. *Okay, now we're cooking.*

She looked around a box at Bobbie and showed her keys. Bobbie nodded looking off at Alex who was still across the room rummaging through Jane's stuff.

Another few seconds and Theresa was behind the post opening the handcuffs. She put her pocket knife in Bobbie's hand, and then patted Bobbie on the backside and headed for Ross.

Bobbie watched Theresa slither like a snake toward Ross. Alex suddenly became quiet and Bobbie turned quickly to see what was happening. He was grinning and chuckling over a box he'd opened. "Bloody Hell, look what we found."

He sat and went through his papers. "Zilpha, stay by the door so you can grab Jane when she comes in. Turn your light out. She won't see my light until she's inside."

Zilpha touched his arm. "Let's go. You have what you want."

Alex's eyes went black as a raven and he shook his head at her. "No…Jane's got to pay for this." He looked over at Ross. "They both have to pay, and Bobbie can watch."

Chapter 36

The Confrontation

They felt the rumblings of the storm occasionally while they waited quietly. Zilpha stood behind the opening side of the door. She thought she heard some footsteps splashing and snapped her fingers at Alex. "I hear something. Cover your light a little more."

The door opened enough for a shadowy form to enter as it closed, Zilpha pushed her back against it, grabbing Jane around her upper torso and wrenching her arm behind her back. Not recognizing the voice and seeing Alex moving closer, Jane tried to get free from the hold that became more painful as she resisted.

Alex came at her waving his papers. Without a word, he lunged and slugged her hard in the face. Zilpha couldn't hold the dead weight as Jane fell to the floor.

Frowning with disgust, Zilpha yelled at Alex. "Are you nuts? You have what you want. Leave them here. No one will find them for days and they'll be dead." She looked over at the post where Alex had tied Bobbie and saw her taking the tape off her face. *I have to make a move here. Bobbie's team must be around.*

Alex sneered. "Oh, they'll be dead but not from being left."

Zilpha drew her gun and yelled. "Bobbie, get Ross out of here!"

Alex stared at her. "What the fuck are you doing?"

Bobbie ran to Ross. "Let us help you, Zilpha."

Just then, Theresa appeared holding her gun. “I’ve got you covered.”

Zilpha shook her head. “Help her get him out of here. Now!”

They each got under an arm and lifted him. Theresa whispered. “We’re closer to the cabinet, but do we expose the rest of the team?”

Bobbie cringed. “I don’t think it matters. Zilpha wants to protect us and reduce the playing field. This was her plan all a long.”

They managed to get Ross to the cabinet door. As the door opened, hands appeared to help him over the ledge.

Zilpha turned on a handheld tape recorder. They heard Alex talking to Edse. Alex said. ‘I don’t give a fuck, kill the bastard.’ Edse then said. ‘Thank you, I don’t know how much more I can take from this love struck piece of shit.’

When the tape stopped, Alex nodded. “So this is what it’s about. I wondered why you had a change of heart about going to New York. You wanted to throw me off guard.”

He moved toward her. She backed up tripping over Jane. Alex kicked his flashlight, drew his gun and fired. “Did I get one of you?” He moved back behind some boxes.

Zilpha helped Jane into the fake walled area. She whispered. “Stay here. He’s mine.”

The tape played over again. Alex laughed. “Hey, I was doing you a favor. Your talents were being wasted. You had no life. You were kissing ass with that fuckin’ kid of yours.”

Zilpha shot at the direction of his voice. She laid the tape down on a box and set it to repeat continuously. “Eleven bullets! Edse and you put in him! That’s a favor?” She fired her gun again at different areas. “That boy was my life.”

Alex shot several times hitting her. He heard her fall. He slowly came out of hiding trailing blood. He turned on his flash light to see her lying on the ground against the wall. He grinned as he slid his leg forward. “We could have been a great team, but…nothing lasts forever.” He stood looking down at her. “Paybacks are hell…” He pointed to his leg. “You almost got me. I’ll survive, but…” He shook his head and took aim. “Sorry, you lose.”

From the dark, Jane threw a crate at him and as he flinched, she grabbed Zilpha’s gun and kept shooting at him. Jane screamed.

"You're the loser! You bastard! Now it's your turn." She emptied the gun. Every bullet hit him somewhere, until he fell to the ground. The cellar suddenly went silent.

After a few seconds of quiet, Jo and Linda dropped down the ladder. The cabinet door opened and flash lights and lanterns lit up the area. Sister Mary Francis had gone back to the chapel to wait for Father James to arrive. The two of them reached the entrance to the cellar as the last gunshot could be heard. The team members helped them over the cabinet ledge. They all converged at the back wall.

As the tape started to play again, Kitty turned off the recorder and put the little handheld recorder in her pocket. Jo knelt next to Zilpha and took her hand. "We have medics coming, just hang in there." She took her pulse and looked up at the Team and gave a sad look shaking her head slightly.

Zilpha opened her eyes. "Is he…?"

Jane took her hand. Teary eyed, she smiled at Zilpha nodding, "Yes, he's dead…You saved my life." She saw Jo shake her head. She took Zilpha into her arms. "You can hang in there. We have a lot to learn about each other."

Zilpha pulled on Jane's sleeve. "My house…is a trap."

Jane dropped her head to hear Zilpha. "What about your house?"

Zilpha whispered. "Code…three codes…" She pulled on Jane's sleeve. "Henry…Punch in… Henry at the front ."

She stared off and then looked at Jane. "Henry's dad…punch in …. cellar."

She shut her eyes. Jo wiped her brow. "You can do this. The medics are almost here."

She stared at Jane again. "Last one…is… a … password for comp…comp , Charlie." Jane felt her relax.

Father James knelt next to Zilpha and took her hand. Zilpha opened her eyes and smiled at the priest. He leaned forward to hear her whisper. "Not enough time to cover my sins…." As if someone had come into the cellar, she put her hand up and whispered affectionately. "Look… Charlie and Henry have come… for me."

Her eyes stared off. Jo reached over and closed her eyelids. "She's gone."

The silence was deafening. After Ross viewed the area, he tried to say 'battle'.

Kitty pointed to the many shell casings on the floor. "It does look like a battle zone."

Taking Ross's arm she motioned to Bobbie to set him on a crate behind her. "I've just called the paramedics to come in now. We had them wait at the end of the tunnel for an all clear. Somehow, we've got to make sure the media doesn't get hold of this."

The door opened, and following the paramedics was their boss, Chief Inspector O'Doul, with two policemen. Looking over the crime scene he gave the men some directions and then shaking his head, he studied Ross. "You look a little worn. Should you go with this run to the hospital?"

Dennis, using Bobbie's shoulder as a crutch, cringed at the sight of his boss. Swallowed hard and whispered. "No, sir, I'll be… all right… after some rest." He watched O'Doul look down at Alex's body.

Ross motioned to Bobbie. "Tell Chief."

Bobbie squeezed his hand. "That's Alex, Chief. He's wearing a mask."

The Chief pointed to the woman's body being put into a body bag. "Is that Jane?"

Bobbie piped up. "No sir, that woman is Mrs. Peckham. You met her at the airport when the bodies were returned from Johannesburg. Her son…"

He frowned at Bobbie. "What! She's the mother of the young man who…"

Kitty interrupted him. "Sir, we will give you a complete report." Then she took Jane's hand and walked her up to the Chief. "Sir, this is Jane."

Chapter 37

Another case to be filed inadmissible

Several days later, the Dream Team, Ross, Bobbie and Jane met at Zilpha's cottage.

Kitty shook her head as she shut the van door. "Who would guess this cottage was owned by a mystery woman." She turned around looking at the beautiful view. "To think we had to evacuate the entire area, until the bomb squad went through the place."

Another car stopped next to the Scotland Yard van. Three doors opened. Jane and Bobbie appeared to help Ross get out of the car.

Ross leaned on his cane. "I wish she'd lived. There're so many questions to be answered." *Especially to thank her for saving our lives.*

Theresa opened the gate. "I for one want to see this place." She stopped short and turned to Kitty, "Do we still have to use the codes? There were three, right? Each one attached to a lot of bombs!"

Jo laughed. "Now, who's being the scaredy-cat?"

Theresa squinted at Jo, who was nodding her head. She mouthed *Fuck you* "Big difference between a rat and a bomb."

Jo put her arm around Theresa as they walked through the doorway. "Come on. See, it's okay."

Jane went to each room absorbing every detail. In the bedroom overlooking the patio, she leaned against the wall. "There's such a feeling of love everywhere." She cringed with embarrassment at talking to herself. Walking out she stroked the bedpost. *I need to keep this for her. I have to buy it.*

She heard a tea kettle whistle and went to look.

Bobbie was in the kitchen. "I think Zilpha would want us to share in her hospitality."

Jane smiled. "I'm sure you're right. Let me help."

Bobbie opened the French doors that led to the patio. Jane followed carrying a tray with eight cups and saucers, a large tea pot, and the usual English accoutrements.

Jane did the honors pouring for everyone. Theresa put her hand over the creamer and whispered, "I take it black." She saw Jane's eyes open wide. Theresa put her hand on Jane's shoulder. "I know what you're going to say. I've heard all the remarks! No true Englishman drinks…tea… black …"

Linda chuckled. "Jane, she's being nice! This time."

Jane stirred her cup of tea looking at each person teary eyed. "I never imagined this day would ever happen…Thank you for overlooking my phobias. I'm so sorry it ended the way it did." *There has to be away I can make this up to Zilpha.*

Ross cleared his throat. In a scratchy voice he said. "I feared the worst. We searched everywhere for you. The nightmares drove me on. Several times I woke during a storm and saw you standing in my bedroom." He put his cup down. "Now that we know about the tunnel, was that you? Or did I only dream it?"

Sheepishly Jane smiled. "The most recent storm…I was soaked and …I snuck up to your room to get a towel and the thunder was so bad it woke you out of your dream. I was so scared I grabbed your sweatshirt from a chair by the door and left before the next flash occurred."

He chuckled to himself. "You were scared! I thought I was losing my mind. I wish you had told me." With searching eyes, he frowned. "Why didn't you?"

Jane shook her head. "Dennis, you'd either be dead or in prison. It was my vendetta." She touched her scar. "Alex thought it was a lark that he'd made a fool out of the Yard. He used the scar as a scare tactic, reminding me, the law wouldn't protect me at all."

Ross stared at the ground and then looked at her. “You’ve done a good job covering it. Can you have plastic surgery?” *Poor girl. She was so attractive.*

Shaking her head, her eyes welled up. “When the doctor told me the scar was probably permanent, implying that many surgeries would be required but still wouldn’t guarantee removal, I knew I had to make a decision, be a slave to his fear tactics or get away from him. I had no clue where he hid his money. The only way I could find out was to go back… That was the hard part, pretending to want and need him.”

Jane dropped her head. “I had a way with him…sexually.” She put her hand over her mouth. “All the times before, I thought he wanted kids and he would say…soon…soon. Then, when I went back, I knew I would use sex to bait him. This was hard because now he hated the sight of me.” She touched her face. “I had to wear a scarf across my face until he turned the lights out.”

Bobbie frowned. “Jane, you really don’t have to talk about this now. We all know it’s been a horrific experience for you.”

Jane walked to the planter wall. She turned to Bobbie. “Yes, I do.”

Sitting on the wall, she absorbed the peacefulness of the green field. She watched the tall grass gently bending as if in a dance. Lifting her head, she closed her eyes to enjoy the slight breeze that had come for a moment.”

Kitty motioned to the group to give her time.

After another few minutes, she turned to all of them teary eyed. “The day before I disappeared, Alex came home disturbed about something. He wouldn’t say what it was. He just wanted to have sex over and over.” She stared off. “It was hard and cruel.” She wiped a tear from the corner of her eye. Straightening her back, she cleared her throat. “Usually he’d fall asleep but this night, he got up, put on his pants, and left thinking I was asleep. I followed him out behind the cottage near the creek. I watched him open the vaults. I ran back and got into bed before he returned and practically leaped on me for more…The next day, I watched him leave and sat with the binoculars watching the road for over a half hour. I then ran down to the creek and forced open each vault. Once I found the papers and read how he murdered Lizzy and why, my heart fell apart and I knew he was evil. I had to be the one to stop him.”

She stared at the cottage. Taking a deep breath she grinned. "I used his money to better myself physically. It took a long time to become resilient. I trained in martial arts, boxing, firing guns. All of my instructors made the comment I didn't need to be trained to focus. It was evident I was filled with hate but I learned how to control my anger. This scar and Lizzy's death became my shield."

"All my training was at camps that provided accommodations. That lasted for two years or more. The few friends I had knew of my plight and would periodically let me know if anyone was looking for me."

Ross bit his lip shutting his eyes. "When did you use the tunnel or know about it?"

Bobbie nodded. "The night we met Zilpha, she told us and showed us pictures of you in Ross's cottage. She suggested that you may have read to Lizzy the history of Godstone and found out about the tunnel."

Jane grinned. "That's right. I did read about it, though I hadn't considered using it until Alex went to prison. It took some time to find it, let alone make the cellar livable. It was a project that allowed me to use all of my training. When Alex was released, I knew the end was near. Father James told me about Karen's call and the chapel incident. I knew then Alex had never left England." She saw the look of surprise on their faces. "Alex didn't share with anyone. Charlie was his only friend. I was confused about the woman being at the chapel, but I knew the man was Alex. Father James described the man's actions to a tee. What gave him away was the way he would stare at you as he decided to let you live or die. Father James said the man had piercing cold eyes. Well, I knew, and thankfully it's over now."

She looked at the team members and then at Ross. "Dennis, you know only too well, had Zilpha lived, you'd be arresting her for a lot of crimes. I played a role in many of the schemes Alex arranged. I don't believe there's a statute of limitation on crime, is there?"

Getting up, Kitty put her cup down and put her arm around Jane. "You're right up to a point. Believe it or not, the law does advocate leniency along with justice."

"What do you mean?"

Kitty sat on the wall and motioned for Jane to sit. "Jane, I can't go into all the details as it would take as long as Ross, Bobbie and I spent in the Chief's office to explain. Let me put it this way…Alex's attorney's found loop holes in the case he was tried for and convicted. These loop holes allowed him to go free based on time spent in prison. Had Alex lived, he would have gone free because of double jeopardy, and you'd probably be dead. Based on the reports that we gave, we all felt his death was a result of self-defense. The fact that he's dead erases any information of crimes past that you may have been involved in, i.e. no collaboration. "

Ross grinned a little. "Yes, but Jane, for this to be permanent, you can't ever talk about this whole incident to anyone outside of us."

Jane nodded. "I understand…Chief O'Doul made that very clear when he came to see me."

The look on their faces made her chuckle. "See, I can keep a secret."

Karen raised her cup. "You're a free woman, Jane! But, you have to come forward and make your mark in the world. Either you work with us or…" Karen grinned at her. "You could do something for the orphanage."

Jane squeezed her hands together and shook her head. "All I have is Alex's money and there is a lot of it. Father James won't take it. I had to go through all sorts of drama just to get that surveillance system in."

Karen piped up. "I thank you for that!"

As Linda picked up the tea pot, several cups raised. She paused before pouring tea into Jane's cup. "Believe it or not, according to Sister Mary Francis, your art works have been sold at the Bedrule's fairs. We've all seen the sketch you gave Ross of Lizzy…Jane, you have a talent. It's a gift. Don't waste it."

Jane looked around the patio and then turned to look at the field behind. She looked back at the group. "You know, if I could buy this property, maybe I could develop a camp for the orphanage and Father James could send a few kids two or three times a year for art lessons." She stood up and pointed. "This is so beautiful and I think Zilpha would approve."

Ross walked slowly to the wall. "Bobbie, tell them the idea you just had."

Bobbie stood next to Ross. "I agree this is a serene place. I thought one way to pay tribute to Zilpha would be to plant some special trees in honor of her son, our Hennessey and her."

Jane nodded looking at her. "Right out there in that flowing high grass. It echoes a sense of freedom and tranquility."

They all lifted their cups of tea to the idea.

Ross made a suggestion. "Before we go, would anyone like to see the other side of Zilpha? It's almost unbelievable. I was here when the Bomb Squad found her secret life. The people that knew her, such as neighbors, her son's law partner, Michael Doone, had no clue. According to Michael, he was sure Henry hadn't any idea his mother was involved in criminal activities."

Kitty reached for the door knob and Theresa stopped her. "Ahh, Boss…Could you put the code in?"

Kitty grinned. "Theresa, all the devices have been defused and removed."

Theresa cringed a little. "Please."

Kitty shook her head and punched in Henry's name on the keypad.

Theresa grinned. "Thanks…" She mouthed to Kitty 'There are two more'.

The team members helped Ross go down the second level of steps and at the bottom they just stared without a comment.

Theresa said what they were all thinking. "Holy fuck! Look at this place."

Blinking her eyes, Linda shook her head. "This… is another world. No one would ever believe us." She turned to Ross. "The Yard isn't going to dismantle this, are they?" She turned to Kitty, "My God, this would be a fantastic aid for the team!"

Karen waved to Patti D. "You're our computer guru. Let's see what kind of data she's got."

Patti D. sat at Zilpha's desk and turned on the computer. The Password sign came up.

Jo nudged Theresa. "Hey, password chick! Aren't you going to panic here?"

Patti D. frowned, “I can bypass this. It’s obvious Zilpha wasn’t a computer geek.” She pointed to the screen. “If she wanted to keep us out she would have…”

Theresa put her hand on Patti D.’s shoulder. “Patti, don’t be a Butthead. Look around this place…Zilpha wasn’t stupid…Humor me, once more, okay?”

“If I must…Jo, what was the last code Zilpha gave us? I just think the computer wasn’t as important as the other stuff.”

Jo cringed. “She gave a code for the compressor. It says on the bomb squad’s check sheet there was a device behind the compressor. They entered the name Charlie.”

Patti D. leaned forward to type. “See…All three codes have been used. I can easily get around…”

Theresa shouted. “Wait…Listen to me… Kitty, her last code words were comp.” She looked at the others. “Remember, she said it a couple of times.”

Staring at Kitty, “She never said the word, compressor. You know that could mean computer and her computer is asking for a password!”

Linda frowned. “Then you’re saying the device behind the compressor is…”

Theresa blurted firmly. “A fuckin’ decoy…” She nudged Patti D. “Put in Charlie for the password…Please!”

Kitty nodded to Patti D... “Put in Charlie. Just to make sure. Can’t hurt anything. They have removed three devices.”

As Patti D. finished and pressed Enter, a light flashed. Then they heard several loud clicking sounds inside of the desk and the word success appeared on the screen, showing balloons around it . They heard Zilpha’s voice. “Hello, you! We’re still here! I can always count on Charlie. Have a great day! ”

Ross shrank with his mouth open. “I think we need to make another call to the Bomb squad from outside. Those clicks began as the code was keyed in. I know for a fact no one from the squad opened anything or moved anything around this desk. Their bomb detector took them right to the compressor.”

Breaking the silence of total disbelief, Jane said quietly. “I want to keep that message. I know it sounds crazy, but it’s the only recording we have of her and I never want to forget the sound of her voice. It radiates such love."

Theresa stood by the desk as the team left. She stared at Patti D. "Don't turn off this fucking computer…Fact is you can stay here until the squad arrives. Don't even get out of that chair until they scan you."

Patti D. laughed when she heard Theresa mumbling, as she went up the stairs. "I've just aged thirty years. These fucking bombs are following me around. The Admiral and now this…"*Fuck!*

Chapter 38

The changing of the guard

Two months had gone by when the same group arrived at the cottage in the town of Crawley. It was time for sweaters and jackets even though the sun was still shining brilliantly. This time, they were greeted by the new owner.

After all the hugs, Jane led them to the patio and pointed. "The landscapers have just left. I told them to leave the final mounds of dirt and the watering. I wanted to share that with you."

There was a tray of glasses on the patio table and two bottles of champagne, chilling in buckets of ice. She handed a cork screw to Ross. "Would you do the honors?"

They each took a glass and walked out to four trees outside of the planter wall.

Bobbie grinned at Jane. "You had a cobblestone walk and stone benches put in. Nice for the times you want to be alone and think…What is the fourth tree for?"

Jane walked up to each tree. "This first one is in honor of Elizabeth Hennessey, your fallen team member. The one behind it is for Henry. I asked the landscapers to plant them close to one another and if they could graft together a branch from each tree." She pointed up and smiled. "You never know?"

She walked across the cobblestone circle to the tree opposite Henry's tree. "This is for Zilpha. It's called a Queen Grape Myrtle…I love it. The hues of blue and violet are so warm." She pointed to the corner window of the cottage. That's my bedroom and I can see the trees when I awake. The landscaper said the foliage will last almost to winter. Then in the spring I will be able to enjoy the beautiful colors in the flowers."

Ross nodded. "That is beautiful…Are you going to tell us what the fourth one is for?"

She stood in front of it. "I love Japanese maple trees. I know it's very common but the color lasts a long time. This tree is very special in that I'm dedicating it to all of you. I want you all to feel this is a haven for you, be it for rest, for fun or even for training. I wanted to keep everything as it was so I was able to convince Chief O'Doul this property could be one of the departments training centers for the Dream Team."

Kitty put her arm around Jane and raised her glass. "I can vouch for the plea bargaining. A lot of red tape was involved. It wasn't an easy battle, but she did it."

Jane smiled and raised her glass. "You not only saved me but have given me the desire to help orphaned children. It will be wonderful for my students to see all the hues each tree will have. When that happens, we will celebrate again. I'm working out a plan with Father James."

Karen raised her glass. "That sounds like a toast to me!"

They turned to walk back and saw a plaque on the back wall. Kitty read it. "The Peckham Cottage." She frowned at Jane. "This is your home now."

Jane shook her head. "No, I'm just the caretaker."

About the Author

The author lives in Rocky River, Ohio, and is a graduate of Ohio State. She taught school for six years and then entered the business world where she still keeps her day job.

Made in the USA
Middletown, DE
13 August 2015